GOLDEN HOUR

GOLDEN HOUR

RACHEL LABERGE

Paperback ISBN: 979-8-9891308-9-4

Editing by Kendra with Curious Minds Editing.

Cover design character art by human artist, Valerie.

Also by
Rachel LaBerge

THE PLAY CALLER SERIES

YOUR PLAY TO CALL
YOUR RULE TO BREAK
YOUR SECRET TO KEEP

THE EMERALD CANOPY LODGE

A LODGE AFFAIR
WHEN THE SNOW SETTLES

STANDALONES

FROM THE SIDELINES
THE ONE BED RULE
a love letter to those who left me behind

Have Faith In Me | A Day To Remember
Daylight | Taylor Swift
Cherry Wine | Hozier
Different Languages | All Time Low
Sink | Noah Kahan
Bloom | Paper Kites
Clearest Blue | CHVRCHES
Space Song | Beach House
Sweet Tooth | Cavetown
Camden | Gracie Abrams
I Want It All | Coin
King Of My Heart | Taylor Swift
Belong | Dashboard Confessional
I Will Follow You Into The Dark | Death Cab For Cutie
The Bottom | Gracie Abrams
Video Games | Lana Del Ray

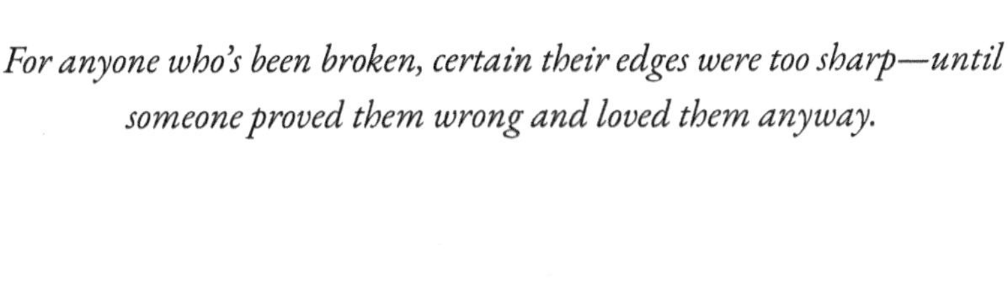

For anyone who's been broken, certain their edges were too sharp—until someone proved them wrong and loved them anyway.

And for Ambar, my sweet friend who made sunset photos our thing.

LETTER FROM THE AUTHOR

Now's the time for content warnings. If that's not your vibe, time to turn the page. Riiiiight now. Or... now!

Seriously.

Last chance.

Don't be mad at me...

Ready?

GOLDEN HOUR is a love story, one that has a special piece of my heart. I always aim to be as transparent as possible with readers, so I want to share a few content notes before you dive in.

This book includes themes of **grief, the death of a parent, anxiety, panic attacks, depression, and parental abandonment**. It also contains **on-page sexual content and graphic language**.

GOLDEN HOUR is intended for readers 18+ only.

Welcome
TO
GOLDEN HARBOR
MICHIGAN

One

COLSON

THE SUN SEEMS TO shine brighter in Golden Harbor, Michigan—and I fucking hate it. I try to pull the blinds down, but they don't stick and immediately roll back up, leaving the window exposed. Kind of like the blinds are giving me the middle finger, acting like nothing more than a magnifying glass for the rays to beam in.

I wish it'd rain. What I'd pay for massive, gray thunderclouds. The kind that rolls in, completely unexpectedly, and shuts the sun up with sheets of rain. One that feels like the start of a storm, catching everyone off guard.

Rubbing my forehead and trying to block the sun, I wish I would've stopped about three bourbons before I did last night. The light feels like a punishment, one I probably deserve.

On cue, my shoulder starts to throb. Being hung over on an eight hour drive where the sun was inescapable wasn't enough. Sure, I could've flown, but that would've taken a plan. Thinking ahead. Something I've not been good at as of late.

Opening the cabinets, the yellow paint hits me and the room starts to spin. Is it the crippling hangover or being back here? Well, *being* here. I only was here once—when I gave it to my mom for her birthday. Me, my mom, and the interior decorators I hired to give her full creative control with this place.

When I was a kid, she always talked about us having a summer place up north. This would be during the times where things were the darkest—me having the last piece of bread with peanut butter on it while she acted like she wasn't hungry. She'd be sitting down with me at the table during the few minutes she had between getting to her next shift. Her next job.

I looked for years, wanting to find something perfect for her. Once I had that solid and promised NBA money in my bank account, I was on the hunt.

That's what brought me to Golden Harbor, Michigan. It's early June; I should be in Chicago, wrapping up the NBA season with my team. But everything fell apart, or maybe I blew it up, and now I'm not sure where I belong.

Maybe it's nowhere.

I pull out three rogue ibuprofens from my pants pocket, pop them in my mouth, and fill a glass with water from the tap. I need to dull the throb in my head and my shoulder.

Slowly, I go back and forth from the car to the guest bedroom, bringing my bags in. Feels fitting for the current state of my life: chaos incarnate, shoved into a suitcase and some duffel bags. I drop the last duffel on the bed—a queen mattress with some blush pink quilt I'm positive my mom picked out—and exhale like it took everything in me to carry it ten steps. My shoulder twinges again.

I grab the remote from the nightstand and hit the power button, needing noise. Any noise. Something to drown out the quiet of this place. The screen blinks to life and I look away, focusing on unzipping my suitcase, pretending I don't hear the familiar theme music. But then—

"—former Chicago guard Colson Burke officially released this week after his on-court meltdown. GM is calling it conduct detrimental to the team—"

My spine goes rigid.

Another commentator jumps in, voice too bright for what he's saying.

"—Burke hasn't been seen with the team since the incident last week, and sources say the organization felt they had 'no choice'—"

I freeze halfway through pulling out a stack of T-shirts. My throat goes dry, and the room tilts—not from the hangover this time.

The incident. It's always said like that. Like it's some unspeakable crime instead of me doing what I thought was the right thing. Instead of me taking the heat so someone else wouldn't lose everything.

I sit down on the edge of the bed, elbows on my knees, staring at a knot in the floorboards while they talk about me like I'm not real.

"—a shame, really. Burke was the star of his draft class after bringing the first championship to his college. A massive contract a few years back. But at this level? Talent doesn't outweigh drama—"

My jaw clenches so hard it aches.

Drama. Right. That's what we're calling it now.

Fuck, if they only knew. I can imagine the headlines if the truth ever came out. I'm sure my old coaching staff will do everything in their power to keep it where it belongs: locked away with no key to be found.

I reach for the remote, ready to shut it off, but my hand stops mid-air. Because part of me wants to hear it, to feel the sting. To know exactly how bad the fallout is. How far I've fallen.

"...some close to the situation say this could be the end of the road for Burke unless he seriously reevaluates..."

I click the TV off before they can finish the sentence. I can't do it. Silence crashes back into the room. Heavy. Too heavy.

I let out a long breath, scrub a hand over my face, and stare at my open suitcase like it might offer some kind of answer. It's just more evidence that I can't handle whatever this all is. Being in the city felt all wrong. No one knows about this place, so I feel like I'm safe here—even if it's only for a few days. Or however long I decide.

My mom would've told me to get up. Keep going. Well, after she verbally kicked my ass for my behavior. It doesn't matter who was in the right or the wrong, she would hate to see me act like that. Hate to watch me be removed from the bench. Tossed like a piece of trash they no longer needed.

But she's not here. It's just me and the sun beaming through all these goddamn windows with too-thin blinds. The only thing louder than the silence is the truth buzzing in the back of my mind: I don't know how to fix any of this. I have no idea what I want. What I deserve. What my next move is.

I grab a throw blanket and toss it haphazardly over the curtain rod, doing anything I can to dim the light. It'll do for now.

Falling into the bed, I close my eyes and let the drowsiness from the drive and the hangover pull me into sleep.

Two

SADIE

"I THOUGHT WE HAD the jelly sandal conversation *last* time?" I ask the nine-year-old that's basically limping at this point.

"They're so cute," she croons, her cheeks pink from either embarrassment or the early summer sun's heat.

She's not wrong—the sandals are adorable. Actually, they bring me back to a time where I begged my parents for them at the store, even though my mom told me how they'd give me blisters. My mom was right, but she could never know. I went through a box of Band-Aids a week that summer.

The little girl stands in front of me wearing a skort, matching tank top, and a legit pink satin bow in her hair. I'm a firm believer that sports are for everyone and this isn't her girly-girl side showing; she's in physical pain from those plastic hellscapes on her poor feet.

"We're almost done for today, but next time, let's do half and half. You can switch into your tennis shoes when these start to hurt your feet, ok?"

She nods before doing a spin and beaming at me. I watch her run back to her 'team' and they all whisper about what we just talked about. The girls cover their mouths and giggle while the boys pretend not to listen. I love watching kids make friends during the summer.

I clap my hands loudly, getting everyone's attention. "Okay, let's finish this with a shootaround outside. Parent pick up starts in one minute."

The kids cheer, run to grab their bags, and race to be the first outside to get one of the basketballs. It's nothing but the sound of dribbling and energy burning from little humans and I take a moment. Slow down, pause, drink it in.

This is the third year I've been in charge of the rec center in Golden Harbor. It's not much when you look at it, but it's these types of moments that really make a difference. Giving parents the option for summer care, because even though the kids don't have school, parents still have to work.

I do what I can to help our small community, one I used to visit every summer when I was a kid. My dad was a college basketball coach at a Division I school a few hours south of here, but Golden Harbor was where we escaped to. Where he wasn't Coach Becker, where he didn't have to watch film or take recruiting calls during dinner. Up here, he was just my dad.

That's why I came back, why I run this place. If I can give even a sliver of that feeling to these kids—the freedom, that summer-magic kind of safety—then it's worth every hour, every budget headache, every minor injury, including today's blistered jelly-sandals incident.

Not only was my dad someone not to share when we'd come here, but I was simply Sadie. There was no one asking me what my plans were when it came to the sport my family practically breathed into my bones.

My mom used to joke that, when she was pregnant with me, I was never calmer than when she was watching my dad coach. The sound of the basketballs, the squeak of the shoes on the hardwood, was the only time I was chill.

Most of the parents have picked up their kids, some of them wishing for five more minutes and others having checked out about twenty minutes in. I have a few high schoolers who volunteer throughout the summer, and they're in charge of check in and out—I get to do more of the fun stuff with the kids.

"Alright! Last round. Get your shots up and put the balls back once you're done!" I shout to who's left.

The kids scatter like confetti, laughing, tripping, picking their favorite spot on the court with only one hoop outside. We're lucky enough to have two full courts inside, so I didn't push when we only had the one out here—we treat it like a bonus spot to hang out, do drills, pass time.

The sun kisses my shoulders and I look to the sky. It's a perfect June day without a cloud to be found. I'm thinking of how I'll spend my night when there's a loud CLANG.

Next door, at the vacation house I know to be vacant, a basketball slams into the side of a black car, one I've never seen before. It bounces off, then rolls into the yard.

"Oh no." I wince as one of the boys freezes, hands still overhead from his overly ambitious half-court shot attempt.

He runs up to me, pulling at my shirt. "Coach Sadie," he whispers, eyes huge. "I need a redo."

A redo. The phrase they learn during their first day with me. Free to be used when you miss your last shot, forget the play we're running, or when you need a minute to try again.

"Yep," I say with a sigh. "But let's hope the owner is chill."

Spoiler: he is not. Because standing there—jaw tight, sunglasses on, expression set to "don't even breathe near me"—is a guy I absolutely recognize, but pretend I don't. Not here. Not with kids around.

Colson Burke, NBA star.

Well, at this point he may be a *former* NBA star. Definitely a current storm cloud.

He turns slowly, eyes locked on the brand-new dent in his car, then at the guilty nine-year-old, then at me. Well, I think at me, considering he hasn't taken off his sunglasses.

And, oh yeah, he's pissed.

I jog over, hands up in surrender.

"Hey! Hi. Hello." I give him my friendliest, most 'everything is fine' smile. "We, uh... may have grazed your car. Lightly. As in, barely. As in, it's probably more of a love tap?"

His mouth stays flat. "That was not a love tap." He has a point. The dent is... visible.

"Coach Sadie, is it okay?" the guilty party yells over as he waits outside his parent's car.

I wave him off so I can handle the six-foot-five thundercloud standing in front of me.

I clasp my hands. "So... we dented your car. But good news, it has character now. One of a kind." I smile, rocking on my heels, trying to get him to crack.

Colson stares at me like he can't decide if I'm delusional or dangerous. "It didn't need character," he says flatly. "It's a BMW."

Glancing at the house, I reply, "Well, for the safety of your stay, may I suggest the garage?" Part of me wants him to tell me what he's doing here, to explain how long he's staying.

Slowly, he looks to the garage and back to me. He lips press into a thin line and it's clear he won't be sharing anything with me.

"This an every day thing? With the bouncing? And the kids? The yelling?" He crosses his arms and rubs his forehead.

I bite back a smile. "We're working on being a quieter bunch, but you know. Kids. Summer." I shrug my shoulders.

Colson exhales sharply through his nose, annoyed but not erupting, and maybe this is the only win we'll have during this interaction.

"Look," I tell him, lowering my voice. "I'm really sorry. We'll make it right. I can have the center cover the repair. We have a small fund for, uh, damages."

He lifts a brow. "You have a fund for this?"

"In theory."

It's really just me pooling any and all leftover funds from the camps and events before personally covering everything else. The rec center is the busiest during the summer. I still run classes and offer the space for other coaches and instructors in the fall, but I also pick up shifts at a local bar. I've even worked at the small, local library when our elderly librarian has needed a day off or two. I'm multifaceted, but he certainly doesn't need to know that.

I stick my hand out. "I'm Sadie. Sadie Becker. I run the rec center."

He hesitates like touching another human might physically hurt, then reaches out and shakes my hand once. Quick. Polite. Over it.

"Colson," he says.

"I know," slips out before I can stop myself.

His jaw ticks.

Cool. Great job, Sadie. Excellent first impression. Car damage and then an awkward interaction that's the equivalent of a root canal.

I clear my throat. "Anyway, welcome to Golden Harbor."

He looks at the lake, at the kids, at the dent.

"Yeah," he mutters. "Thrilled."

I smile because I don't know what else to do. The thing about Golden Harbor is that most people are genuinely happy. It's like this is a small piece of the public who have remembered what it means to be a community. To help each other out. To see the good in others. I'm not sure Colson Burke shares that sentiment.

"You'll be here for a while?" I try to make the question sound as light as possible.

Colson turns, his dark hair flopping onto his forehead. He waits long enough that I wonder if he's even going to answer.

"Yeah. A while. Something like that." He says the last part as he walks away, back to the house.

Didn't have this—an NBA player posted up next to the rec center—on my bingo card for today. One thing's for sure. It feels like this summer is about to get even more interesting.

Three

COLSON

THE FUCKING SUN IS still out with a vengeance, but at least it doesn't feel like my skull is cracking open. Progress. The hangover's gone, but the rest of it—the ache in my shoulder, the weight in my chest—is still annoyingly here.

I make my way into the kitchen and open the one cabinet I put food in yesterday. I brought some essentials from my place in my packing frenzy. Scanning the slim and really random options, I land on something tried and true.

PB&J.

It might be pathetic for a six-foot-five professional athlete, but it's familiar. Automatic. Something I ate a thousand times as a kid. Something I ate a thousand more times while I was broke and hustling for a contract.

I spread the creamy peanut butter, then the raspberry jelly, on the bread I brought from my apartment and turn on the TV, a little desperate for background noise.

Big mistake.

ESPN blares through the quiet of the house, and before I can switch the channel, the familiar headline flashes across the ticker.

BURKE'S SIDELINE OUTBURST RAISING SERIOUS QUESTIONS FOR CHICAGO

My stomach drops.

They cut to *the* clip—the clip I've seen more than enough times, but apparently not enough to stop tormenting myself with.

There I am during a nationally televised game, standing at the edge of the bench, yelling at one of the coaches. A teammate trying to step in. My face twisted in frustration. My arm in a sling, my season circling the drain. The moment everything tipped from bad to catastrophic.

I know I look unhinged, like I've completely lost it. But no one knows the full story. I'm not sure if my head coach knows anything about what's going on, but I doubt it. I always thought he was one of the good ones, which is why this hurts so bad.

The commentators start in, their voices too sharp for this early in the day.

"...immature reaction..."

"...lost the trust of his coach..."

"...behavior you don't bounce back from easily..."

I swallow hard, sandwich hovering halfway to my mouth.

I remember every second of that day. The rough rehab and physical therapy session. The looks from a select few of our staff which made it feel like I wasn't doing enough. Seeing a teammate get hurt but the staff wanting him to risk it to go back in the game. The fear that everything I'd worked for since I was a kid was slipping away.

And I'd snapped. Publicly. Spectacularly.

I shut the TV off before they can play it again. The replay hasn't quit in my head so there's no need for the echo chamber.

Dropping into a chair, I stare at my sandwich like it personally offended me when my phone buzzes.

A text from Kevin—my old teammate-turned-friend, one who definitely still has a spot on the team.

Kevin

hey

where'd you go

I stare at it. My thumb hovers but I don't know what to say. My fingers have nowhere to go. What am I supposed to say?

Yep, just reliving my greatest disaster minute by minute. Living the dream up here in exile. I'm surrounded by heartache and pain that goes deeper than this fucking shoulder injury and public humiliation.

The screen goes dark and I take a bite of my sandwich, chewing slowly, tasting nothing.

Then my phone lights up again—this time, a call.

Howie. My agent. While I entertained the possibility of texting Kevin back, there's not a cell in my body that's thinking of taking this phone call. Hell no. Not today.

It goes to voicemail. And then it rings again. And again.

On the fourth time, I almost throw the phone at the wall, but my shoulder emits a sharp warning pain and I rein it back. It brings me a murky sense of judgement. Like 'think again, you idiot.'

I answer on the final ring, voice flat. "What?"

His sigh is a mix of frustration and relief. "You can't keep ignoring me, Colson. We need to talk about your options."

"I don't have any options," I mutter.

"There are overseas teams that—"

"No," I interrupt. The thought of going from my dream to a step down overseas makes my stomach turn. Even though there's no one keeping me here, now that my mom is gone, I can't imagine it.

His voice is quieter and that somehow makes it worse. "You can't disappear."

"Watch me." Silence crackles on the line.

He lowers his voice. "The longer you hide, the worse it looks."

I close my eyes. The worst part? He's right. He's always right. And it still doesn't help.

"I'll call you later," I lie and hang up.

Before anyone else can call or text, I turn my phone off. There's nowhere for me to be, no one who actually needs me. Without basketball or my mom, there's nothing else.

Even May stopped reaching out. She was my on-again, off-again girl-friend who eventually turned into a long-term relationship. We were together for two years. When everything happened with my mom, she stuck around for about as long as it's acceptable before looking like a garbage human. After that date expired, she was gone. But really, she was gone long before that.

I know I was the shell of the person she met. The person she loved. The person she hoped would change my mind about getting married. No part of me needed a wife, or had this desire to be someone's husband, but May had other plans. She thought she'd be the one to change me. Little did she know she reinforced my opinion, made it so that doubling down felt right.

May got tired of waiting for me to come back to myself. While part of me doesn't blame her, the other part is glad she left. I could've never given her what she wanted and even though I clearly communicated that, she always held out that it'd be different.

Fuck, this hurts.

The kitchen feels smaller. Tighter. My chest feels the same. I rub a hand over my face, exhale, and glance out the window toward the driveway. The dent in my car catches the morning sun.

A snort escapes me. I honestly couldn't care less. A dent is nothing. A dent can be fixed.

I wish the rest of my life were that simple.

I take the last bite of my PB&J, toss the plate in the sink and brace my hands on the counter, letting the quiet settle. I'm not hungover. I slept. I ate.

I should feel better. But I don't. I glare at my cell phone, powered down but still like a little traitor on the table. This morning, I didn't hate myself right off the bat. I was trying to take it one step at a time, and then it was like everything closed the gap and ran back to catch me.

The clock on the oven tells me it's not even eight in the morning. I wonder when the rec center opens and the sound of kids screaming and the basketballs bouncing off things—hopefully not my car—will fill the outside. Or when I'll hear her yelling about plays and drills.

Part of the reason I came to Golden Harbor was to get away from basketball. The universe seems to be playing some cruel joke on me, like I've not been through enough. Naturally, a rec center would be right next door to this place.

Sadie. Ridiculously bright in a way that feels offensive given my state—sunshine in human form, all energy and ease, and that stupid, effortless smile. The kind of brightness that makes people notice.

I don't need that. I don't want that.

I need something dark, something quiet; something that won't pry open the parts of me I've been duct-taping together. But instead, I'm stuck in a house that feels like a shrine, with its yellow cabinets and someone like Sadie next door.

The hits keep on coming.

Four

SADIE

IT'S BEEN THREE DAYS since the dent in Colson Burke's car happened and I haven't heard from or seen him. Well, that last part is sort of true. I saw him peeking through the curtains yesterday morning when the kids started getting to camp. His car isn't in the driveway anymore, which is probably best for everyone.

I'm not sure I've ever seen anyone in that house before now. Sure, there was some maintenance, like someone was checking on it, but no one living there. That's a shame, considering it's absolutely gorgeous. It was on the market for a bit, but it was way out of my price range. I know that it sold at asking price, based on the app I was practically stalking for new properties.

Today, there are no kids at the rec center. It's Friday and most of them end up calling off anyway, going to do summer things with their families. So it's only me and my long to-do list of admin things that waits for me until the end of the week.

Like my grocery list.

I head to the little market off Main, the one which always smells like apples and overripe peaches, with a cart that wobbles like it's been in a bar fight. I'm scanning the produce when a familiar shape comes into view from the corner of my eye—tall, broad shoulders, baseball cap pulled low.

Colson.

Of course he looks like a commercial for T-shirts and bad decisions, with his muscles straining against the baby blue fabric.

For some reason, it feels like I should hide. I seriously consider ducking behind the apples, I really do. But then a voice—too loud, too excited—cuts through the aisle.

"Oh my God, it is him," a college kid with hair falling into his eyes, in a neon-pink T-shirt, whispers not-at-all quietly to his friend. He lifts his phone. "I'm totally getting a video."

Before I think, I step right between his camera and Colson.

"Hey!" I chirp, too brightly, waving like we're best friends reunited in a sitcom. "Didn't expect to see you here."

Colson blinks up at me, thrown. "Uh. Hi?"

The tourist lowers his phone, annoyed that I've ruined the shot.

I keep my smile plastered on and tilt my head. "Do you mind?" I ask the tourist sweetly. "He's just trying to buy groceries. Like a normal human who needs...avocados."

Colson's mouth twitches like he's fighting a smile.

The tourist grumbles something and wanders off, defeated.

Once they're gone, I step back and immediately the store feels too small. "Sorry," I offer. "He was about to film you like you were the new animal at the zoo and it didn't feel right."

He huffs a laugh. "Is that...a common comparison for me? An animal?"

"Only on Thursdays," I shoot back. The second the words leave my mouth, I'm wondering why I said that.

He pauses, looking at me fully, with a lazy-quiet intensity that makes my pulse stutter a little. "So you're my bodyguard now?"

"Only part-time. And only because I still owe you for the dent." I gesture vaguely, as if the dent is floating above us. "How's the car?"

"Still dented," he answers, but his tone feels a touch warmer, like the icicles on the edge are starting to melt. His eyes catch mine like ice caps on the lake.

Well. That does something to my insides I absolutely do not permit.

"Great grocery store." I look around the space.

Colson's brows knit together, following my gaze. "Isn't it the only grocery store?"

I shrug. "Unless you count Big Joe's farmstand."

"Big Joe?" His brows knit a deep line in his forehead.

"Everyone knows Big Joe." I shrug again, knowing I sound like an idiot because clearly, this man doesn't know him.

An awkward pause pulls between us, like cheese from a mozzarella stick that's about to fall on the floor and be completely inedible.

"Do we count that?" The confusion layers over the top of his words.

Because I've dug myself a hole, I keep going. "Only when it's sweet corn season. Then Golden Harbor has *two* grocery stores." I put my hand up with two fingers showing, like a peace sign.

What am I even saying? Where did the extra side of cringe come from? I put my hand behind my back, afraid to put up any more numbers or who the hell knows what.

Sadie. Get it together.

Colson looks at me for a beat too long, like he's deciding whether to say something or maybe he's planning his escape. Hell, he could be looking for the emergency exit sign.

"Got it," he says, pushing his cart, slowly but enough for me to take the hint.

My brain short-circuits for half a second before my feet betray me and follow. I pull out my grocery list and set it inside the front compartment of my cart.

"What are you doing?" he asks, turning to see my cart almost in line with his.

"Shopping," I answer, acting like this is something we've done a hundred times. "I, uh... also need groceries. Which are... here."

Brilliant, Sadie. Truly groundbreaking logic.

Colson blinks once. Twice. His cart wheel squeaks in the silence, and I swear it's judging me too. He stops, taking me in before continuing. He runs his hand through his hair, his arm thick and muscular.

Something warm—and terrifying—settles low in my stomach. He smells like soap and sun-warmed cotton and maybe trouble. Definitely trouble.

I have the sudden sinking realization that I've invited myself into his personal space and there's no socially acceptable way to back out now without faking a phone call or my own death.

Awesome.

I'm back home, standing in my tiny kitchen with the door still half-open like I forgot how to walk into my own apartment. I press my palms to the counter, trying to steady myself, but my mind keeps circling back to the way he looked this morning—rumpled, brooding, irritated at the world and somehow still magnetic.

Colson Burke. In Golden Harbor, Michigan of all places. It doesn't make sense. Guys like him don't disappear into sleepy lake towns unless something's wrong, and everyone who follows anything sports related knows exactly what's wrong: the bench blow-up, the shouting match with his coach, the endless commentary dissecting his character like he's on trial.

I wonder who owned this house before him? Maybe he's renting it? It was clear someone was renovating, but no one seemed to stay after that. Not all the way surprising when it comes to towns like this—millionaire CEOs with their lake house, on another lake, to match the ones scattered about their favorite vacation towns.

After putting away all the groceries, I stare at my small kitchen table and think back to the entirely painful interaction with Colson. I know this is something my brain will play on repeat for many years to come: an anxiety-induced feature film titled, "Remember when you made a complete ass out of yourself in front of the gorgeous NBA player?"

The thing about Golden Harbor is that it's predictable. All the locals know how to move around each other. Tourists come and go, cluttering the streets, but it's like the unwritten bargain you come to terms with when you live in a lake town. A local would never try to get a video of someone while they were here. That's tourist behavior and why I stepped in.

Colson Burke seems unpredictable. Why isn't he in Chicago trying to smooth things over with his team? Or trying to find another roster spot? Maybe he's stepping away from the game? And why did my heart do a weird, traitorous flip the second I got close to him?

I haven't dated anyone in the last two years. I mean, I've gone on dates—typically horrible and nothing to be repeated—but haven't seriously seen someone more than a handful of times. The idea of being alone has been one I've latched onto because I'm barely all the way together after my last failed relationship.

Nick was the master at taking pieces of me, ones he made me feel like I should want to give, and others he had no business to. Hindsight is always 20/20.

My skin prickles as the memories try to come roaring back. I practice pushing them down, tucking them away, doing my best not to let them pull me under. The feeling of not being wanted. Discarded. That's what happens when the man you thought you'd spend forever with calls off the wedding.

There are days where I still have a hard time believing it. My mind replays it back: me with my ribbon bouquet, gathered from my bridal shower gifts, pretending to walk down the aisle, and Nick blurting out words I never thought I'd hear. *Sadie, I can't marry you,* which hurt all on their own, but not as much as *I don't want to marry you.* I thought it was a cruel joke or maybe he was having cold feet. I was right about it being cruel.

I don't know if there's anything quite as earth-shattering as sending back wedding gifts. Like, thank you for the monogrammed gift but these are not my initials and I can't even think of a fun acronym to associate with it, so, here you go? What will you do with it? Believe me, I know the answer is nothing.

Something warm and terrifying settled low in my stomach when Colson looked at me, like recognition of risk. Someone complicated, bruised, dragging a city's worth of scrutiny behind him, storming into the town where I've found safety and happiness. His shadows mixing with mine seem like a bad idea. The shadows I've done my best to tuck away, move on from, and try to smother with the good things I know are out there.

And yet, standing here in my quiet kitchen, I can't shake the feeling that whatever brought him to Golden Harbor isn't something he plans on sharing... and that somehow, I won't be able to stop myself from wanting to know anyway.

Five

COLSON

I'm crossing the street after grabbing the mail, minding my own business—well, trying to—when I hear her voice cut through the morning air.

"Colson!"

I close my eyes. Of course. Of course she'd show up the second I try to disappear back into the house. The last few days have consisted of me binging shows on Netflix; something I didn't have time for during the season or training. I'm not doing any of that now. I turn around slowly, deliberately, because if I move any faster it might look like I care.

Sadie jogs toward me—ponytail bouncing, cheeks flushed from whatever work she's doing. While I'm dreaming of coffee in an IV, she's clearly been up for hours. She looks like the embodiment of morning. I look like someone who could barely survive this one. Fantastic match up.

"What?" I ask, not bothering to hide the rough edge in my voice.

"I, uh... need help," she admits, and I'm already irritated because she looks nervous about asking me. Like I bite. Which, fine, maybe I do.

"With what?"

"A heavy cabinet in the storage room. Like ridiculously heavy. And the kids can't get to the equipment until it's moved."

I try to get past the interaction. "I'm busy."

Sadie looks at me with the mail in my hand, and her eyes linger longer on my somewhat disheveled hair. Like she knows I'm going to do nothing but rot in my bed.

"With mail?" she presses.

I stare at her. She stares back, trying to look unbothered but clearly bracing for me to double down on no. Not because she thinks I'm lazy. Because she thinks I'm *mean.*

"Don't you have a boyfriend who can help you?" I ask because the last thing I need is some guy getting in my shit over something like this.

Sadie blinks slowly and time stretches between us. It's like the mention of the word brings her down a notch—almost like a trick I may need to keep in my back pocket.

She breathes in, holding it for a second, before blowing it out—like she's trying to keep her cool. "No, Colson. *I don't* have a boyfriend."

I don't know why but that surprises me.

I should say no. I should *absolutely* say no. But I hear myself grumble, "Where is it?"

Her whole face lights up like I did something heroic. Christ.

Inside the community center, the air smells like gym floors and craft glue—like a childhood I didn't really get to have. She walks ahead of me, talking with her hands, and I try not to notice how her hips sway or how she smells faintly like orange slices and something warm.

We step into the storage room and I take one look at the cabinet.

"This thing's ancient. Why do you even have it?"

"Historic," she corrects immediately. "And we're a community based rec center. We take any and all donations... well, almost all. Once, someone tried to donate a bunch of mismatched shoes and how does one even end up with individual shoes—"

I sigh, looking at her, and it's enough to get her to stop as soon as her eyes meet mine. They're light, almost the color of brown sugar.

If I use my legs, and my good arm for the lifting, I should be okay. My other arm can simply guide and keep it in control. I was only wearing the sling when I was with the team, needing to protect myself from a rogue ball coming my way.

"Where are we moving it?" I ask, hands on my hips, taking in the orderly chaos around me. Plastic bins with kids' names on labels, ones that probably change as the year goes on. Shoeboxes with extra socks. A desk off to the side where she probably works every once in a while.

"Like ten feet that way," Sadie points, past the door to where it will no longer be blocking the door.

Nodding, we crouch down to lift. Slowly we stand, keeping eye contact to maintain the same pace. She smiles through the concentration as we start to move—me walking backward, her forward—and fuck, she's pretty.

Her face lights up and she says, "This is good."

We slowly lower it to the ground and right before I'm in the clear, a bite of pain nips at my shoulder. I clench my jaw through it.

She notices. Of course she notices. "Shoulder okay?" she asks, all soft and concerned.

Part of me wants to ask her how she knows it's my shoulder, but if she knew who I was, I'm guessing she knows about my injury. "It's fine."

Sadie raises a brow like she doesn't believe me for a second. "You're compensating."

That makes me look at her. Really look at her. "Let me guess, when you're not wrangling kids at the rec center, you moonlight as a doctor?" I ask.

She shifts her weight to one leg, hands on her hips, and shakes her head. "My dad was a college basketball coach. I grew up listening to him talk about player injuries and seeing them first hand."

Okay, I didn't expect that. Didn't expect her to understand anything about the hell of recovery. It looks like she was going to continue but she stopped herself. Something shifts in me—something I don't want to name.

Before I can respond, the hallway erupts with the door opening and then complete kid chaos.

"Oh my gosh, it's him—"

"COACH SADIE—"

"He's SO TALL—"

I freeze like someone pulled a fire alarm in my chest. Sadie leaps in front of them. "No ambushing strangers. Outside please!"

They scatter, still whispering about me at full volume. I drag a hand over my face. I don't know what I thought would happen when I got here, if I'd be able to hide away and be a secret recluse or what. I'm not even sure what I wanted.

"Sorry," she says, a little breathless. "They're excited." She shrugs her shoulders. "Older group, so there are some basketball fans, some that may recognize you, I'm guessing." She gives me a sad thumbs up that I think is supposed to make me feel better.

"Whatever you say."

Sadie tips her head towards the antique cabinet. "You're surprisingly helpful for someone who scowls as a hobby," she teases.

I should ignore that. I should walk away.

Instead I hear myself say, "It's a talent."

Her smile hits me like a chest blow. I recover quickly, stepping back, putting distance between us before she can make me do something else stupid—like smile back.

"Thanks," she says quietly. "There's a door if you want to sneak out the back." Sadie points down a hallway.

I grunt something noncommittal and head for the door.

And the worst part? I can feel her watching me walk away. I hate—*hate*—how much I want to look back.

I've been in Golden Harbor a week and have only left my place once to get groceries. The only place I've existed is in the confines of this house. One that's starting to haunt me. Looking for a coffee mug, I put my hand deep in the cabinet, pulling one from the back.

I expect it to be one of the matching mugs I've used previously—clearly a set my mom purchased. But instead, I'm looking at a picture of me and my mom. A mug I got her when I was probably twelve that features the two of us at one of my basketball league championships. I'm all awkward and too tall for my age and she beams, still wearing her shirt from waiting tables at the diner.

My mom loved coffee mugs. She always seemed to collect them but would still stick to her same three to four favorites, this being one of them. The idea of her keeping it all this time has me grasping at air, fighting for it.

Grief is a funny thing… in the sense that it's not funny at all. It's dodging uppercut punches and kicks to your teeth while you're scrambling back. Grief doesn't care how strong you are or how many minutes you played last season or how many times you pretended you were fine on national television. It just hits. Without warning, without mercy.

Taking a step back, my back hits the kitchen island and I slide to the floor, leaning against it. I pull my knees into my chest and put my head between, trying to get air. My hands tremble as the tightness digs deeper into my muscles, infiltrating the ligaments and tendons—the things that keep me physically together—and I feel the sharpness of its nails.

Rubbing my hands together, I try to steady the shaking. My chest keeps tightening, compressing, folding in on itself like a collapsing tent. I can't get in a deep enough breath. My throat burns. My eyes sting.

I press the heels of my palms into my eye sockets, willing myself to get it together. To breathe. To not fall apart in a kitchen painted the exact shade of yellow she picked because she said it made her feel like the perfect summer day.

It's been months and I haven't cried since the funeral, haven't let myself. Crying feels too final. Too much like admitting she's really gone and that this house—this stupid, bright, too-quiet house—is all I have left of her.

The mug stares back at me from the counter like a dare. Like a reminder. Like the wound you forget about until you hit it just right.

A sound escapes me—something between a breath and a choke. I pull my knees tighter, trying to cage the shaking before it gets worse.

It doesn't work. I bow my head, fingers digging into my hair, and let the weight roll through me. The regret. The pressure. The loss. The stupid, suffocating ache of missing someone who saw every version of me and loved me anyway.

The sting behind my eyes finally breaks, tears dripping down my cheeks. I don't wipe them away. What's the point?

I don't know how long I sit on the floor, letting myself finally shatter in a place where no one will see me.

No cameras. No teammates. No commentary. No one.

Just me, a picture on a mug, and the kind of grief that comes in waves—a current you can't swim against.

When the shaking slows, I drag in a breath—thin, jagged, enough to keep me upright. My head thunks lightly against the cabinet behind me, the wood cool against my overheated skin.

I stare at the mug again. A memory buried in the decades. And even now, I can hear her asking me, "What are you going to do?" That was what she'd say every time I came to her with something she thought I was capable of handling. Most of the time she was right.

"I'm trying," I whisper to no one. To her. To myself. "I'm trying."

I'm not sure if that's a lie or a promise.

Six

SADIE

"What a dick. You should've duct-taped him to the bleachers," Maren groans, shoving a bouquet of peonies into my arms like emotional support flowers.

"I can't duct-tape a grown man onto town property," I mutter.

"You could. You absolutely could. I've seen you duct-tape a broken table leg to a cooler for an entire tournament weekend."

"That was different," I protest, adjusting the stems. "The table didn't have free will."

Maren—my best friend and owner of Harbor Blooms, purveyor of gossip and unsolicited encouragement—gives me a pointed look over the counter. Her braid is messy, her apron covered in dirt, and she still somehow looks like a walking magazine spread.

"Who quits two hours before practice?" she asks.

"Coach Dave," I say dryly. "Apparently he and his family landed a last minute rental cabin in the Upper Peninsula. *Too good to pass up.*" I mimic his sad excuse for leaving me high and dry.

"And he couldn't have told you yesterday?" Maren lightly moves daisies into the three arrangements she's working on.

"He texted me a canoe emoji," I deadpan.

She winces. "That's brutal. And dickish."

"Now I've got thirty kids and no assistant coach. And you know how last time went when I tried to do a full scrimmage solo."

"Six crying children?"

"Seven. And that wasn't even counting me!"

She tosses a rose petal at me. "What's your plan?"

I exhale hard, leaning against the counter. "Panic. Briefly. Then… I don't know." I pinch the bridge of my nose. "I need someone who can talk to kids, keep a drill running, lift a ball without throwing out their back, who knows the basics of the game."

Maren slowly raises an eyebrow. "So… like your conveniently planted NBA-playing neighbor?!"

I stare at her. She stares back.

Her eyes widen. "Oh God. You're thinking about asking him."

"I am not thinking about him," I lie, much too fast.

She lets out a laugh, clapping her hands and pointing at me. "You're busted! I said about *asking* him. You're over here daydreaming about Colson Burke."

"I'm not busted, I'm desperate," I hiss. "There's a difference." I wipe my hands on my leggings. "And I'm not daydreaming about anyone."

"Desperate enough to ask the six-foot-five smoke show with the permanent scowl?"

I groan. The thing is, Colson could do this in his sleep. If he could act like other humans weren't a virus he was trying to avoid.

I grab my keys. "I'm not doing this because I want to."

"Of course not," Maren says sweetly. "You're doing it because you have no choice, and also because he's hot."

"It's for the kids," I insist, trying to convince her, and maybe myself.

"Coach Hot Rage!" she calls after me. "Let me know!"

I'm standing in front of Colson's front door, about to knock, and this is the moment I question every life decision that brought me here.

My hand hovers and when I finally have the guts to knock, it's louder than I hoped.

Through the window, I watch him walk toward the door. He swings it open, brows knitted, clearly wondering what the hell I'm doing here.

"Car's in the garage if you have a bat or something you want to hit it with." He jokes, but no sign of a smile touches his lips.

I stand with my hands on my hips. "I'm kind of in a bind."

A few short seconds pass before he says, "Hard pass."

"You don't even know what I'm asking."

"I do," he retorts. "And it's a no."

I inhale. Count to three. Resist the urge to run away and put an end to me asking for anything ever again.

"My assistant coach bailed," I explain anyway. "I have thirty kids inside and I need a second adult before they burn the place down."

"No."

"Come on. One practice. You can even scowl the whole time."

"I'm not coaching."

"Because you can't... or?"

"No."

Before I can argue, a tiny voice pipes up from behind me.

"Coach Sadie? All the balls are on the rack. Just like you asked." The kid—little Evan with glasses too big for his face—peers up at Colson like he's staring at an actual Avenger. Evan's mom needed to drop him off early so she could get to a meeting, and I always try to accommodate when I can.

Now, did I ask Evan to wander over to interrupt this conversation? No. Am I mad that he did? Also no.

Colson freezes.

Evan blinks. "My brother said you were the best playmaker in the whole league."

Colson looks like he's trying to pretend he didn't get metaphorically punched in the stomach.

I fold my arms. "In the whole league? Wow!" I say to Evan, side-eyeing Colson.

"My mom told me if I can get A's and B's this year, I can get a new jersey. I showed her one of yours. The special city jersey from this year." He rocks back on his heels and my heart warms from sweet Evan.

A muscle in Colson's jaw ticks and for the first time since I met him, he looks... guilty. Probably has something to do with his future in the NBA being in shambles.

Evan puts the nail in Colson's grumpy coffin when he asks, "Are you helping us today? I'd be the coolest kid in my grade if I can tell them I got to hang out with Colson Burke this summer." His eyes are wide and honest.

I try not to smile, pressing my lips together, but I can't help it. My lips tug up at the corner. I couldn't have drawn this up any better. And it's like I can feel his icy shell melting.

Colson rubs his hands over his face and drops his shoulders in defeat. "Just for today."

"Yay!" Evan yells so I don't have to.

"See you in ten minutes," I call over my shoulder as Evan and I walk back across the yard to the rec center.

My stomach flips and I can't tell if it's a surprise from him agreeing to help me. Or something else.

Something else I refuse to acknowledge.

Seven

COLSON

I CAN'T BELIEVE I'M actually walking toward the rec center. Actually, I can. It's Evan's fault—tiny human with his too-big glasses and the story about his mom bribing him with my jersey. Him talking about his mom had my chest cracking open.

Then it was his brother, and his class; how excited he was to be in front of me was like a glimmer of light in the darkness. For a moment, I wasn't the guy who yelled at his coach on national television. I wasn't the screwup or the potential has-been. I was somebody's favorite.

And you don't say no to a kid who says something like that. Not when your mom once saved up her tip money to surprise you with your first NBA jersey when you were about his age.

Now I'm here, standing outside the gym, hands shoved deep in my pockets, giving myself one last out. I could turn around right now. Walk back to the house. Make it clear this was nothing but a momentary lapse in judgment. Hell, they probably expect me to back out.

As if he has the best timing to ever exist, the door opens and Evan's face peers through. "Coach Sadie told me to make sure you weren't stuck out here. Said you might need a little encouragement."

The way his tiny voice almost stumbles over the word *encouragement*. I'm definitely not going back to the house. *Coach Sadie*. Fuck, how does she know me like this?

"No, I'm not stuck. I'm coming in," I say, and with each word, the little boy's eyes light up.

Evan opens the door further. "I told her you would. Colson Burke wouldn't let us down."

I'm going to melt into this floor. Evan is being too fucking nice to me right now. Part of me wonders if this is truly all him or if he had some specific coaching before he came to find me.

I take a couple steps in and the second I'm all the way inside, the chorus of small voices nearly rattles the windows.

I sigh, mutter a curse under my breath, and muster all the energy I'll need for this.

"Say hi to Coach Colson." Sadie's sing-song voice cuts through the excitement.

And like they've said it a hundred times, all the kids call in unison, "Hi, Coach Colson!"

I lift my finger up and mouth 'one time' to Sadie. She nods, her dark blonde hair in a ponytail kissing her shoulders.

Sadie blows her whistle and all the kids' eyes go to her, like their heads are on a swivel. She looks at me over the top of the clipboard, eyebrows raised like she can't believe I showed. When she flashes me a smile, my knees try to wobble.

Fucking traitors.

WE'RE WARMING UP AFTER a halftime snack when I see a kid who hasn't made a shot all day.

"Hey, keep your elbow in when you shoot," I tell him. "Makes your release more stable."

He tries it. The ball arcs perfectly and swishes. His entire face lights up. It's like the made shot took a piece of my resolve with it.

I drift from kid to kid, giving quick tips and gentle corrections. They're eager to hear from me and are more patient than I was at this age. This used to be one of my favorite things—working with kids at the camps my team would offer. I used to be one of those kids. My mom would sign me up for anything and everything basketball related—scraping together all of her leftover tip money from waiting tables to fund it.

My body remembers how to do this—how to teach the basics, how to encourage without overthinking it. My heart remembers, too, even though I wish it didn't.

When I straighten up after making my rounds, talking to each of the players, Sadie's watching me. In a way that makes me feel seen, which is dangerous territory.

She walks over and says, "You're good with them."

I grunt. "It's just one practice."

"Mm-hm." Her brows press into her forehead.

"I mean it."

"Oh, I believe you," she lies cheerfully.

I want to argue, but then someone's hands tug on my shirt.

"Can you come back tomorrow?" a little girl asks, blonde hair in two pigtails, who did a couple cartwheels while waiting for her turn during a drill.

Jesus Christ. The timing.

I swallow. "We'll... see."

The little girl smiles, while trying to dribble the ball between her legs a few feet ahead of us.

The next hour flies by. The kids leave sweaty, red-faced, and carrying the kind of happy exhaustion only three hours of running around can cause.

When it's only us, Sadie waves at me. I start walking toward the back door, kids and parents still out front probably getting situated. "So…" she calls after me, "see you tomorrow?"

I don't turn around. "I didn't say I'm coming tomorrow."

"Right," she answers, voice bright and almost echoing through the gym. "I'll mark you down as *Definitely Showing Up.*"

I stop at the door, fighting the urge to smile. "I'm not coming tomorrow."

Her hands lift in faux surrender. "Absolutely. I'll make sure the back door is unlocked in case you want to sneak in."

I shake my head, push open the back door, and step into the afternoon sun.

I'm not coming back. I'm not. Probably not.

Fuck.

Okay, yeah, I'm screwed.

Eight

SADIE

GOLDEN HARBOR (LOCALS ONLY) - Thread

Carla B.: Does anyone know the young man behind the rec center?? He is GRUNTING VERY LOUDLY and flinging what looks like ropes?? Should I call someone??

Terry P.: Carla, sweetie, they're called battle ropes.

Carla B.: Well he is battling something back there.

Donna R.: Pretty sure that's the new guy who moved in next to the center. The tall one.

Carla B.: No one with arms like THAT is allowed to have sad eyes.

Moderator: Reminder: Please refrain from speculating about neighbors' emotions.

I snorted when I saw the thread. It took me about five seconds to figure out exactly who Carla was talking about. And another five to walk to the window and peer through to see for myself.

Colson. In his backyard. Sweating. Working on ropes that are tied to a tree. The backyard slopes down so he's awkwardly on an incline.

The grunting makes sense. Catching the attention of some locals like Carla, who has never missed a chance to be publicly thirsty in her life. I swear, she used to walk up and down the beach whenever she heard there were attractive older men here with their families. She'd deny it, but I'm all over it.

He has a jump rope lying on the grass, a couple of free weights, and a resistance band. His T-shirt clings to his back, and his arms flex as he moves the ropes.

Colson, who *did* come back to practice. Who keeps telling me we won't see him the next time but every day at the last minute, he strolls in. I don't know who is even giving him the details on the practice schedule. Probably one of the kids. He's slowly becoming one of their favorites.

I stopped before I meant to, caught between assessing his form and staring like an idiot. Before I could talk myself out of it, I'm out of the rec center and walking toward Colson.

He's been showing up for us. Now, I can try and show up for him. Hopefully he'll see it that way.

Gently, I try to greet him. I definitely don't want to scare him. The headline you don't want to see is *NBA Player Has Head Injury After Local Trespasses, Startling Him.*

He's wearing earbuds, which makes sense as to why he can't hear me. Or, maybe he's doing his best to pretend like I don't exist.

Stepping in closer to him, I wave my hands, doing my best not to look like a creep. It's not until I'm almost within arm's length of the rope that he picks his head up, sees me and stops.

Not before donning that perfect scowl.

As he takes his earbuds out, sweat dripping down his face, his brows knit together.

"Uh, hey. Hi." I try to sound unaffected. Like, who has the right to be this gorgeous? "Tough terrain out here."

His hands rest on his hips as he tries to catch his breath. "Ummm..." Colson looks around. "Sure?"

The pause is as awkward as the unlevel ground beneath our feet.

"What's up?"

Colson is talking while I look around, wondering if Carla or any of the local lurkers are anywhere close. Maybe peeking out of their windows or taking a long walk, including a specific street.

"Sadie..." He waves his hand. "Do you need something?"

Before my brain catches up to my mouth, I reply, "You." To make it worse, I clap and point.

Colson says nothing, but his brows push into his forehead and his mouth twists into the start of a grimace.

"No, not you. That's—" My fingers touch my temples, like I have the ability to turn back time. "Let's start again." I take in a deep breath and sigh it out. "You," I emphasize, "should come work out in the rec center."

"You...want me to come work out?" he asks slowly, like he's translating my words from a different language.

"Yes," I reply. "One, your backyard is a death trap. Two, we don't have any kids today. Three, we have those big industrial fans that make you feel like you're in a Nike commercial."

He seems to soften with each reason. I mean, the fans are legitimate, considering it's unseasonably hot for early June. It's only going to get hotter.

Colson wipes his face with the bottom of his shirt—flash of abs, hello—and nods once. "Give me two minutes."

He grabs his water bottle, coils the ropes, and jogs inside behind me. His shoulder gives the slightest hitch as he slings the jump rope around his neck, and I pretend not to notice.

Inside the rec center, the hum of the lights fills the quiet. No squeaking sneakers. No echoing yells. Just an empty court with one overhead light shining in the center.

The moment I push the door fully open, the automatic fans along the ceiling roar to life, sending cool air down in slow, sweeping waves.

"Wow," he admires, glancing up. "You were right on the fans."

"I told you. Nike commercial." I toss him a ball from the rack, then grab my own.

We walk out onto the court, the fans ruffling our shirts, the whole place ours. It reminds me of my college days when I'd grab a friend and we'd screw around for a few hours… waste time in the place that held all my hopes and dreams.

Colson wanders to the rack of balls and I pretend not to notice. He switches balls, testing the new one with a bounce, the sound echoes throughout the empty gym. I walk over and do the same.

And then it feels like I'm home. Me and a basketball.

We both do our own thing on separate sides of the court. It feels good. Time seems to run when I'm on the court, like I used to do before the injury that took me out. The one I agonize over when I'm feeling particularly pathetic and need to throw myself a pity party.

I take a few dribbles and pull up for a gentle jump shot. The ball arcs perfectly—every coach I've ever had would be proud—and smacks off the back rim, bouncing hard to the left. My right knee twinges as I land. Still. Six years and I can feel every weather change.

Colson's eyes track it. Of course they do. His gaze flicks down to my brace, then back to my face. It's the first time I've worn it in front of him, considering it's not something I need to coach—only when I'm getting as close as I can to the sport that built me.

"You over-rotate a little on that knee," he remarks. Not unkind. Not pitying. Just noticing. "You been rehabbing it lately?"

"Define lately." I force a smile, jogging after my rebound. "It works. Mostly."

He doesn't push, but I catch the wave of what feels like concern in his expression. For a man who thinks nobody sees him, he sure sees everything.

He steps back to the three-point line, dribbles once, and goes up for a shot. His form is textbook—until the follow-through. His right shoulder tightens, his face pinches, and the shot sails short, clunking off the front rim.

I blink. "Was that… on purpose?"

"No," he mutters.

"Cool. So we're both disasters."

His mouth twitches. Barely, but it's there. A ghost of a smile.

We fall into a slow rhythm—rebounds, easy layups, lazy passes that don't test his shoulder or my knee too much. The fans push air over us as our shadows streak across the shiny court.

I see him watching me so I pass him the ball. He catches it—just one, and tosses it lightly back to me. "I used to hit those threes in my sleep," he admits, nodding toward the spot where his shot bricked. "Now my shoulder...."

His words drift off and it feels like I'm on the verge of something. Like he's about to crack open the shell and let me peek inside. But he stops, and I don't feel like pushing him today.

I dribble in place. "Well. Lucky for you, today is just us. We're allowed to suck."

He exhales, quiet but almost a laugh. "Didn't realize that was on the schedule."

I spin the ball on my palm. "It is now."

Colson stares at me for a second too long before a smile hits his lips and he looks to the floor, almost as if he's hiding from it.

Part of me wants to see if he's going to commit to helping me out. I should know, for the kids, or that's what I keep telling myself.

I walk to the bleacher that has my phone and say, "Should probably exchange numbers?" My voice comes out wobbly and unsure. "Since you're my new assistant coach. And we still have to get the dent in your car fixed."

Colson eyes me, holding the ball in the crook of his elbow, the other hand resting on his hip. "I'm next door." He says this in a way that makes it feel like he doesn't want me to have his number. "And I'm not your assistant coach."

I decide to leave the coaching details fuzzy—enough that he might actually bite and continue helping me. "For how long though? No offense but you seem a bit like a flight risk. Maybe I'm not there to step in at the grocery store next time and the tourists run you out of town." I shrug my shoulders, melting into the facade of the joke.

"Then you'd be off the hook," he answers, so matter of fact.

I roll my eyes. "And you'd leave me with that guilt? No way. No thanks." I walk closer, about to give him my phone.

I swear he's going to smile, but he doesn't. Instead he takes the phone, enters in his first name and number, and hands it back to me.

We stay in the gym for I don't know how long. This wasn't in my plans today and I'm actually surprised he decided to take me up on the offer.

That's the thing about Colson Burke, though. He seems like he's full of surprises.

Nine

COLSON

I STARE AT THE messages from Kevin and my stomach turns. Today has been rough. Without the distraction of practicing with Sadie, or the kids, it's like the only thing creeping around me is the uncertainty of what's next.

For the first time since being out here, I miss the city, my friends. The coffee shop I'd run to on the weekends when I wasn't traveling for an away game. The late night diner we'd go to after having a couple drinks. Familiarity. Comfort. Little pockets of the city that didn't care that I was NBA Player Colson Burke. To them, I was just Colson.

What now? Is there a next team? Do I want there to be? Is it even a possibility?

I know I'll have to come clean about everything that led to the public blow up. I don't expect my behavior to go unchecked, but it all feels impossible.

Kevin is one of my closest friends. The guy who I love to do nothing with. I text him back because I don't want him to worry.

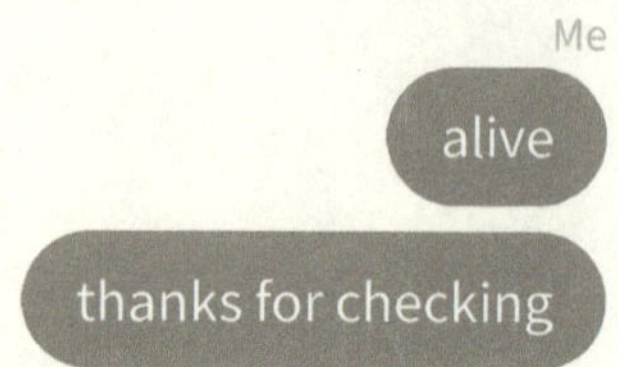

That's all I have in me. I don't tell him about the shoulder rehab and he doesn't ask. Another reason why I know he's one of the real ones. He's always had a knack for being interested in me as a person, not only the NBA version of me.

Once I'm sure the messages go through, I turn my phone off. The curtains aren't closed all the way and I can see the sun is about to go down. I've wasted a whole day.

I've done nothing besides slather peanut butter and jelly on bread, sleeping on and off, and feeling like I'm in a vice grip at the hands of life. Or maybe it's grief.

Closing my eyes, I try a technique a sports therapist gave me this season. Envisioning the sound of the waves, my feet in the sand, the water pulling in and around me. How the water feels on my skin. What does it sound like? Anything I can smell?

The thoughts keep crowding me. The beach and grounding sounds are too far away. Each time my mind wanders it's like a kick to the dick, making me even more frustrated.

I'm in walking distance to an actual lake. Fucking idiot. Why are you trying to think about it when you could do it? I throw the blankets off me, put on socks, walk down the stairs, and put my shoes on.

I have a general sense of where the water is. I can figure this out.

Starting in the backyard, I move toward the water. My mom and I did this once, when I gifted her the house. She was so excited to be this close to water. Seeing her face light up was one of my favorite parts of the trip. I even took a picture of her—she's standing with her feet in the water, almost to her knees, her arms out to her sides and head tipped towards the sky. I had no idea that would be the only time we'd be together in this place. The one she dreamed of.

Fuck. I wish she was here.

While I'm beating myself up and trying not to let the darkness suck me in, I'm practically running on the sand. My breath is quick and barely like I can grab enough air. Pain travels from my shoulders down to my fingers.

I lose my socks and shoes and get my feet in the water. The cold takes my breath away but feels like it could soothe the burn I simply can't shake.

I've always known what comes next. The goal was always the NBA. I made sure I played two years in college to go in the first round of the draft—I was picked second, not first, but it was more than I could've hoped for. After that, it's been growth and building a reputation, so I can stay in the league as long as I want.

Everything else came after. I thought if I could keep basketball, grow that success, anything else would sting less. For a while that worked. It's like, even if I didn't get exactly what I wanted or if things went south, at least I still had basketball. The game kept me together until it absolutely ripped me to shreds.

It feels like there's something on my thigh. Looking down, I see it's nothing but my trembling fingers. Couldn't tell it was my own hands—they're numb from holding a fist. I try rubbing my fingers together and feel nothing, the pads of them numb.

It's shocking but the sky is what catches my attention. Streams of pink, orange, and the glow of yellow as the sun sets. Almost like pieces of summer days, chasing one another.

The brightness reminds me of my mom on the one day we made it out here. A single day. All that time we had and I couldn't make the trip more than once. It's not that we had a lot of time, but it makes me feel like I'm spiraling out of control.

I wasted almost an entire day today. What have I done the last few weeks? The thought of time, life, all of it slipping away is enough to beat me down. It's enough to bring me to my knees. So, that's what I do. Practically crumble into the water, leaning on my knees.

I let my hands fall to my sides, the fingertips grazing the water, waiting for the feeling to come back. The waves push in and around me, soaking my shorts with the lake water.

There's nothing but the sound of water pushing into the beach and then pulling away. The water crashes, sloshes, and brings the icy bite with it. I look to see if I've somehow run into a tourist trap, but some quick glances show me a few people about a half mile down the beach.

It's just me.

And good thing. Because I am a fucking mess.

I can't even cry. The only thing I can do is feel the raw cut of helplessness, darkness, fitting for the sun going down.

The cold should pull me out of it—shock me, shake me, *something*—but it doesn't. It keeps creeping higher, threading around my legs, curling like a hand around my ribs. And somehow that makes the emptiness worse. It seems the lake is trying to remind me that I can still feel, but only the parts that hurt.

My chest feels hollow, scraped out. Not even a bruise. Just...space. Vast and echoing.

The water chills deeper, sliding against my skin until my whole body feels like it's dissolving into it. It's almost a relief—how the cold numbs everything in the way I wish I could numb my thoughts. The ache in my throat, the pressure behind my eyes, the exhaustion that's been dragging at my bones for weeks—it all folds under the weight of that freezing water. Like I'm disappearing inch by inch.

I stare out over the lake, watching the colors drain from the sky, and it hits me how easy it is for something beautiful to fade right in front of you. One moment warm, the next swallowed by gray. I don't know why that makes my stomach drop, but it does. Maybe because I feel like I'm doing the same thing—blinking in and out, losing pieces of myself so quietly that no one would notice until there's nothing left.

My breath comes out harsh, a ghost of steam in the cooling air. I wait for emotion to hit—rage, grief, anything—but all I get is a heavy drag of nothingness settling in my chest. Like the cold has seeped all the way through me, iced over everything that used to spark or burn or matter.

The waves push again, harder this time, and the cold punches up my spine in an almost personal way. My body shudders, but inside I'm still locked up. Still stuck in that dark, hollow space where even my thoughts echo back empty.

I close my eyes, letting the water climb a little higher on my shins, and the only thing I can think is that I don't know how I got here. Not just on this beach, not just in this moment—but here, inside this version of myself that feels scraped raw and used up and...gone.

The lake keeps moving. Keeps breathing. And I sit here, frozen in place, wishing I felt alive enough to do anything.

Ten

SADIE

"Some of us are not professional athletes. Slow down," Maren whines from behind me.

Turning, I look at her over my shoulder. "If one of us hadn't made us late, I wouldn't need to speed walk. Now get moving, you beautiful butterfly, otherwise we're going to miss it."

Maren, being overly dramatic, huffs and then says, "You act like we don't live here. Like. We could do this every night if we wanted to."

"The clouds are going to be working overtime for us tonight." I kiss my fingers like I'm a chef. "I told you, my summer goal is to see more sunsets near the water. I didn't do it nearly enough last year."

That's the thing about summer; it slips away before you can adequately get your hands on it. That was something I definitely felt last year, and it hit me much harder than expected.

I had a great season with our summer rec program—growing both the classes and sessions we offered, the volunteers that helped make those possible, and had more kids than we'd ever had. But I felt empty, burn out singeing my edges. There were other things going on that I'd tried to push down, but they only play nicely for so long.

When fall crept into Golden Harbor, I made a list of things I wanted to try and do over the next three hundred sixty-five days–it was part of pulling myself out of the hole I hadn't realized I was in. That may have been the scariest part.

Not knowing how much I was struggling until I was already knee-deep in it. Something I've always been good at is getting through the lows; at finding ways to grow and view them more as an opportunity than a setback. Not in a toxic positivity way, but more like if I could find a way to spin it in a positive light, then the negativity couldn't take more from me than it already had.

It works until it doesn't.

Maren, wanting to support me, made her own list. Honestly, I feel like it's one of the reasons her flower shop has leveled up the last few months. It's mostly about consistent marketing, which we know is the key to moving the needle, but knowing and doing are two wildly different things.

She catches up with me, bumping her shoulder into mine. "My summer thing is to eat more ice cream. So, let me know when we're making my dreams come true this week, ok?"

We make quick work of the walk and I can feel the smile that's pinching my cheeks. I'm always happiest on the beach—I remember that even from being a kid.

The sun is starting to dip and paint colors across the sky. I'm thankful the beach isn't crowded, a rare occurrence for warm summer nights in Michigan. I put the blanket on the sand, and Maren and I get situated.

I pull my knees to my chest, clasping my fingers in front. The lake has no business being this dreamy right now. The water looks like that fresh, deep blue as perfect waves tip and crash onto one another, pushing in far enough on the sandy beach.

Each second pulls the sun further and the colors start to show. Sunsets are all about clouds. Some people think having a clear day would create the best type of sunset, but they'd be wrong. Clouds are responsible for reflecting back the colors of the sun—which is all of them—and the higher the clouds, the better. Even the mid-altitude ones will work but once you start getting into the low hanging ones, they're more of a deterrent than anything.

The sun keeps dipping and even though it was hot today, there wasn't a ton of humidity—another win. A little humidity is okay, some water droplets not making a ton of difference, but when there's a significant amount, it literally steals the light and the colors. Humidity is a thief.

I watch the sky closely, in complete awe and happiness. Colors spill across the horizon—lavender fading into apricot, gold edging the blurred streaks of clouds like brushed-on light. The sun sits low over the lake, a glowing coin sliding as its reflection stretches across the water in a long, glittering path.

The lake catches every shade, rippling with rose, tangerine, and a burst of coral that look almost painted on. There's no high humidity or fog to blur the edges; everything looks sharper, more substantial.

Maren and I sit in complete silence with a few of the other beachgoers. It's like an unwritten rule, and everyone seems to keep their conversations hushed and close. The feeling of the beach seems to wrap itself around me and it's a sensation I'll chase all summer.

Dusk is quick on the sun's heels, dropping the temp as soon as it gets the chance. It's not until then that Maren bumps into me, pointing down the beach.

"Now, I don't have my glasses on, but I'm wondering if the thing I thought was a rock is actually your almost seven-foot NBA player, moonlighting as a rec league assistant coach."

I look to where she points. She's right. Colson. He's sitting in the water, shoulders rounded with his head tipped down.

Everything about this feels wrong. Seeing him like this. Him feeling whatever it is that's got him in the lake. It's like we're stumbling on a moment that's private.

We stay put for a few minutes—Colson does pick his head up eventually and look down the beach. His side profile was what I needed to know it was 100% him.

"Well, I'm going to walk back," Maren announces, standing and wiping sand off anywhere it may cling.

"No, I can drive you." I stand, pulled out of my wondering why Colson looks like he's mourning on this beach.

She grabs my hand, squeezes, and replies, "You and I both know you're not going to leave him like this."

I squeeze back because she's right.

Maren is on her way back to town, which is only a few minutes' walk, as I stand and contemplate what to do next. Do I wait for him to get up and then call it a night? Do I check on him? Fuck, he'd probably hate that.

Before I can convince myself otherwise, I'm walking toward him. The beach is almost empty now, nothing but the sounds of the water's rhythmic crash and feeling of unease with each step.

I can't explain it; even though I'm almost sure to be met with classic Colson push-back, it's not an option to leave him out here alone.

Ditching my shoes, I leave them on the sand as I step into the warmer-than-expected water. Trying to be quiet, I slowly walk through the waves pushing into the beach.

When I'm next to Colson, I slide down, the water now cooler as it kisses my skin. I don't say anything and I don't even look at him.

But I can feel him look over to me. A minute of silence passes between us, like waves slowly pushing something to shore.

"It was pretty, wasn't it? The sunset." I offer something neutral and try to act like the wind hitting my face isn't about to make me shiver. "Never gets old. No matter how many times I see it."

I see him nod out of my peripheral vision.

When he doesn't say anything, I finally look at him. His cheeks are pink from the wind, but also glistening from tears. He didn't try to wipe them away or hide them, even when I sat down next to him.

His shoulders are rounded and his chin dips almost to his chest. The man looks like he can barely hold himself up. Whatever it is, he's going through it.

A few more long minutes pass and the darkness continues to creep over the lake–some of the stars eager to show off. "Are you okay?" My words are quiet, barely loud enough to be heard over the water.

This time, Colson turns to me, and his eyes feel like they have the power to break me in half. They're practically dripping with sadness. "You don't have to stay here."

"I know. But, I'm already in the water. Sort of committed." I try to make a joke as the nervousness wraps around me.

Shaking his head, he pushes back with, "I didn't ask you to do that."

"I know you didn't. But I couldn't leave you here."

"Why?" He asks like he already knows the answer. Like I'm not the only person who knows the pain of being left behind, in a way much deeper than this beach visit.

"Because I just couldn't. I can't really explain it."

He nods and finally wipes his tears with his sleeve, eyes facing out to the depths of the lake. I try to see what he's watching and the push and pull of the lake soothes me. I get why he's out here–I've done similar things when everything has felt impossible.

We sit for a few more minutes and then Colson stands. He offers me a hand, which I take, both our hands chilled from the lake. He helps me up and without another word, we walk back.

The beach is empty besides the two of us. Colson keeps my hand for a beat longer than he needs to, thumb brushing once against my knuckles before he lets go. It sends a surprising flicker of warmth through me, cutting through the lake's chill.

I pretend I don't notice the way my hand misses his the second it's gone.

Eleven

COLSON

I'm in the car, travel mug full of coffee and nowhere to actually go. But I'm driving. This is something I used to do when I was struggling and I lived in the city—just slip behind the wheel and disappear for a bit. Change the scenery, change the story in my head. No reason I can't do it now.

I have no plan. Drive until I want to stop. Pull over when it makes sense. Try to get space. Maybe find some clarity. Lick my wounds of embarrassment from yesterday.

Last night roars to the front of my mind—the perfect storm of Sadie being there and seeing me. There was no going back from that. Once she saw me like that, we were in it and there was no way I could walk it back.

My phone is connected to the car, playing some of my favorite music. The windows are down and the air whips through. It's early morning—the kind where Michigan feels like it's stretching awake right alongside me. Morning mist clings low over the trees, and the lake looks like brushed glass as I pass it, sunlight skimming across the surface. The air smells like dew and holds the promise of a fresh day.

I wish that feeling reached me.

Instead, something in my chest is tight. Basketball used to be the answer. The one thing that kept me pointed somewhere. Now I don't know if I'm holding onto it out of love or out of fear. What does it mean if I walk away? What does it mean if I don't? Either choice feels like losing a part of myself.

I take another sip of coffee, grateful for the caffeine even though I slept for basically twelve hours after my time at the lake. I was spent. Emotionally and physically The road curls around a line of tall pines, their shadows flickering over the dashboard as if they're counting the seconds I've been avoiding the truth.

And then there's Sadie.

She sat with me on the beach last night—sat in the cold water, let the waves soak her until she was pretending not to shiver, didn't flinch when I fell apart right next to her. She could've walked away. Most people would have. But she stayed, and the way she looked at me... like she wasn't scared of the mess I am.

The way she stayed... It knocked something loose in me, leaving me open in a way I'm not used to.

It's not just last night. She's always like that. Selfless in a way she doesn't even notice. The kids at the rec center adore her because she pours everything she has into them—energy, time, patience. She remembers the little details like the stories they tell, their favorite snacks, and what they need to work on. She lifts them up without expecting anything in return. Seems like that's who she is. Kind for no reason. Kind even when no one's watching.

And for some reason, she's been that way with me, too.

I think about her tall frame beside mine last night. How we worked out at the gym. Her long dark-blonde hair fell down over her shoulders before she pulled it up and away from her face. Golden. I noticed that more than I should've. I notice a lot more than I should. Like how she lights up when the kids are in full force or how she laughs when something is actually funny.

The road opens up again, sunlight flooding the car. I breathe in slowly, and it still feels like something big is shifting. Fuck. I need it. It's like I'm desperate to figure out what to do next.

I'm a thirty year old basketball player. I've made more money than I could ever spend. Honestly, I could walk away from a financial standpoint. That's always been the loudest one. When you grow up with nothing, it's a different type of security.

My shoulder will fully heal. My reputation? I'm not so sure.

The thing I know I'd have to share is the truth about what happened. That day. My recovery. Everything is messy and intertwined and would honestly be people taking my word for it—though I'm not sure how much value that has at this moment.

Do I want to go to that effort? Or do I let everyone think I'm the asshole the team is making me out to be and start over? Move on?

Fuck. I don't know.

But right now, as I'm driving along the lake shore, it feels like I can finally start thinking through some of these questions. Maybe start getting to the bottom of it.

AFTER MY DRIVE, WHILE looking for a piece of paper, I find one of my mom's notebooks. She always seemed to have one with her. Jotting down ideas, to-do lists, things she wanted to get back to. It's pretty unremarkable in the sense that it's just a plain black notebook, one she would've kept in her purse if she had the chance.

Expecting it to be empty, I'm surprised to see her feminine and loopy writing inside. The title has me smiling and is like a punch to the gut at the same time: Golden Harbor Things for Colson.

There's only a few things under the title, but it's clear she was thinking of things we'd do together when we made it back here. During the off-season, I was planning to come up for a two week stretch, get a proper vacation. The thought of her making this list, taking up the space on the first page of a notebook, also means it was probably going to be her summer journal.

My mom loved keeping a journal for each season—I have a whole box of them packed up at her house. When I started going through her things, packing boxes to keep or donate, I found a spot in her closet where she kept them all. She managed to fill them almost all the way up, some having more empty pages in the back than others, but this was one of her most consistent habits.

My lips turn up through the wave of sadness running over me, trying to take me out at the knees. It makes me happy, seeing her writing, thinking of her planning things for us.

The page reads:

-cherry pit-sunset-floral arrangements at harbor blooms-the basement

I don't even know what "cherry pit" means but I have this rush of needing to figure it out. I may have been looking for a piece of paper to make a to-do list, small projects I wanted to do around here, but it seems like I found something else.

There's no reason I can't do these things now. Right? It would've been better with her, that's for damn sure, but it's like fate kind of gave me something to look forward to.

And for now, that seems like enough to keep going.

Twelve

SADIE

Why is Colson waiting for me?

I'm pulling into the rec center and can see Colson, his back against the building. He keeps tucking his hair behind his ears, like he might be a little nervous. My stomach flips when I turn the car off.

It's the first time I've seen him since we were at the beach. It was the weekend, the rec center was closed, and I had no idea if he'd show up again. But here he is, bright and early on this Monday morning.

"What do I owe this pleasure?" I ask, putting a little smile on my lips.

Colson takes a few steps toward me, grabbing one of the bags hanging from my shoulders as I put my key in the lock at the front door.

"Wanted to catch you before you got too busy." His face is softer than I'm used to, blue eyes switching between me and the ground.

The lock clicks, so I push in prop the door open, needing to let some fresh air in the gym.

We walk to my office, where I set everything down, and then I ask, "What's up?" I rest a hand on my hip, needing to do something with them before I start to fidget.

Colson rubs his hands together and then jumps in. "Thank you. For the other night."

"It's no problem. Seriously. Someone has to protect you from rogue waves—Golden Harbor takes its hospitality very seriously," I joke, lifting my hands up.

He lets out a small laugh, breaking the tension a bit. "I don't really know what I'm doing here. This house was my mom's. It was one of the only places I knew to go once everything happened." Pausing, his eyes hit the floor before locking on mine.

I nod, wanting him to continue. His mom... Was. Oh no.

"And, I know I've been rough. Or pouty. Or—"

"You are a master scowler, but continue," I interrupt.

"You've been kind to me. In a way that you didn't have to be. And you keep doing it. And... I just wanted to say thank you."

My chest warms as he strings the words together. It feels like a type of conversation he's practiced. Or at least thought through. Not to be performative, but for him to be more comfortable.

"I'm going to be better. Or, I'm going to try. Fuck, I have a lot to figure out. And scowling actually wasn't getting me all that far."

"Well, if your scowl can't do much, not sure anyone's could. Like I said... master level." I shift my weight on my heels.

He rubs his chin like he's trying to stretch out the muscles, or see if he can feel the lines from said scowl. He should know better; those kinds of lines are invisible and run through your soul.

I knew it before, but Colson standing here in front of me proves it: he's in pain. Something we all are too familiar with in one way or another. It makes me want to wrap him up, pull him close to me, but that would be wildly inappropriate, so I don't.

I have to give it to anyone who wants to try. And right now, Colson Burke is doing just that.

I tip my head to him and he smiles back at me. Fuck. It's almost full, like he really means it, and I swear it steals the air from my lungs. Colson Burke's smile is even more perfect than his scowl—but I don't dare tell him that.

"You're welcome. If there's anything I can help with, in regards to the scowling, let me know."

He nods in a way that ends the conversation.

I walk out to the gym, needing to get things ready for the day. Standing next to the rack of basketballs, I start testing them, seeing which ones need air. Colson sees what I'm doing; when I get one that's a tiny bit flat, I pass it to him, and he pumps it up.

It's comfortable silence as we work through the tasks before the kids get there. We turn the fans on and get the fresh air blowing in, fill up the water coolers with ice, and get some cones out for drills.

"You hanging out today?" I ask as we get dangerously close to the early birds getting dropped off.

"If that's okay, I'd like to." Colson's voice is smaller than I expected.

I nod and reply, "You're always welcome here. The kids love having you."

He lights up a bit when I mention the kids. It's true. He's only been a few times, but when they see Colson, the energy is different—in a good way. Part of me wonders if they're trying to crack him, see the goofy side of the NBA player who showed up for their summer program.

I choose to ignore the piece of myself that's screaming how the kids aren't the only ones. I also like having him here. Obviously, it's easier to do this with more than one adult. But it's a lie to say that's the only thing.

It's Colson. There's something about him. I can't put my finger on it. And I'm happy to have him around until I figure it out.

TONIGHT IS ONE OF those where the clock moves like it's wading through mud. Slow. Dragging. It's the kind of night which reminds me that it's just me and comes with a whole bunch of loneliness. During the day, it's the kids, the rec center, keeping all those things smooth and moving. But now that I'm home, it feels a bit empty.

I pour myself a glass of cherry wine from one of my favorite Michigan vineyards and open my laptop. Staring at the search bar, I don't even know what to enter. After my fingers hover over the keys for an embarrassingly long time, I finally type in "small business ideas".

I end up in a flow of reading stories about people who needed a change, had an idea, and brought it to fruition. Some people opened bookstores, started a food truck, or a storefront with something they made that they decided to sell.

Maybe if I read all these success stories, it'll spark the creativity I've been searching for. I love running the rec center, truly. I make enough to live comfortably in one of my favorite places, and that's not nothing.

I love living somewhere as tight knit as Golden Harbor. As much as I love summer, fall is a close second. Not because of the gorgeous colors and chilly air off the lake, but that's when I get to jump into other businesses whenever they need help. Bartender? Hostess? Barista? All of those things are possible. It's like beautiful chaos and opportunity.

But it's not enough—and I'm not surprised.

Ever since the fallout with Nick, since my life blew up right in front of me, I knew this season would come. The one where I'd have to stop and ask myself what's next.

What Nick took, what's still hard to put into words, was the carefully built vision of our life together. We asked the hard questions. Made real compromises. Bent and adjusted in ways meant to keep both of us happy.

When something like that collapses without warning, when there's nothing you can do to stop it, it's jarring. Devastating.

So I went into survival mode. Built a life one piece at a time. The goal was simple: don't get ahead of yourself. Take on what you can. Function. Reevaluate when you have the energy.

I did the same thing after I tore my ACL. The dream of playing in the WNBA was gone in a second. Well, a lengthy recovery simply proved I wasn't the same player with the same type of ceiling. I was damaged goods and I knew I'd never make it back to the court the same way.

Even now, anxiety hums under my skin, my stomach flipping if I sit with it too long. I used to bargain with myself—if I hadn't torn my ACL, I never would've met Nick, never would've had that life.

But that argument doesn't bring much comfort anymore. Because the man I loved doesn't exist now. At least, not the version of him I'd built my future around.

I close the laptop and set it on the coffee table, the screen going dark. My apartment is quiet in the way it always is. Just me, the low hum of the refrigerator, the soft glow of a lamp in the corner.

There's a sadness which settles in when I'm alone like this and my brain is searching for answers. Not heavy enough to knock the air from my lungs, but persistent. The kind that slips in when no one's watching. I don't cry. I sit with it, letting it take up the space it needs.

I think about all the versions of my life I once planned so carefully. How certain I was. How sure I felt. Now everything ahead feels grayed out. Undefined. And that scares me more than I like to admit.

I curl up on the couch, tucking my feet beneath me, wrapping myself in the quiet. For tonight, I let myself be a little sad for the woman who thought she knew where she was going.

And then I turn off the light, leaving the future for another day.

Thirteen

COLSON

"This may be a dumb question, but does the phrase *cherry pit* mean anything to you? Other than the literal?" I ask Sadie as the last kid gets picked up from camp. I've been helping out over the last few days, and somehow we've fallen into this easy rhythm—moving around each other, working together, trading jabs that feel way too natural.

I've put my mom's list on the fridge–the things I want to try and get to. The first thing on there is *cherry pit* and I still don't know what that even means. I wouldn't say I'm off to the strongest start but it's better than nothing.

We're walking back into the gym to close up when she responds, "Cherry Pit. It's a place. Have you not been there yet?"

"Considering I just asked you what it was, how could I have been there?" I poke, mostly to see that little eye roll she does.

"It's a Golden Harbor staple," she explains. "Every Thursday during the summer, they have these contests... like who can make the best thing. Whatever it is that week. Think cherry jams, cookies, juice, salsa—"

"You did not say cherry salsa. That sounds like a hell no from me." My brows pull together and I definitely judge.

She stops walking and shakes her head at me. "Do not knock it until you try it. Salsa is one of the things that gets two Thursdays! There are so many people who want to participate that they break it up into two different weeks. And it's delicious."

I lift my hands in surrender. "Okay, okay. Whatever you say. No judgement."

We start putting the basketballs back on the racks when Sadie asks, "So, are you free tomorrow night?"

I stop, hands on my hips, the gym suddenly feeling smaller. Her eyes are on me—curious, hopeful in a way that hits unexpectedly hard.

"For what?" I ask, trying to sound casual even though my chest tightens.

Sighing, she rolls her eyes. "Cherry Pit. It's Thursday. The whole thing we just went over," she grumbles while pointing between us.

Wait. What? Does she want to come with me?

"You—ugh." I put my hand through my hair until it reaches my neck. I pull at the skin. "Want to go?"

She side-eyes me long enough for me to think about it. To wonder if that's a flash of disappointment.

"Relax, Colson. It's cherries. Not a marriage proposal."

Her face almost pales on those last two words. I watch her swallow past whatever it is.

"Cherry pit. Yes. Let's do it."

Sadie smiles as she pushes the racks back so they're ready to go for us tomorrow morning.

Us? Who am I? I've found it easy to kind of melt into her rec center schedule. That can't be all that bad, right?

Fuck. Probably.

I don't know. It's easier to let *that* be the thing determining what's on my schedule. The short term version of what's next.

Do you know what I like best? I'm Coach Colson—not NBA player Colson Burke. I know some of the kids and their parents know who I am, a few bringing some things for me to sign in the most quiet and respectful way I've encountered.

No one's blown it up yet. Nothing has been leaked.

After everything is put away, ready for another day of basketball chaos, Sadie's locking the door when I ask her about it.

"Did you tell people? To keep me here a secret? Or something?"

Her eyes catch mine, and in the sunlight it's like they're made of gold. "No, not really. I lightly reminded the older kids to be respectful, the ones who I thought could pick you out of a lineup. But nothing else. Why?"

"People still don't know that I'm here. I was expecting a few days of keeping it under wraps, but it's been weeks."

"You're not the only person who has needed a break, Colson. They get that. Golden Harbor has good people." She says this like she's telling me the time—so sure and clear.

I nod because otherwise it doesn't make sense. Back in Chicago, I've been bombarded at a coffee cart where people were being so aggressive that they bumped me, spilled my hot drink, and one of them tried to sue me for damages. It's hard to envision a place where they let me be.

Maybe Golden Harbor is it? I bought my mom this house because I thought it was something she would love, a place worthy of her. Never thought I'd be the one who also needed a little Golden Harbor in my life.

The universe has a funny way of lining things up.

"Also, maybe they're afraid of you." Sadie shrugs her shoulders, putting the gym keys in her bag. "You have mastered that *leave me alone or else* look."

The air is thick, like it's clinging to my skin. Quietly, I laugh as her hair blows in the summer wind. "Never seemed to work on you."

She pauses, dramatically turning her head to face me. "Nope. I'm not afraid of you, Colson Burke." She pokes me in the chest playfully, and I find myself taking a step back.

It's like something cracks, shakes free. Something I can barely put my finger on. But it feels like someone loosens the ropes tied around me.

Like a reflex, I grab her finger and she laughs. Like we're both on the inside of a joke. The way she fills the space between us has me grinning back—I like that I surprised her.

And then everything slows. The wind almost dies down and a piece of her long blonde hair is stuck to her lips. Without thinking, my fingers delicately reach to her face, pulling the hair from her face and tucking it behind her ear.

What the fuck am I doing?

I cough, letting go of her finger and stepping back, turning it into me going back to my place.

"See you tomorrow, Sadie," I call over my shoulder, trying to hide the grin through my words.

Because I barely know her. But being around her feels like I've finally come up for air.

Fourteen

SADIE

I SWEAR I'M NOT a dramatic person. Not typically. But tonight is definitely challenging that claim.

Because I've been standing in front of my mirror for fifteen minutes, trying to decide if my hair looks better down or half-up. Which wouldn't be a crisis except for one tiny, humiliating detail: Colson tucked my hair behind my ear. Once. And I simply haven't recovered.

Maren walks in and I know it's her because the click-clack of her heels, after the shut of the door, is one of her staples. She comes up behind me and rests her hands on my shoulders.

"You better spill. You're making that face," she announces.

"What face?"

She sits up and points her phone at me like a weapon. "The one that says you have a secret."

"I do not make a face." I do everything I can to soften whatever look I'm giving her.

"You absolutely do. It's rare, considering how we tell each other everything."

I groan and flop my head forward into my hands. "I hate you."

"No you don't," she teases, patting my back. "You hate that I'm that good. Now, let me guess—does this have something to do with Mr. Hot Rage."

I lift my head. "He tucked my hair behind my ear. It wasn't even romantic."

Maren squeals and I'm trying my best not to let the flush hit my cheeks.

She grins. "You like him."

"No, I don't."

"Liar."

"I'm not lying! I don't even know him all that much."

"Okay, then explain why you're acting like you're about to make a life altering decision with your hair." She gestures to my hands that are holding half of it up, again, as I try to determine what looks best.

I stare at her. "Because I want to look presentable."

"Presentable?" She repeats it like it's the funniest word she's ever heard. "Babe. Aren't you going to Cherry Pit? They've had events where they encourage people to leave actual cherry pits on the floors and tables."

"That was one time!" I'm amazed at my best friend's ability to remember almost everything.

She's right. I just don't want her to know that. Something changed that night at the beach. I'd be lying if I wasn't around town that weekend, hoping I'd casually run into Colson even knowing that would be the absolute last place I would find him.

He could've played off the whole thing at the beach as if it never happened. Never bring it up. But he didn't. And the way he was thanking me... I didn't expect it. Maybe that's why this is catching me off guard.

It wasn't a throwaway comment. He meant it. And this could be the start of the steep downfall I feel I may be plummeting towards when it comes to Colson Burke.

I let out a strangled groan and hide my face in my hands, mostly trying to hide my expression. My cheeks hurt from smiling. I hate how much they hurt.

"He's hard to explain," I mutter into my palms. "Like, he's intention-al."

Maren scoots to the edge of her hair, elbows rested on her knees. "Intentional?"

I peek at her. "You know what I mean."

"Sure I do."

"And he's kind. Like unexpectedly kind."

She wiggles her eyebrows. "And tall."

I give her a side eye glance, "He's an NBA player. Typically, they are tall."

"And hot."

I glare at her. "I didn't say that."

"You didn't have to. I'm happy to fill in that blank that you always seem to neglect to mention." Her words drip with the happy type of sarcasm I typically love her for.

I throw my head back, eyes on the ceiling. "I'm doomed."

"Completely," she agrees, "but in a fun way."

My phone buzzes. The screen lights up with a notification for a message from Colson. Maren looks at me and immediately starts to clap. "Girl. I'll get out of here so you can get to your date." She rubs her hands together like she's an evil scientist and her plan is finally going to work.

Blowing out a breath, I argue, "It's not a date."

She puts her hands on my shoulders and lightly shakes them. "Keep telling yourself that."

The realization of the unanswered question hangs between us and I can feel the weight pulling on me from the inside out. Thoughts rush through like they have somewhere to be. Dating. Relationships. Feelings. Leaving.

Maybe that's part of this? Yes, I've been on a few dates since Nick, but nothing has really ever happened that I'd consider serious, or significant. Honestly, I've spent more time with Colson than anyone other than Maren.

When did that happen? One minute he's the ass next door and the rec kids are denting his car; the next I'm meeting him downtown. In between are all the hours in the gym. It sort of came out of nowhere and my brain can barely make sense of the way I'm looking forward to seeing him tonight.

My face must give me away because Maren is all over it. "Are you okay? You know I'm only giving you a hard time, right?"

I nod, unsure of what my voice would sound like if I used words.

Her eyes feel like they're looking into my soul when she gently says, "If you're thinking about Nick, don't. It's been more than enough time and that dickbag deserves no more of your energy."

Like a true hype girl, Maren makes sure to include an insult for one of her least favorite people. I wouldn't say she was ever a Nick fan, but she was happy that I was happy. They bickered whenever we were together and she loved standing up to him, having the upper hand.

A few months before he called off the wedding, she brought it up a single final time. It was like I was living in a romcom and the maid of honor was giving me an out, telling me she'd drive the getaway car. No questions asked. She promised she'd never say "I told you so," a promise she's still kept. When she asked, there was a seedling of doubt, one I chalked up as normal, something everyone harbors when entering into a new phase of life.

Turns out I should've listened to my intuition, because it wasn't long before he was telling me that he loved me, but he fell *in* love with someone else. Have you ever heard such a thing? The casual "I love you, but" and saying it in a way that was meant to feel it wasn't that bad.

Spoiler alert: it was that fucking bad. For some reason, all the feelings of not being enough creep up, like when you're trying not to be embarrassed but everyone can see the crimson of your cheeks like the biggest fucking tell.

Maren lightly shakes me, bringing me back to the moment. "Babe, quit doing that. I can see it. No need to relive, especially now. You're having a fabulous hair day, some hot professional athlete with biceps you could fall into is about to meet you, and Cherry Pit serves booze."

She shrugs and pinches my cheek, touching where they ached a minute ago.

"You're right." I try to shake off the depressing trip down memory lane, like I'm willing myself back to the moment.

She's smiling, looking at my phone, where the unread notification lights up my screen. "Go! Before he thinks you bailed and starts emotionally spiraling like the sensitive king he is."

I smack her arm. "He does not spiral."

"He absolutely spirals."

Her hands land on my shoulders, steadying me. "Deep breath. Have some fun tonight. You are allowed to do that every now and again." Maren wraps me up in a hug.

"Okay," I exhale. "Okay. You're right."

She grins. "Text me updates. Or emergencies. Or if you see him naked!" She's halfway out the door, yelling the last part over her shoulder.

"Maren!" I yell after her, trying not to laugh.

I come back to the mirror, running my hands through my hair another time and solidifying the choice to leave it down for once. It's like the universe knew I needed a pep talk, or whatever Maren was trying to accomplish.

Still blushing, still nervous.

Still hopelessly, stupidly excited.

Fifteen

COLSON

We're meeting at Cherry Pit because the thought of asking Sadie if she wanted me to pick her up was enough for me to break out in a clammy sweat. Instead, I suggested we meet there. Safer.

I know I'm reading into this much more than anyone should. She's being nice. Last week she watched me have a fairly public meltdown and she's trying to make sure I'm not going to spiral. She wouldn't want to lose her assistant coach.

Or that's what I keep telling myself.

I'm walking up to the street, looking for a bench where Sadie said she'd be. The streets are busy with a mix of locals and tourists for the summer. Everyone has somewhere to be, a plan to get to, but there's smiles and an easy type of energy surrounding us.

I love Chicago. It was the first place that ever really felt like home after Michigan. But the energy there, most days, is chaos and business. Nowhere near as much as New York or LA, but people are trying to get to the next thing.

Not in Golden Harbor. People move slower here, walking hand in hand, lingering at a restaurant's host stand set right on the street, smiling as they ask how long for a table. String lights flicker on above the patios. Somewhere, music drifts out of an open door, soft and familiar.

It's only a few more steps until I see her.

Sadie's sitting on this bench, the wind off the lake whipping through her hair which shines with the help of the sun. She's wearing a dress, long and loose, the top kind of scrunched and pulled together. It's this light green color and shows the rosiness of her skin where the tops of her shoulders have been kissed from the sun.

I'm not blind. Sadie in her athletic or coaching attire is attractive, in a way that I can't tell if she knows it or not. But seeing her now? Her face tilted up to the sky, the sun hitting her cheeks, her hair loose and dancing over her shoulders? She's remarkable.

And like she can feel me, her eyes open and light up when she sees me.

"Colson, tell me are you ready for your first Cherry Pit experience?" Her hands rest on her hips and I can't help but stare at her lips shiny and plump.

"I think so?" I nod along. "You... You look–" My words get stuck in my throat.

Sadie tilts her head, eyes like warm honey, and looks down at her dress before catching my eyes again. "Yes?"

I can't help but laugh at myself at the awkwardness. I am the middle school version of myself with the stumbling and words falling on top of each other. Slowly, I swallow past the unease and say, "You look really pretty. That dress. I like the color."

When she beams, I know giving the compliment was the right move. There was no question—my mom made it clear that was a non-negotiable. Something she used to tell me was you never know how hard someone's day was, or how our simplest words could make an impact. I try to carry that through now.

"Let's go pop your cherry," Sadie jokes, a blush creeping over her cheeks.

I can't help the head shake as I follow her inside.

CHERRY PIT IS BIGGER than it looks from the street. Once you're inside, it opens up—long wooden tables, strings of lights overhead, and wide doors pushed open to a patio spilling toward the water. The lake stretches out beyond the railing, blue and endless, like it's got nowhere better to be.

It seems like Golden Harbor does this a lot—hides the good parts until you're already in.

Sadie heads straight for the patio, nodding at someone behind the counter who greets her by name. They know her. They tip their head to me, like they know me too—maybe they do, maybe they don't. Hell, maybe I'm just the random guy out with Sadie tonight. But no one stares. No one whispers. It's like the town has collectively decided to let me breathe.

I didn't realize how much I needed that until I do. Part of me wondered what it'd be like when I got here, ventured out into the city, but the people of this lakeside town have done nothing but let me exist. Fuck, the way I needed this.

We grab seats at a high-top table facing the water. The breeze carries the lake air and the smell of sand, in a way that has me itching for a beach day.

"So," I say, eyeing the paper tasting menu, "you said cherries. You did not say wine."

Sadie smiles like she's been waiting for this. "I absolutely implied wine."

"You absolutely did not. You said *cherries*. That could've been pie. Jam. Or literally anything that doesn't involve me pretending to understand tasting notes."

"Colson," she says gently, "this is Northern Michigan. If there are cherries involved, wine is never far behind. Plus, it's basically juice with a college degree. It's delicious. It's local. You can't go wrong."

She takes my menu, putting it on top of hers on the corner of the table. "Plus, no one knows what the cherry item will be until you get here. It's a surprise."

I look around the patio which is almost full. "Wait, you mean to tell me people show up and don't even know what kind of thing they could be tasting?"

Sadie nods eagerly. "You got it. Unless you have an in with someone who works here and they're feeling gracious. But, it's one of the parts of town that feels charmingly old school. No social media posts. Nothing to check. Just show up and see what's going to happen."

When our server comes, Sadie immediately orders for us. We each get a full tasting flight and an order of fries to share.

"Anything else for you, Colson?" the server—Birdie, based on her nametag—asks.

Hearing her say my name catches me off guard. "No, that should be good," I offer with a small smile.

Birdie turns, wearing a kind of lightness which makes me settle into my chair a bit more. I can still see her walking through the restaurant when Sadie says, "Yes. She knows who you are. No. I didn't tell her."

"Wow. So different from back home," I reflect, sitting back in the chair. The word home feels foreign when it rolls from my lips. Like I'm telling a lie.

She notices my shoulders loosen before I do. Her smile is gentle, almost protective. "Golden Harbor's good like that," she boasts, and the look she gives me makes it clear she's never doubted it for a second.

When the first tasting glasses arrive—deep red, lined up neatly—Birdie explains the lineup: Montmorency cherries from Old Mission Peninsula. Balaton cherries grown farther north, closer to Leelanau. Different soils. Different sweetness levels.

Sadie listens like she's taking mental notes. I pick up my glass and sniff, immediately feeling like an idiot.

She watches me with open amusement. "You look like you're trying to remember how to parallel park. I promise you, it's not that deep."

"I'm being respectful," I reply. "I don't want to offend the cherries."

"They've been through worse," she says. "Trust me."

I take a sip. The wine is tart, bright. Sharp in a way that makes my mouth wake up.

"Well?" she asks.

"I don't hate it," I admit while watching the crimson liquid swish around the glass. What I don't tell her is that it's actually good. Like, I'm wondering if we'll get an opportunity to buy bottles at the end.

Her eyes light up like I've told her a secret. "Wow. Mark the calendar."

The second wine is darker, smoother. Balaton cherries this time—sweeter, richer, less bite.

Sadie nods after tasting it. "These are my favorite. They're kind of overlooked, but they're smooth with enough of a bite."

I glance at her. "You just described yourself."

She snorts. "Better be careful, Coach Colson." She gives me a side-eye glance as she brings the wine glass to her lips.

"I meant it as a compliment."

She studies me for a second, like she's deciding whether to believe me, then lets it go with a small smile.

Birdie drops the fries at our table, including a container of a dipping sauce. She must notice I'm trying to figure it out when she jumps in, "Cherry honey mustard. A staple here."

Sadie has her hands in the hot fries and is dipping them into the sauce before Birdie is even leaving the table.

"Oh my god. This is my favorite," her eyes roll back as she revels in the fries.

Hesitantly, I follow her lead. I take a fry, dip it in the cherry honey mustard, and take a bite. I'm kind of expecting to not like it but it's the exact opposite. The cherry isn't too sweet and seems to be a solid pair for the honey and then brightness of the mustard. It's fucking good.

"Your face is giving you away," Sadie teases, raising her brows. "You love it, don't you?" she questions me as she takes another fry.

Shrugging my shoulders, I agree by taking another fry, heavy on the dip.

"It's good. I'm surprised." I lift my hands in a fake surrender, like she caught me.

She smiles slowly. "You do that a lot," she says. "Pretend you're undecided when you're already in."

Her words have me pausing for only a second. I reach for the wine, taking a small sip.

Because she might be right.

CHERRY PIT HUMS AROUND us—glasses clinking, someone laughing too loud at a nearby table, the smell of cherry in the air. We've got a basket of fries between us we're pretending is communal, even though Sadie's definitely winning.

She's suggested we trade questions and it seems fair enough—or maybe that's the wine convincing me.

"Okay," I say, leaning back in my chair, trying to keep this low-stakes. "Easy one. One place you'd love to vacation."

She doesn't even hesitate. "Italy."

I smile. "Yeah?"

"Yeah," she replies, popping a fry into her mouth. "The fact that carbs are considered a lifestyle choice and not a weakness? Done."

"That's a compelling argument."

She grins. "I would simply eat my way through the country and call it cultural immersion."

I lift my glass. "I respect it."

She clinks hers against mine—and then, without missing a beat—

"Did you ever actually date that model? The one—what was her name—Lena Cross?"

I choke. Just a little.

She watches me try to recover. "Too much?"

"No," I answer, wiping my mouth, heart thudding for reasons that have nothing to do with surprise. "Just... bold."

She shrugs, unapologetic. "Hey. You agreed to trading."

"That escalated quickly."

"That's how I like it," she says, reaching for another fry. "So?"

I study her for a second—how her cheeks pinch when she smiles, the way the string lights catch in her hair, the absolute lack of fear in her eyes.

"Briefly," I admit. "Like a single, almost horrible date. Definitely not in the way the internet decided."

She nods, satisfied. "I thought so."

"You thought what?"

"I don't know," she says lightly. "I feel like it didn't fit."

I laugh before I can stop myself. "What makes you say that?"

"Is that your next question?" Sadie pauses, the wine glass in front of her lips.

Well played.

And I realize I'm already thinking about what I'm going to ask her next—something less safe.

Sixteen

SADIE

THE THING ABOUT TASTING wine is that you never really know how much you've had until you realize you've maybe had too much. Or just enough. Depends on who you ask.

I'm sitting across from Colson and we've had a full tasting, plus a glass of our favorite kind. I'm trying to hide my pure amazement over him. With each minute that passes, it's like he becomes less and less skittish. He seems more relaxed. Comfortable.

His cheeks are also pink. Probably from the wine.

"Okay," he starts, "my turn."

I smile. "Uh-oh."

"You ask about internet gossip," he says playfully. "I get to ask about your last relationship."

I laugh once, surprised, and lift my glass. "Bold."

"Fair," he counters.

I consider skipping it or even talking about another failed date, then decide not to.

"Alright," I answer. "I raise you one very public model date with a called-off engagement."

His brows knit together. "Wait—"

I finish the rest of my wine before he can stop me, the glass clinking as I set it down. "We were together for three years. It felt like the next step."

He already looks like he regrets asking.

"And then," I do my best to keep my voice steady, "he fell in love with someone else."

The table goes quiet for a beat. Not awkward—real.

"I'm okay talking about it," I add, gentler now, because his face has gone careful. "It's been a few years. It sucked but you have to move on."

He nods slowly. "I'm sorry."

"Yeah," I deflect, reaching for a fry. "Me too. But I'm good."

He watches me like he's checking that I mean it.

I do.

The music swells somewhere behind us, laughter floating on the warm air. I glance at him, smiling a bit.

"My turn," I say.

He exhales, half a laugh, half ready to accept the challenge.

OUR FRIES HAVE BEEN long gone. Birdie brought us some fresh bread with cherry apple butter when she brought our glasses of wine—kind of like she knew we'd need something to soak this up. Cherry Pit really only serves bar food during the summer—they're so busy that a full menu hasn't ever done them any good.

I can't stop looking at Colson's mouth. His lips. The way they seem to almost pull into a full smile. How he presses them together when I ask him questions.

A TV in the corner starts playing the NBA Finals. Game seven, winner takes it all. I catch myself watching for half a second too long, and he notices, turning to see what pulled my attention. When he looks back at me, it's like he's wrestling with something. His fingers curl around the stem of his glass, then loosen. Then tighten again.

He moves like someone who hasn't quite landed yet. Like the ground shifted recently and he's still figuring out where to place his weight.

I don't want to watch him bleed over something he can't control. Not tonight.

"So," I start carefully, softly enough that it doesn't feel like a trap. "Ready for the next adventure?"

He blinks, surprised. Not defensive; more like he's been caught.

The game roars behind us, the room reacting in waves, but our table stays quiet. He looks down at his hands like they might have an answer for him, trying to hide the flinch.

"The next adventure? What do you have in mind?"

I stand from the table. "I'm sure we can figure something out."

His eyes lift to mine, searching. Something tender settles there, something grateful and a little stunned, like he didn't expect me to meet him right where he is.

I wave him to follow as we walk outside, the warm summer air wrapping around us. The sun hangs low, stretching everything long and gold, like it's not ready to call it a day yet. Kind of the perfect parallel when it comes to me.

I don't want to go home—not yet.

The wine has settled into me in a pleasant, lazy way—warming my chest, loosening the edges of my thoughts. Everything feels a little softer, a little brighter. It's almost like this June night is leaning in instead of closing down.

We walk through the crowds, nothing too busy but enough to remind me the tourists are still around. Sandals scuff on pavement, laughter spills out of open patios. Someone weaves a little too confidently down the sidewalk, arms wide like they own the night.

Colson stays close without touching, his presence steady at my side. I can feel him even when I'm not looking, like my body's keeping track for me.

The lake flashes between buildings, dark now but still catching the last of the daylight. I match my pace to his without thinking. It feels like we've slipped into something familiar without either of us noticing when it happened.

I should be thinking about tomorrow. About responsibilities. About going home.

Instead, I find myself hoping the night keeps giving us excuses.

"I get it."

Colson looks at me as I say, "Get what?"

"Why you love this place."

His expression softens like it was something he didn't expect to notice. "The lake is hard to beat. Like, the sound of the waves. Having it right there? A dream." He gestures to the water.

I glance at him, catching the faint pink still clinging to his cheeks, the way his mouth curves when he listens. We go to cross the street and I'm not paying enough attention, the curb coming up faster than I expect. I stumble, barely, but enough to break my stride.

Colson catches me without hesitation. His hand wraps around mine, warm and sure, like it's the most natural thing in the world. Like he never even considered not doing it.

"You good?" he asks, steadying me.

"Yeah," I reply, even though my pulse is suddenly everywhere. "I'm good."

But he doesn't let go right away.

His thumb presses lightly at the inside of my wrist, grounding, familiar in a way that makes my chest ache. I can feel the calluses there, the strength he keeps contained, the way his grip is careful instead of tight.

My body feels the sparks. The weight of his hand, the quiet claim of it, the way the world narrows down to this small point of contact. Us on the street, unmoving as people carry on around us.

When he finally releases me, it's hard to hide the disappointment.

I step forward anyway, hoping he didn't notice the way I slow, like I might intentionally stumble again if it means he'll reach for me once more.

The sandwich shop is only a few steps away and I'm immediately grateful for their summer hours.

"Any requests?" I ask as I have one hand on the door.

Colson smiles, shrugging, "No. Whatever you like is good."

Part of me wants to tell him that I'd prefer him. His hands. Anywhere.

Fuck, maybe I did have too much wine.

Seventeen

COLSON

THE THING I LIKE most about Sadie is that she doesn't feel the need to fill the silence. We can just be. That's how it feels tonight, or whenever it's only the two of us together.

We make our way down to the beach as the sun dips lower, the sky stretching itself out in bands of gold and pale pink. The sand is still warm from the day, holding onto the heat like it doesn't want to let it go yet.

Sadie had us stop at her car, grabbing a blanket like this was always the plan. Like she didn't even question whether we'd end up here.

She spreads it out over the sand. I watch her do it, the ease of her movements, the quiet confidence of someone who belongs to a place. I sit when she pats the spot beside her, close enough that our shoulders almost touch.

She opens the brown paper bag, containing whatever she grabbed at the shop. Sadie hands me my half.

Peanut butter and jelly. Cut clean down the middle. A bag of chips between us.

My chest tightens. I pick up my half, turning it over in my hands like it might vanish if I don't pay attention. "How did you know?"

She shrugs, like it's no big thing. "You bring it sometimes when you're coaching at the rec center. Wait, is there an issue with the jelly or something? Is it that you're very specific about a very generic sandwich?" Sadie waits for me to tell her that something isn't right.

I swallow hard. "No, no. Absolutely not. This is perfect. Thank you."

It's such a small thing. A nothing thing. But it feels like proof that I exist in her world even when I'm not standing right in front of her.

I take a bite. It tastes like comfort, like childhood. Like the kind of meal you eat when you don't need to impress anyone.

She smiles, leaning back on her hands, watching the water instead of me. Like she knows better than to make a moment feel heavy.

The sun slides closer to the horizon, turning the lake into something molten and unreal. The air cools, brushing against my skin, and for the first time in a long time, I don't feel like I'm waiting for the next hit.

I don't remember the last time I did something like this. Just... let the night happen. Let myself land in the next thing without a plan or an escape route.

I'm still piecing myself together; it wasn't too long ago that I was at the edge of this lake with a sadness too enormous to contain. Tonight is completely different.

Sitting here, with Sadie beside me, it feels like maybe I don't have to have it all figured out yet. Maybe a piece at a time is enough.

Sadie's dress rides up a little as she settles in, knees bent, sandwich balanced easily in her hands. It's unintentional, the kind of thing she doesn't think twice about.

That's when I see it.

A pale scar curves along her left knee—clean, deliberate. Not old enough to be forgotten, not new enough to still be angry. The kind of mark that comes from something that stopped everything.

I've never seen it before. At the rec center she's always in leggings, hair pulled back, moving with purpose. This feels like a glimpse of something unguarded.

She catches me looking and follows my gaze down, and smiles, small and knowing.

"ACL," she explains. "Senior year of college. We were playing in the NCAA championship, the elite eight. I should've been sitting out but my coach had this thing about not resting starters, even if we were up big."

I look back up at her. "Damn."

She nods. "Yeah."

That's all she says, like it explains everything it needs to.

I glance back at her knee, then up at her face. "You were good," I remark. It's not a question.

She lets out a slow breath. "Good enough that the next step was the WNBA."

Not *in* it. Close enough to touch. My shoulders slump at the realization—the injury took her out.

She nods. "That was the plan. Training camps. Summer workouts. I loved it. If the timing had been different..." She trails off then shrugs, like she's made peace with the sentence ending there. "I tried to rehab and come back, but by then the coaches who'd been talking to me were gone. I was damaged goods." She laughs to herself but it's sad and a bit faded.

Playing with the edge of the blanket, she continues. "Pro sports move fast. If you miss your window, they don't wait."

Something shifts in my chest. Because suddenly it clicks.

Sadie Becker. The way it's always sounded familiar. Not because of her dad—though that didn't hurt—but because I've heard it before. On game recaps. On lists. Whispered with respect.

She was *that* Sadie.

Something tightens in my chest.

Because I know that feeling. The way you obsess and love something. Thinking it will be there for you until you're ready to walk away. The way it still grabs hold of you, even when it's not yours anymore.

Maybe that's why losing my spot with the team hurts the way it does. They took the thing I've loved my whole life. And before that? They wanted me to risk it.

I watch Sadie, the easy certainty in the way she says *I loved it*, and realize something that catches me off guard. I miss the thing that felt like it was in my control. And for the first time since everything fell apart, I let myself admit how much I still want it back.

The sun dips lower, the lake turning molten and still. I don't tell her I get it. But for the first time, I realize I don't only understand her loss—I recognize it.

She leans back on her hands, close enough where I feel the warmth of her through the blanket. I think about how long it must've taken to get back here. How much patience that kind of healing requires. It makes my shoulder injury feel like a papercut.

"How's the shoulder feeling?" she asks.

I stretch my neck, side to side, and then roll both shoulders. "Much better. Needed a little more time for it to heal. But, it didn't really matter after all."

In this moment—when she looks at me without saying a single word—I know I'm going to tell her everything. She's going to be the first person who gets the full story. Given how she told me about her failed engagement, it almost feels like I owe her a little more of myself. Fuck, maybe I even owe it to myself.

"So... the shoulder," I start. "That's part of why I was dismissed from the team." I pause, trying to get my nerves under control, then keep going. "The head athletic trainer wanted me back sooner than I was comfortable with. And I don't mean mostly healed. I mean—" I take a breath, swallow it, and force myself forward. "He wanted injections. Pain meds that we don't talk about. Enough that I wouldn't feel it during the game and could deal with whatever came after."

Her eyes soften immediately. "Oh no."

I nod. "Yeah. He didn't care about the long term. We were finishing the season strong, talking postseason. That was all that mattered to him."

I stare out at the water for a second, grounding myself. "I told him no. More than once. And he made it clear it wasn't something I was supposed to talk about, so I didn't. I kept it to myself."

My stomach drops as the memory surfaces—us in the training room, the way he'd assumed he had leverage. Like I'd fold.

But I wasn't a rookie. I knew my body. I still had years left on my contract and every intention of seeing it through. I was thinking big picture.

He wasn't.

"It was the right call," I say quietly. "I wasn't even close to ready. I could barely lift my arm high enough to brush my teeth. Being on the court wasn't anywhere on my radar."

Sadie doesn't interrupt, doesn't rush to fix it. She listens.

"That must have been hard," she says softly.

"It was."

"So, he got sick of you telling him no? Is that what happened at the game?" She asks this with honesty, like she's trying to understand.

Sadie may be the first person to do that. No agenda. No news outlet to report to. Simply trying to understand what happened during the viral video clip that seemed to take my reputation down in a matter of seconds.

"One of our second-year players pulled his hamstring," I reveal. "It had been lingering for a couple months, but he tweaked it again during the game. We were tied going into the fourth quarter, and it was basically a must-win."

I shake my head. "I overheard the trainer leaning on him. Telling him to keep going. Not to give up on the team. Not to let anyone down."

Sadie drops her head into her hands, and something in my chest tightens—like she already knows where this is headed.

"He's a kid," I continue. "Can't even legally drink yet. And here's this grown man, someone in a position of power, trying to bully him into playing through it. I could see it on his face—how badly he didn't want to go back in. But he started to agree anyway."

I swallow. "That's when I lost it."

I glance down at my hands, then back up at her. "What happened at the end of the bench—that was me stepping in. Standing up for someone who didn't feel like he could do it himself. A player who was legitimately injured and had no business being back on the floor."

I exhale slowly, the weight of it still there.

"And I'd do it again."

Sadie loops her arm around my bicep, easy and sure, like it's the most natural thing in the world. She leans her head toward my shoulder, her warmth radiating through the thin fabric of my shirt.

Something in me gives. Melts. Like I've been bracing for impact and suddenly realize it's not coming.

"Colson," she says quietly. "I'm so sorry."

There's no judgment in it. No attempt to smooth it over or reframe it into something easier to swallow. Only understanding. Space.

Her thumb presses lightly into my arm, grounding, steady. It tells me she believes me. That she sees what it cost me to do the right thing—and how unfair it feels to be the one carrying the consequences.

I let my head tip the rest of the way, settling against hers. She doesn't shift or flinch. She simply stays, solid and warm, like she was ready for it.

For the first time since everything happened, I feel... steadied. Like maybe I wasn't completely in the wrong. Sadie doesn't push for more. Our question game drifts away, unfinished.

For a moment, I wonder if this is the end of the night. But instead, we sit. Quiet. The way we did the other night.

Sadie shows up. The way she has since the first day I met her.

Eighteen

SADIE

Maren doesn't even wait for me to sit down before she asks, "Tell me you kissed him."

I blink. "Hello and good morning to you, too."

She wraps both hands around her coffee, eyes bright with purpose. "Did. You. Kiss. Him?"

"No," I answer, a little too quickly.

Her smile turns slow and smug. "Interesting."

"There's nothing interesting about it."

"Now *that* is interesting," she says over the steam of her coffee cup.

I sigh and lean back in my chair, staring up at the exposed brick ceiling like it might rescue me. "We didn't kiss. We watched the sunset. We talked. It was nice."

Maren tilts her head. "You're glowing."

"Am not."

"You're all smiley. And bright. All sunshiny for an early Friday morning."

I roll my eyes because, no matter what, Maren will not stop until she knows every single detail. It's one of the reasons I love her so much. I pretend to focus on my latte. The café hums around us, but my mind keeps drifting back to last night.

Our makeshift picnic on the beach. The way the sky went soft around us. Colson opening up about everything that happened the night that changed everything.

"Okay," Maren says, tapping the table. "Then what *did* happen?"

I hesitate. That's mistake number one.

Her eyebrows shoot up. "Oh god. What did you do."

"We held hands," I share, wincing.

Maren freezes. "Held hands?"

"It was barely holding," I rush to clarify. "More like... at the end."

Her eyes light up. "Explain."

I sigh. "He walked me to my car. We were talking about nothing, the kind of things you say when you're not ready to say goodbye yet."

I pause, remembering. We'd stopped beside my door, the night quiet around us. There were a few people out on the streets but we stayed on the beach for a while. Neither of us reached for the door handle. Neither of us stepped back.

"And then," I continue slowly, "he reached for my hand. Just... took it. Like it made sense."

A flashback of last night settles in, gentle and warm.

The heat of his palm. The way his fingers laced with mine, unhurried, deliberate. The squeeze—light at first, then firmer—like he was grounding himself. Or maybe grounding us.

I'd squeezed back, my thumb brushing his knuckles without thinking. Not desperate. Not dramatic. Then he thanked me for a good night—the first one in a long time—according to him. I'd be lying if it hadn't sent a jolt of electricity through me.

Back in the café, Maren is staring at me like she's watching something secret be revealed.

"You loved it," she states.

I smile, thinking back. "I really did."

She grins. "Did you squeeze back?"

"...Yes."

"How long?"

"I don't know," I say weakly. "Longer than necessary."

She presses a hand to her heart. "I am unwell."

"It wasn't about kissing," I insist, suddenly serious. "It didn't need to be. That moment felt... complete."

Maren softens, nodding. "Sometimes it is."

I look down into my cup, smiling despite myself. "It was enough."

She lets out a dramatic sigh. "Please explain why I'm kicking my feet over this. I fully expected a steamy make-out story, and instead I'm getting misty-eyed over a damn hand squeeze." She swipes at the corner of her eyes. "I even went to Cherry Pit and asked Birdie about you two."

"Maren," I groan. "That's cheating."

She shrugs, unapologetic. "Sue me. I was excited. And a little bored, okay?"

I roll my eyes and pretend to be annoyed, but I'm not. I take a long sip of my latte, trying—and failing—to hide my smile. No matter what, I love that I have a friend who cares enough to do slightly unhinged things like this.

"Anyway," she continues, eyes wide again. "Birdie told me she heard a lot of laughing from your table." She shimmies her shoulders in a way that has me stifling a laugh.

"We had fun. We did the thing where you trade questions–"

She presses a hand to her chest, already emotional. Maren cries about everything. "Stop. That's my favorite."

I can't help but roll my eyes at her. I love her forever but I know she's about to deep dive. "It was nice. He shared more than I thought he would."

"Of course he did," she adds, voice wobbling. "You know you fucking deserve it. After everything."

I hear her words. I really do, But part of me is afraid to lean into it too far. I don't want to get my hopes up.

Maren lifts her mug in a coffee toast. "To the hand squeezes that ruin you for everyone else. And the bad bitches who deserve them."

I WALK ONE OF the local trails, letting the quiet of a Friday morning settle around me. Each minute that passes brings us closer to the rush of tourists on their way—the inevitable swell which comes with summer in a lake town. Right now, though, it's still calm.

The sun is already warm, amplifying the scent of sunscreen on my shoulders as it heats my skin. Not a cloud in the sky. It's going to be a hot one. I smile to myself, thinking about the local vendors setting up for the day, about cool treats and overworked food trucks, about people giving in to takeout because leaving the beach early never feels worth it.

The trail curves, familiar under my feet, and before I realize it, I'm passing the spot where Colson and I watched the sun sink into the lake.

My steps slow.

A prickle of nerves sit beneath my skin, then comes the smile, the one I don't bother trying to hide. It carries a feeling I haven't let myself have in a long time. Too long.

Hope.

It's the kind that sneaks up on you when you meet someone and suddenly the space you didn't know was empty starts to feel... noticed. Like maybe there's room again. Like maybe the thing you've been missing hasn't been lost after all.

The thought makes me nervous. But as I keep walking, breathing in the warmth of the morning, I let myself wonder if maybe it's time.

Which is quite the jump, considering I have no idea what last night was even about. Neither of us confirmed it was a date. It was simply us spending time together. Me showing him around.

The way he opened up about that night with his team. His injury and the pressure to come back too soon. Colson didn't just open up but he started telling me secrets. Surprising, considering getting him to share anything real about himself has always been a struggle.

I've not talked about my ACL injury longer than I can remember. All the locals know the story, there wasn't anything else to tell. My time as an up-and-coming basketball player is so far in the rear-view mirror that it felt like a completely different life.

Do I miss being part of a team? Sometimes. I think it's the feeling of belonging, being a piece of something bigger and working toward a shared goal. Spending time with people who challenged me, pushed me, made me better.

Tearing my ACL ended my basketball career. It also quietly unraveled most of the friendships that came with it. I still keep in touch with a few former teammates, but it isn't the same. Without the game, the connection thinned.

I came back to Golden Harbor because it felt safe. Like the beach knew me—like it could help soothe the burns left behind by the fallout. I know, deep down, that my next step probably isn't here. But every time I think too hard about what comes next, my stomach twists in on itself.

There's a time and place to face that. This isn't it.

Right now, I need to figure out how to get Colson to agree to help coach the summer tournament.

I started it last year, mostly as an experiment, and it turned into something better than I could have ever imagined. I reached out to a handful of rec centers within a few hours of mine and pitched a basketball tournament. Each center brings teams for three age groups, and we run small brackets for each one.

Last summer it was hosted about thirty minutes away. This year, it's here—in Golden Harbor.

Colson has no idea this is a thing. I feel a little guilty springing it on him now, but if I'd told him upfront, there's no chance he would've agreed. Honestly, the commitment alone might've been enough for him to say no to helping at all.

I need teams confirmed. I need coaches. I need backup plans.

So I add one item to the top of my to-do list:

Get Colson to say yes.

Nineteen

COLSON

I'M ON A LADDER stenciling house numbers above the garage while I think about the third note tucked into the mailbox.

MAIL HARD TO DELIVER. PLEASE FIX VISIBILITY.

I snort under my breath. Like the other two weren't clear enough. How much mail am I even getting here?

I'm situating the stencils, making sure they're straight, before I grab the onyx paint. I step down a rung, tilt my head, then adjust the stencil by half an inch. Can't really screw this up without a ton of cleanup so taking my time seems like the move.

I'm trying to be annoyed at the ask for the address numbers to be visible, but honestly, it gives me something to do. A distraction. So I'm not running through the same thing over and over again.

Last night.

Sadie, sitting on the beach with the sunset painting the sky, reflecting into the water. The way she listened. The way she didn't rush me when I started talking. How easy it felt to open my mouth and not regret it immediately after.

She was gorgeous. Not in a trying-to-be way. In a grounded, unguarded way that made it hard to look away once you noticed. It's not the first time I caught myself staring, but it was the first time it was only the two of us for a while.

I climb back up the ladder, happy with the stencil placement, and set the small can of black paint and paintbrush within reach. Carefully, I dip the brush and start filling in the stencil.

I'd rested my head against hers, made it okay for us to be like that. That alone feels dangerous to think about.

Sadie Becker. I won't pretend I didn't Google that name last night and read a ridiculous amount of news articles, even watched some highlights. Fuck, she was a special kind of player. One that could've made a difference for the sport. My chest squeezes when I think about how an injury, a fluke, took her out with no whisper of a warning.

My shoulder feels really good today, serving as a reminder of how I'm still capable. This will fully heal and I could come back to the court. To the game.

Maybe I could.

That's the difference between me and Sadie. I kept thinking about how if I hadn't seen the scar or asked her about it, I'd have never known. I've been so wrapped up in all my shit that I quickly realized I don't know a whole lot about her. Her life was supposed to be different, but here she is, smiling like it's her job and spending her summer with kids. The contrast isn't hard to decipher. I'm a moody bastard and she's gracious, full of a glow I can't quite put my finger on.

"Wow," a voice says from below. "Didn't realize you were an artist."

I freeze. Like an idiot, I wonder if I've thought about her too long and she's simply appeared from the universe.

I look down to see Sadie standing at the end of the driveway, sunglasses pushed up into her hair, carrying a tray of two coffees and a brown paper bag. As always, her smile is absolutely unapologetic.

"You—" I clear my throat. "How long have you been there?"

"Long enough to confirm you have more talents than advertised," she says.

I scoff, finishing the number I started, then set the paintbrush down. "It's a stencil. Not much talent required."

She laughs, stepping closer, shading her eyes to look up at me. "You look good up there." Her voice is velvety smooth.

The bag is stamped with the bakery logo, matching the coffees. The lightbulb goes on as I cross my arms across my chest. *She's going to ask me for something.*

I climb down, suddenly aware of the ladder, the house, the spot of black paint on my index finger.

She looks around before her eyes land on me. "I was actually coming to find you," she admits. "Wanted to ask you…"

My stomach tightens on instinct. I knew it.

"Dangerous sentence," I say.

She shrugs. "You'll live."

She takes a breath, suddenly more careful. "We have a basketball tournament. A few local rec centers come together to play against each other. A few weekends in August. And I was wondering if you'd help coach."

There it is.

I hold back a laugh as my chest goes tight. My mind races ahead of me, already inventorying ways I could mess this up. Commit and not be enough. Say yes and disappoint her. Get too close to the thing that still hurts.

"I don't know if that's a good idea," I say slowly.

She nods, like she expected that, but something shifts anyway. Small. Tucked behind her eyes. "You don't have to answer right now."

Sadie sets the bag and the tray down, grabbing the coffees, and offering me one. I take it carefully, our fingers brushing for half a second too long before she pulls back.

Too quick.

"I mean—I get it. It's a lot," she continues, talking faster now. "A few weekends is a commitment, and you've got things going on, obviously. And I probably should've mentioned it earlier instead of just showing up here, like you don't have anything to do. Clearly, there are things on your list." Sadie gestures to the ladder.

She laughs, but it doesn't quite land. Her weight shifts from one foot to the other. She won't look at me.

"I thought it could be fun? But it's totally fine if you don't want to—" She finally looks up, eyes searching. "—or if you don't want to spend that much time... here."

With me, hangs unspoken between us.

My chest tightens. She thinks I don't want to spend time with her.

"Sadie," I say gently.

"Seriously. I can ask someone else. I have other options. Don't feel like you have to-"

I interrupt her again. "Sadie."

She stills.

I take a breath, hoping to still the shaking fingers I know are about to show themselves. "I don't want to let you down," I admit, the words tumbling out before I can overthink them. "That's what this is."

Her brow furrows. "What do you mean?"

I grip the coffee cup, trying to get a hold of myself. "I'm afraid if I say yes, I'll find a way to screw it up. You need someone you can count on and I'm not sure that's me."

I look at her then. Really look. Her eyes seem more understanding with each word, soft and hopeful like your morning coffee. The silence that follows me coming clean about my anxiety is different.

"It's not about not wanting to be around you," I continue quietly. "It's about being scared that I'll disappoint you if I am."

Sadie exhales slowly, some of the tension leaving her shoulders. "Oh," she says. "Okay. That's... not what I thought."

"I gathered that." I bring the coffee cup to my mouth, taking a sip.

A small smile returns to her mouth—careful, but real. "I think you're someone I can count on." She swallows past something, taking a step closer to me. "The fact that you're worried about it shows me you're the right person to ask."

Her words swirl around me, like when you're trying to get warm in the winter and the blanket on your shoulders finally helps. Sadie, with the right amount of pressure to make a decision.

She thinks she can count on me. Fuck. That means more than it probably should.

"Honestly," she says, gentler now, like she's giving me an out on purpose, "let me know when you make a decision. Either way, I'll take your assistance—any way you can offer it." Sadie tips her head toward the rec center, sunlight catching along her cheek, her collarbone, the bare skin of her arms. The morning light hits her just right, warm and unfiltered, like it's trying to make a point.

Something in my chest tightens; not with fear this time, but with the urge to step into the space she's offering. To say yes because I want to be near her. Because I want to see that smile again when things go right. Because I want to be part of something that feels hopeful instead of heavy. Because I like how I feel when I'm around her.

She gives me one last look, patient and kind, before offering me the brown bag. "Cherry scones. They're almost impossible to get unless you're there when they open." She shrugs her shoulders.

Her thinking of me this morning is enough to push me into a decision. I can't imagine telling her no.

"You're good at this." I tip the coffee to her before opening the bag, the smell of sugar and cherries making my mouth water. "I'm in. I'll help you with the tournament. If it's possible, don't put my name on any coaching roster or anything."

"People will recognize you. You know that right?"

Nodding, I reply, "Yeah. I do. Hopefully by August, I'll have things figured out."

I kind of like the idea of having an internal timetable—the thing that will make this situation different. Everyone will know that Colson Burke has been hanging out in Northern Michigan. I'm not sure it even matters, but flying under the radar has definitely made things more manageable.

I take a bite of the scone and it's better than it smells. The tartness of the cherries mixes perfectly with the sweetness of the base. Crunchy sugar is on the top.

"Tell me how good it is," Sadie says, waiting for my confirmation. Her mood has completely shifted from the nervous and panicking woman a few minutes before. "You've got—" She gestures to the corner of my mouth.

My hands are full with coffee and the bag in one and the scone in the other. I try to use my shoulder to get it but Sadie laughs, meaning I'm probably unsuccessful.

Her fingers lift, hovering for half a second like she's checking herself. "Can I?"

I nod. I don't trust my voice.

She brushes her thumb lightly against the corner of my mouth. Slow. Careful. Like she's aware of exactly how much that touch matters. Her hand lingers a beat too long.

Everything slows. The pad of her finger is still close to my bottom lip.

The space between us shrinks. My focus narrows to her eyes, like glinting amber. I tilt forward without meaning to. I swear, she does too. The urge to kiss her runs deep, as if it's something I've pushed down more than I'd care to admit.

For a split second, I'm sure this is it. We're a breath away, so close, I can almost taste her.

Her phone buzzes loudly between us. We both flinch and step back.

"I should go. And you," she takes another step back, "have stencils and paint."

Desperate to respond, I say, "Thank you. For the coffee."

"You're welcome." Sadie smiles, turning to leave, glancing back at the last minute. "Try not to fall off the ladder, Coach."

Twenty

SADIE

THE GYM IS CLOSED for the Fourth of July, but the building doesn't care about holidays. Neither does the weather.

Rain pounds against the roof hard enough that I can hear it even over the echo of my footsteps on the court. It's been coming down for hours now—steady, relentless—and the forecast says it's not letting up anytime soon.

I stand barely inside the doors, keys still in my hand, watching water drip from a seam near the far corner. Not a flood. Not yet. Just enough to make my stomach twist. I know there will be a similar situation in the storage closet. That's how it's always been when we get lots of rain, like we are right now.

In my dream world, we'd have permanently fixed it, but that hasn't been in the budget. The center has been operating on razor-thin margins ever since I took over.

Drip. Drip. Drip.

I grab a bucket from the storage closet and slide it under the leak—the one I was right about—the sound changing pitch as the water hits plastic instead of hardwood. The room smells damp, the kind of air that settles in when rain finds a way inside. Finding the other buckets, I grab them and head out to the gym to catch the others.

Maren's out of town. Birdie's husband, the one other person I'd usually call for help, texted back saying they were a few hours away. I scroll through my contacts anyway, knowing it won't change anything.

Colson. He's next door and could probably lend a hand. My finger hovers over his contact before I decide against it, putting my phone back down on the bleachers.

I don't want to push him. Not after everything. Not after I showed up to his home, with coffee and a snack, asking him to give up even more of his time to help coach for the tournament.

This I can figure out on my own.

My gaze drifts to the court, to the painted lines and empty bleachers, and my mind slips back without asking permission to when the kids found out he'd be coaching the summer tournament.

The way the room exploded—cheers, disbelief, kids jumping up and down. Colson stood there with his hands in his pockets, trying to play it cool. He didn't want it to be a big deal but the kids were so excited.

"Settle down. It's only for now," he'd said, shrugging like he wasn't lighting the whole place up just by being there.

But I saw it. The way he softened when they crowded around him. The way he smiled when he thought no one was looking. Like the game still had its hooks in him in a way he may not have thought about.

I don't want to be the reason he feels obligated. I don't want to ask for more than he's already given. Even as part of me wishes that he'd walk through the doors anyway, like he belongs here.

And if I'm busy thinking about him with the kids, then at least I'm not spiraling over the almost kiss. Me, standing in the middle of his driveway, basically holding his hand hostage so he couldn't deal with that rogue crumb. Honestly, I couldn't have planned it better if I'd tried.

There was nothing else at that moment. Just me. Colson. My thumb brushing past his lip. The way he dragged it through his teeth right after, like he was trying to ground himself. I swear he could hear the way I swallowed—past the nerves, past the anxiety—trying to hold on to it all.

Now, is this the first time I've thought about kissing Colson? No. Not really.

But those thoughts usually belong to my dreams, where he has a habit of showing up unexpectedly—sometimes with a shirt on, sometimes very much without. Apparently, my subconscious spends a lot more time thinking about Colson than my awake, supposedly reasonable self, ever admits.

It wasn't even the *almost* kiss. It was the wave of disappointment that hit me as I walked away—the tightness in my chest, as if something was pulling and pressing all at once, mirroring the drop in my stomach. The walk home along the trails was spent wondering what it would feel like to give in.

Something slams against the outside of the gym—probably a rogue branch—and snaps me back to the present. The rain hammers harder against the roof now, wind howling around the building.

I exhale and grab another bucket.

This is part of the job, I know that. Facilities. Maintenance. The unglamorous stuff that never makes it into the highlight reel. Still, standing here alone, watching the building fight the weather, the quiet presses in a little heavier than usual.

I need tarps. The realization hits me and I'm annoyed I didn't think about it in the first place. The issue is that the tarps are outside in the tiny storage shed. Reluctantly, I go to my office, grab my rain coat and zip it up.

Maybe the forecast has changed.

That's the hopeful—and slightly delusional—thought I have as I open the weather app for probably the tenth time today.

A red banner flashes across the top of my screen: **SEVERE WEATHER ALERT.**

I exhale through my nose, already bracing.

Severe thunderstorm warning. Flash flooding possible. Hail expected.

I stare at it for a second longer than necessary, like if I wait long enough it might revise itself. Downgrade. Apologize. Tell me that I don't have to go outside, wrangle the tarps and get them situated.

Instead, the rain hammers harder against the roof, punctuating the message.

"Of course," I mutter, slipping the phone back into my pocket.

The building groans lightly around me, water finding new paths no matter how many buckets I line up. Whatever hope I had that this would be a quick fix drains away with every roar of thunder.

This isn't going to stop anytime soon.

Twenty-One

COLSON

The sky has that look to it, the one that matches the weather alert that popped up on my phone.

I've lived through enough Chicago summers to recognize the shift: the air goes heavy, the wind changes directions and acting like it's fading, only for it to sprint back. The unexpected thing about living near a lake is how quick the wind picks up and turns a bad storm into something personal. I move through the house on autopilot, checking windows, latching the loose one in the back, pulling the garbage cans into the garage.

The rain comes down in sheets and is almost sideways. It pounds against the glass, louder than it feels like rain should be. I'm tugging the last window shut when I see her.

Sadie's crossing the parking lot toward the rec center, jacket zipped up, hood pulled tight around her face. She's wrestling with a blue tarp that's clearly winning. The wind snaps one corner loose, yanking it sideways like it's got a mind of its own.

She stumbles but quickly regains her footing. I think she's going to leave the tarp behind, get inside, but she doesn't.

"What the hell?" I mutter.

She's trying to juggle the tarp and the door at the same time, rain pelting her in the face. Another gust catches the tarp and sends it billowing, the plastic cracking loud enough that I hear it even through the glass.

My chest tightens. Why wouldn't she ask for help?

Without thinking, I move. I'm bolting out the door, barely getting my rain jacket on, the wind slamming into me the second I step outside. Rain needles my face as I jog toward her.

"Sadie!" I shout.

She turns, eyes wide in surprise as the tarp tries to take flight again. I reach her in two strides, grabbing the loose corner and anchoring it against my side.

"What are you doing?" I ask, having to be loud enough to fight the wind.

"Just need a tarp. I've got it." The wind shifts, making us turn our faces in order to catch our breath. "I've got it."

"You're kidding. You do not have anything!" I yell, taking her place in front of the door, holding it open and giving her the leverage to get inside.

Once we're inside, dripping water in the gym entrance, something is heavy on my chest.

She laughs breathlessly, half-relieved, half-exasperated. "I was managing."

"You were losing," I say flatly.

Thunder cracks overhead, closer this time. Sadie takes the tarp, trying to shake the water out. She uses a towel to try and take care of the rest of the rain water on the tarp, struggling to handle the awkward size of it. Still, she doesn't ask for help as she takes a few steps into the gym.

Her water-drenched shoes are quick to slip and I'm thankful I'm following her, so I can catch her.

"Sadie. What the hell are you doing?"

She barely acts like I'm there, not making eye contact, focused on the task. "There's a few leaks, no big deal. I'll put the tarps under the buckets and we'll be good."

Scoffing, I say, "No big deal? You were almost airborne with that tarp out there. And let's not forget you almost falling on your ass, cracking your head open, with your wet shoes." My tone is sharper than I mean. "Did you call me and I didn't answer or something?"

I try to make sense of her doing this on her own. Especially when I'm right next door.

"I can handle a leak or two. Didn't want to bother you."

Something tightens in my chest at that. Not anger, exactly—something closer to regret. Like she decided somewhere along the way that needing help from me was asking for too much.

I rub my hand over my face, still damp with rain. "Next time," I urge, softer now, "you ask."

She looks up at me, rain clinging to her lashes, jacket plastered to her shoulders. "Okay," she says quietly.

I look past her then and see a few buckets spaced across the gym floor, water tapping steadily into plastic.

"You asking for help isn't bothering me," I insist, more to myself than to her.

I take the tarp from her hands before she can argue, fold it tighter, already turning toward the doors. "Where's it coming in?"

She points, surprised, and I head that way, rain still thundering overhead.

It comes easily, stepping in like this. And with it comes the realization that sticks—I don't want her carrying things alone because she's afraid of asking me.

BY THE TIME WE finish getting buckets and tarps set up inside, it's clear the storm hasn't let up.

We push through the doors and I stop short. Water is already creeping across the road in front of the rec center, pooling where it shouldn't be, swallowing the curb line completely. The rain turns the asphalt into a moving sheet, reflecting flashes of lightning like it's alive.

The rec center sits low. My place—the summer house—is farther up, perched on a small rise that suddenly feels a lot more intentional than aesthetic.

Sadie pulls her hood tighter and glances toward her car. "I should probably head home while I can." She pulls her keys out of her pocket.

I turn to her, disbelief crawling through my chest. "You're kidding."

"What do you mean?"

"There's flooding. You're not driving through that."

She pauses. "It's not that far."

"That's not the point," I argue, sharper than I mean to.

She hesitates, clearly uncomfortable, then says, "I don't really want to stay here."

I scrub a hand over my face, irritation flaring—not at her, but at the fact that I even have to say this.

"You're not staying here," I say flatly. "And you're not driving."

She looks at me, rain plastering her hair to her jacket, eyes searching like she's trying to figure out the least inconvenient option.

I sigh heavily. "For the second time tonight, let me remind you... my place is next door." I gesture towards the house, my words sarcastic and annoyed—exactly how I meant them.

Her eyebrows lift. "Colson—"

"I'm not arguing with you about this. Driving through flooded streets isn't safe, especially with a bunch of tourists who are doing god only knows what. Now, don't make me carry you." I gesture in front of me, wanting her to move, as the rain continues to fall, cool on my skin.

Thunder cracks overhead before a strike of lightning quickly follows, close enough that she flinches. Sadie exhales slowly, resignation mixing with relief. "Okay. Fine."

I nod once and follow her as soon as she starts making the way toward the house. I'm annoyed that I had to offer. More annoyed that she was about to do her second careless thing in a matter of minutes.

And even more annoyed by how right it feels to make sure she's safe.

Twenty-Two

SADIE

I've seen Colson simply detest the existence of the world, be annoyed at the smallest things, like the sun being out in the summer and he can't find his sunglasses. But right now? His annoyance, or whatever he's feeling, is next level.

And it's my fault.

Right now, I'm trying to distract myself from this fact and focus on the things around me. I've never been inside Colson's house until now. And one thing's for sure—this isn't what I'd ever expect. Everything is so light and has the type of put-together colors and patterns that screams this wasn't his call. Like, there's no world I live in where Colson asks for these lovely yellow kitchen cabinets.

There's nothing besides the sound of my teeth chattering together and the rain dripping down my back, soaking me to my bones. My cheeks sting from the wind, viciously energized from the lake.

I'm looking around, cataloging the details of the parts of the house I can see, when Colson hands me a towel. I pull at my jacket zipper and he helps me take it off, hanging it on a few of the entryway hooks.

I pull the towel around my shoulders, trying to warm up. Looking down, I see my shirt is sticking to my skin. Damn. The wind and rain were no match for my jacket.

The tension between us is smothering; I'm almost afraid to move. Maybe I'll dry out in the entryway and Colson can go on with his night before the storm and I crashed it.

"Are you really just going to stand there?" he asks, as I'm contemplating how long I think I could stand in a single spot. He puts a kettle on the stove.

"As soon as it's safe," I say quietly, "I'll head home."

Colson's head snaps up. "Why?"

I shrug, embarrassed heat creeping up my neck. "Because I am not your problem. This isn't your problem. And because"—I gesture vaguely—"you're clearly mad."

"I am mad," he agrees with me.

My stomach drops because knowing it and hearing someone say it are two different things. "I know. I'm sorry."

He laughs once, sharp and humorless. "You don't even know what I'm mad about."

I frown. "I think I get it." It's hard to look at him, so I get a quick glance before focusing on the kettle heating on the burner.

"No. You absolutely don't get it." He steps closer. "You, standing out there in that storm?" he says. "That's what I'm mad about."

I blink. "I was handling it."

"No," he says immediately, "you were risking it."

"It's not that big of a deal."

"That's bullshit. We're talking about taking cover sort of weather and you're out there and then you're about to drive home?"

The words land heavy between us.

He continues, voice tight. "I watched the road flood, and when I think you're finally going to realize it's too much, you don't. You have your keys in your hand and all I can think about is how much you would rather risk instead of asking me for help."

I cross my arms, defensive. "I didn't want to push."

"Why?" he asks.

The question is quiet. Dangerous.

"I didn't want to be a burden," I admit. The words feel small and almost pathetic on my lips.

Something breaks across his face.

"That," he says, shaking his head and pointing to the words as if they need emphasis, "is the part I can't stand."

"Believe me, I know there's a lot you can't stand."

Colson scoffs, puts his hands on his hips, and looks around the room like he's looking for the next move. The puzzle piece. When his eyes are on mine, I suddenly can barely breathe. They are like waters I dream of swimming in.

He goes still. For a beat, the only sound is the rain hammering the roof. He says nothing as he walks toward me; when he's standing only a step away, all I can think about is how I wish I could get my teeth to stop chattering. His face softens as he takes a breath. "You know what I can't stand? How much it hurt for me to see you out there. How panicked I was. How the only thing I could think about was getting you inside and keeping you safe."

The words are honest and clear. His eyes scan my face like he's trying to find the tell. The way he looks at me is like the answer should've been obvious all along.

He cares.

My chest tightens as his hands grip my upper arms. When they rub the towel, like he's trying to keep me warm, he continues, "I don't know when it happened, but you matter in a way I wasn't prepared for." He looks around like the words may or may not be on the ceiling.

And then he says, "You fucking matter, Sadie."

Did I feel a pull to him? Yes. But I never thought it was something he also felt. My dreams were the only place a version of this conversation could happen.

"I do?" The question feels rhetorical but I'm trying to keep this all straight.

"Yes. You do. And I can't sit back and watch you do things like that." He tips his head toward the outside.

His chest rises and falls quickly, matching his breathing. My hand, pruny from the water, lightly rests on him, the feel of his muscles underneath my palm grounding me to the moment.

Silence crashes down, thick and trembling. I stare at him, the truth finally clear in a way I can't ignore.

Gripping the front of his shirt, trying not to lose my nerve, I say, "Then take care of me, Colson."

Before his name is off my lips, Colson is kissing me.

Twenty-Three

COLSON

I couldn't take it anymore. Or at least that's what I'm telling myself.

When Sadie leans into me, her hips pressing flush against mine, the groan that tears from my chest surprises us both. I'm moaning into her mouth, into this kiss that's turning messy and desperate in the best way. Her lips part a little, and I take the invitation without thinking—brushing my tongue against her lower lip, tasting her. Then she meets me, her tongue sliding against mine, slow at first, then sure.

A brief, breathy sound escapes Sadie, right into my mouth, and it does something reckless to me. It's almost unraveling the knots in my chest that have been pulling each time we've been together.

She loops her arms around my neck, pulling me closer, like she's afraid of the space. Believe me, she's not the only one. I let go of her wrist and slide my hands to her waist, my thumbs pressing into soft skin, which is pebbled with goosebumps, anchoring her there.

Like she knows exactly what I'm about to do, she dips slightly. I lift her, her body fitting against mine like it's always belonged there. Her legs wrap around my waist without hesitation and her fingers slide into my hair. At first they're gently combing through, but then she tugs, enough to make my breath hitch.

I don't break the kiss. I can't. I turn us, moving through the kitchen and down the hall to the bathroom, muscle memory and need guiding every step. She pulls back barely, long enough to catch her breath, her forehead brushing mine.

"What are you doing?" she asks, voice gentle but curious, like she already knows the answer.

I steal another kiss before I reply, slower this time, deliberate. "Taking care of you."

Her laugh is quiet, shaky, but she doesn't argue. I set her on the counter, my hands lingering at her hips as I step back only enough to turn on the shower. The sound of rushing hot water fills the space, steam already beginning to curl into the hallway—warm, promising, and full of what comes next.

I step between her legs as her hands run up and over my chest. I rush to taste her and she bites at my bottom lip. She uses her hand to push me back, her eyes taking in the scene around her.

"Is this real?" A grin pulls at her lips.

I answer her with a kiss and my hands on each side of her face, like I can't touch enough of her. I stop only to say, "Yes, this is real."

The way Sadie smiles into the kiss is something that cracks my chest open. Makes me *feel* from the top of my head down to the tips of my toes. It's in this moment I know this is different. This kiss is everything. It's hot. It's running deep. It's the kind that has me in deep fucking trouble.

At the end of the kiss, she's trying to hold back. "Arms up." I say, giving her the room to make a choice, tell me if it's too much.

Sadie tells me yes when she doesn't hesitate, lifting her hands from my shoulders and holding them above her. Her lips pull up one side, like she's daring me; one I'm happy to accept.

My fingers find the hem of her shirt, soaked and sticking to her skin. Slowly, I pull it up and off of her.

She grabs her elbows like she's trying to stay warm. Or maybe she's trying to hide behind them? Sadie's wearing a black bra and she's fucking gorgeous. Her eyes go to the floor. Fuck, maybe she's embarrassed?

I step closer and hook two fingers under her chin, lifting until she's looking at me. Her lashes flutter like she's bracing for something.

"I've dreamt of this moment," I admit quietly, honestly.

"You have?" Her voice comes out breathy, unsure, like she doesn't quite believe she could be the thing haunting anyone's thoughts.

"Obviously." My mouth curves, but my gaze doesn't soften. I let myself really look at her—at the creamy stretch of exposed skin, her tense shoulders, the way her forehead dips again like she's trying to fold in on herself.

I lift her chin once more, this time stepping in so close my nose nearly brushes hers. My voice drops. "Don't do that. My sunshine girl." I press my forehead to hers for a beat. "I don't want you hiding behind anything. I want all of it."

She inhales in short, shaky breaths, eyes flicking up to mine and then holding there. Something shifts—fear giving way to want, uncertainty softening into trust.

"Sunshine girl?" Sadie asks, and she's fucking beaming, the nickname landing perfectly.

I move before she can retreat, placing a kiss at her collarbone. Just one. Slow. Reverent. My hands brace on the counter on either side of her thighs, boxing her in without trapping her. I trail my mouth across her skin, following the line of bone and heat, each kiss deliberate, unhurried, until I reach the top of her breasts.

My tongue tastes her skin, warm and familiar already, and I feel her react—feel it in the way her body leans toward me without her even realizing it. My hands slide to her thighs, fingers digging in like I need the anchor.

I lift my mouth and move up, lips brushing her ear as I whisper, "Are you okay with this?"

Her hands move to her back and she unclasps her bra, pulling the fabric from her and tossing it. She props herself on her hands, leaning back a little, showing off.

"That's my girl," I murmur while dipping down, putting a nipple in my mouth. Immediately her hand finds the nape of my neck and she pulls me even closer.

One of my hands grips her waist, feeling her muscles flex and flinch underneath me. I love feeling her respond to me this way. I use the other hand to pinch the nipple I'm not tasting. The contrast between rough and soft causes Sadie to moan through the pinching as my tongue laps at the other.

My dick throbs against my briefs. I step back, pick her up off the counter and hook my fingers in the waistband of her leggings. I start pulling them down before she starts to help.

A black lacy thong is staring at me as I'm on my knees to help get her naked. Fuck. She tries to hide the shiver.

I stand, taking off my pants, and her eyes jump to me straining against my briefs.

"You can't look at me like that," I joke.

"I just... I mean—" She pushes her lip through her teeth. "You're—"

I don't let her finish. I step in and kiss her, slow and deep, stealing the words right out of her mouth. Then I trail my mouth up her neck, unhurried, deliberate, until I reach her ear. I bite gently at her earlobe, enough to make her gasp.

"Take your panties off," I murmur. "Get in the shower."

She listens. She always does.

It takes *everything* in me not to drop to my knees right here and ruin us both on the bathroom floor. Instead, I force myself to breathe, to watch as she slips past me and steps into the shower.

Steam is already curling through the bathroom when I step inside. She's standing under the spray, arms wrapped around herself again—not hiding this time, bracing against the heat. Water beads on her skin, tracing paths I want to memorize. I peel off my briefs and step in behind her, the door pulling shut with a quiet finality.

The water hits my shoulders, hot and grounding, and she leans back instinctively, her spine finding my chest like it's always known where it belongs. My hands come to her waist, steadying the two of us. I can feel her warming up, melting into me.

"Still okay?" I ask, low, close, my mouth near her temple.

She nods, breath hitching as my thumbs brush slow, reassuring circles into her skin. I hold her, facing the water, and when she's no longer shivering, she turns to me.

Her hands touch my chest and when she looks up at me, eyes bright and sparkling with honesty, I know it's fucking over.

In this moment, it's clear. Sadie Becker is mine.

Twenty-Four

SADIE

The way Colson looks at me is something I've never experienced. It's like he's taking mental photos, trying to remember every detail. It makes me feel confident. And like there's no such thing as too much time with him.

Each look, kiss, touch has me falling under his spell.

I turn to face him, letting the water hit my back. His hands move my hair from my forehead, fingers warm from the water. I might be five foot eleven but Colson still has six inches on me. He tips his head down until his nose is almost brushing mine, his thumbs on my cheeks and his eyes keeping me in place.

His thumbs brush against my skin and I can barely breathe. The steam surrounds us and I ask, "How do you do that?"

"Do what?" The soft skin between his brows knits together.

"Make me forget how to breathe," I say.

The promise of a devilish smirk threatens his lips and he takes one of my hands, putting it on his chest. "Feel that?"

My fingers against his chest, his muscles, is quite the fucking sight. I let my fingers feel before I realize he's talking about his heartbeat. His racing heartbeat.

"That's what it's like to be around you." His voice is breathy. "You make me want to…" The words fade as he looks away.

"What?"

"Touch you," he admits, like he's telling me a secret. "Everywhere."

His words wash over me, the water having no chance to be as impactful.

I kiss him like he's something I need, something I can't go without. I bite at his full lower lip. When I pull away, I swear I can see flames dancing in his deep blue eyes.

"Then do it," I dare him.

A searing kiss is shared between us as his hand trails down my body and I bite at his lip. His hand lightly cups me until he tests my wetness with the tip of his finger.

Colson's mouth pulls from mine and he bites at my ear.

"Wet. Like a fucking dream."

I can't help the moan that escapes my chest.

"You, Sadie Becker, are a fucking dream."

My knees quiver; they're struggling to hold me up. I know Colson would never let me fall. Fuck, why is that so hot?

"You good?" he asks, his finger teasing me.

"Yes." I can't answer fast enough.

Slowly, he inserts a single finger. He gives me a little bit before pulling out, the pace too slow. My hips tilt, trying for more.

Colson adds another finger and I keep using my hips.

I'm so desperate for him to go faster so I take things into my own hands. I reach down, wrapping my fingers around his dick, which is hard and heavy in my grip. He pumps his fingers inside me and I jerk him.

His lips kiss my neck and when my fingers squeeze him, he groans. I love making him react this way.

"I want you."

"You have me." His voice is breathless as I work him.

"I want more. I want—"

"Tell me what you want," he interrupts.

"I want you to fuck me. I have an IUD so you don't need a condom." I'm so nervous proposing something like this. It's all risk and need but that's exactly how I feel.

"I'm safe for you, baby," Colson says, eyes locked on mine.

I bite my lip and that's all it takes. He lifts me, carefully pushing my back against the shower wall. He kisses me, hard, and even though I have him, it doesn't feel like we're close enough. I want him everywhere.

Colson Burke is about to fuck me in the shower.

That's the brief realization I have when I put my hands on his shoulders. His muscles tense as he situates himself.

He positions his cock at my entrance. "I hope it fits," I whisper. The words surprise me; I think I meant to keep that as an internal thought and it fucking slipped through the cracks.

His mouth is ravenous, tongue tangling with mine. And when he pulls away, he says, "Baby, we'll make it fit." His jaw is tense and his words would have me dripping if I wasn't already. "This pussy? It's mine," he growls.

It's almost like he's telling me the sky is blue. Yes. Obviously.

I kiss him, whimper fresh on my lips, and he lets gravity do some of the work. I knew he was big—my eyeballs and my fingers around him proved that—but when he's stretching me, I find myself sucking in air.

Colson keeps me up against the wall, pulling out then pushing into me a little further. He keeps letting gravity pull me further onto him. The way he starts to fill me is unreal. I've never been with someone like this.

"You're so fucking tight." He pulls out, giving me a break, and pauses. "Are you okay? Do you want me to stop?"

"If you stop, I will *not* be okay," I whine, scratching at his shoulders.

He gives me more. And more. It burns in a way I can't get enough of. I'm squeezing him and he's got an angle that has me about to see stars... and it feels like we're barely started.

"That's all of it, sunshine girl. That gorgeous cunt taking me so well," he groans.

His mouth? I'm a goner. I tip my head back, catching a look of Colson, all muscles and not a scowl in sight. I almost have to pinch myself to prove I'm not dreaming. Because he's looking at me like I'm special. Something to treasure. Like he can't bear to miss a second.

Then he starts fucking me the way I've dreamed of. My back is pressed tight against the wall, and my arms help hold some of my weight as he thrusts into me. He lifts me like I'm nothing. Fuck, it's so hot. I've never been with someone this strong, who has me feeling light as a feather.

He pushes in deeper, stretching me, but it feels like I'll never get enough. The spot in my low belly aches and is about to catch fire. Pricks and sparks are on the verge of taking over.

A moan creeps out before I can help it.

"Oh, fuck. I'm close." Colson's eyes roll back a minute but he doesn't stop.

"Colson—" I whine, desperate for him.

My fingers scratch down his chest and he captures my mouth with his. He bites at my lip, harder than I expect, and it brings me closer to the edge. The one I'd willfully toss myself over. Pleasure threatens to kill me at this rate.

"You saying my name..." One of his hands pulls at my hair before finding my ass, kneading it with his fingers.

"Colson..." I tease, stretching out each sound of his name.

His pace picks up and I'm holding my breath. My heart hammers in my chest, loud and unrelenting, like the way my pussy aches around him.

My orgasm tears through me, damn near violent and aggressive, but I wouldn't want it any other way. I can barely catch my breath as a scream rips from my throat and bounces from the walls. It's like I have pinpoint vision but can feel everything a thousand times more intense.

He grunts with the final thrusts and I'm spiraling around him with my climax. I feel his cock twitch and throb, and Colson stills as he pours his release in me, the steam from the shower enveloping us.

I hold on to the edge of my orgasm as it pulls me through another dimension, and I feel Colson's cock still inside me.

"I'm never getting over you. I hope you fucking know that," Colson groans, kissing me hard and promising.

He's not the only one.

Twenty-Five

COLSON

My mom had a couple candles around the house, ones that have never been lit. I find a matchbook in a drawer and hand them to Sadie, who starts lighting the ones she can find.

You're not supposed to open a fridge or freezer when the power goes out but luckily, I don't really have any food that can go bad. I pull out the block of cheese and preserves, and get to work on the one thing I can really offer Sadie: a peanut butter and jelly sandwich plus cheese and crackers.

Once a few candles are lit, she sits on the counter, legs swinging, watching me like this is the most interesting thing she's seen all day.

"PB and J?" she asks, amused. "You really know how to impress a girl."

"Careful," I say, spreading peanut butter like it's a sacred ritual. "This is a *craft*. Balance matters."

She laughs, the sound warm and easy. The room shifts as the glow spreads, casting soft shadows, gold light catching in her hair. It feels quieter somehow. Like the house is holding its breath.

I line up the cheese and crackers on a plate, then add a spoonful of preserves on the side.

"Now, the real question is," I can hear the smile behind her words, "what is your preferred sandwich shape?"

I hold the knife above the sandwich, stretching out the answer like it's something that holds weight.

"The right way," I say as I cut the bread diagonally. I offer her a plate; when she goes to take it, I pull it away and lean in. My lips find hers and she laughs into it.

Sadie hops down from the counter and takes the plate, her fingers brushing mine briefly, but it's enough to send a spark up my arm.

"Thank you," she says, quieter now. She takes a bite, eyes closing for half a second like she's really savoring it. "This is perfect."

I lean back against the counter, watching her eat, feeling like I'm right where I'm supposed to be. If you would've asked me two months ago where I'd be in July, there's no way I could've called this: my mom's summer house, in the middle of a storm, with a woman who is like sunshine incarnate.

Sadie wears one of my T-shirts, baggy on her, and a pair of my socks. That's all she requested. I need someone to tell me how this woman looks this fucking drop dead gorgeous in my kitchen right now. Her hair is damp, towel dried, and she's fresh faced.

I swear, it's like Sadie can soften the edges. All the things I'm uncertain of, all the shit I haven't dealt with yet—it feels less when she's around.

"Don't forget about the charcuterie." I nudge the cutting board in her direction, which has a single type of cheese and cracker.

She doesn't hesitate when she eats a piece of cheese and exclaims, "Ah, you got the good stuff." Her brows lift and push into her forehead as she continues to taste. "This is definitely from Tom's."

"No, it's from—" I stop to look at the wrapper on the counter. "The Cheese House," I declare, proudly showing her the label.

She laughs and nods. "Yes, that's Tom's place. He's the owner and the only cheese monger Golden Harbor has to offer. Did you get it from there or from the store display?"

"Cheese monger?" I laugh at her. I know it's the formal title for someone who runs a cheese store, but again, I didn't expect the conversation to go to Golden Harbor's residential cheese monger.

Shaking my head, I continue. "Damn. You seem to know everyone." I put a piece of cheese on top of a cracker and pop it in my mouth. "I grabbed it at the store."

"Oh, Colson." Sadie's hand goes to her hip; the way she says my name has me paying extra close attention. "You're missing out. Samples! We have to do a cheese tasting."

We.

I'd be lying if there wasn't a warm feeling running through my chest, reaching my fingertips and stretching down to my toes. She's making plans.

Wind howls and whips around outside, slamming branches into the windows. It makes Sadie jump. I pull out my phone to check the weather app, and see the same types of alerts. I show the screen to Sadie.

Her shoulder slump as she says, "Wow, nothing like a soggy Fourth of July weekend. We get storms like this but they're usually short lived."

Sadie walks to the front windows in my living room, peering out. The roads glisten as lightning strikes, water still rushing over parts of it. When she turns, worry knits into her features. I'm sure she's thinking about the rec center next door. But out of all the things we can't control, weather is at the top of that list.

"Don't worry. We'll take care of it together." I tip my head toward the general direction of the place I know is pulling at her.

Sadie doesn't say anything but I can tell she's still thinking about it.

She changes the subject. "Doesn't look like I'll be leaving any time soon." She comes back to her sandwich, taking a bite.

"What a shame," I joke, catching her eyes with mine. "You'll have to stay here tonight."

As if on cue, she yawns. I gather the dishes, put them in the sink, and reach for her hand.

"Come on," I say and try not to smile too big when she puts her hand in mine.

I lead the way up the stairs to my room. She follows without saying a word. The only sound is the rain and wind pummeling the house. If it weren't for that, I'm almost certain she could've heard the heartbeat that pounds in my chest, echoing throughout my body.

I keep my grip loose, like I'm giving her an out, even though my chest tightens at the thought of her taking it. At the top of the stairs, I hesitate—only for a second—because this all seems too easy.

But she's still there. Still warm. Still choosing this.

I open my door and step aside, gruff and careful, like I'm handling something breakable. And for the first time in a long while, the quiet doesn't feel empty—it feels full of something I might actually want to keep.

Twenty-Six

SADIE

My bones are exhausted and my muscles feel like they're about to give up but I can't stop smiling anyway. Colson holds my hand until we're in his room. Even in the dark, it's there—soft and unguarded—as I step inside and turn on my phone's flashlight. The beam sweeps over pale walls, clean lines, wide windows which let in light from the lightning. The space feels open, airy which is so unlike the man hovering in the doorway like he's bracing for impact.

I let the light wander. "This place is... bright," I say, smiling so he knows it's a compliment. "Even with the power out. Those yellow cabinets downstairs? They're kind of perfect." I tilt my head at him. "You don't strike me as a yellow cabinet kind of guy."

He huffs and drops onto the edge of the bed. Putting a hand to his chest, he says, "Who? Me. Are you sure?" The question is flat and rhetorical.

I follow him, tucking my legs beneath me, the mattress dipping as I settle in. He shifts, fidgeting with the blanket, tugging at the edge like it's suddenly not right.

Colson takes a deep breath, one I can feel in my own chest.

He looks outside, gazing through one of the wide windows when he continues, "It's not really mine. The place..." he says after a boom of thunder. "This was my mom's place. Her summer house."

"Oh," I reply, warmth blooming despite the dark. "So is she—here? Or coming up later?" I can't help but let the excitement run into my words. The thought of meeting Colson's mom has me almost kicking my feet.

His hands still. Then he scrubs one over his thigh, his gaze fixed on the floor. "No," he answers quietly. "She died last fall."

The words land softly but firmly. I turn the flashlight off without thinking, the room going fully dark again, and reach for his hand instead. Suddenly the brightness makes sense—the yellow, the open space, the light that lingers even when everything else goes out.

Poor Colson. That's all I can think. How the man isn't so much grumpy as he is sitting in his grief.

I shift closer and wrap my arms around him, careful at first, like I'm not sure he'll want it. Colson does. He exhales and folds into me, one arm coming tight around my back, the other lifting to thread slowly through my hair. The touch isn't rushed but it feels like he needs it, pulling me closer to him.

"Do you want to talk about it?" I ask, my mouth close to his ear, resting on his shoulder.

He squeezes me tighter but I push back, wanting to see his face.

"The diagnosis came out of nowhere. She made an appointment because she was ridiculously tired. She couldn't sleep enough. But she was an active person. Always running to this club, doing this thing, meeting this person. Flying to my away games." His voice shakes when he shares that last part.

After a moment, he continues, "I thought she was burnt out. It turns out that stage four pancreatic cancer will also do that to you." His thumb brushes the same spot near my temple again and again.

My heart feels like it's about to crack open.

"I went with her to her first appointment with the oncologist." Colson's voice is jagged and rough. "At that point, we had no idea what to expect. There was this feeling of fight and hope that she brought with her. Like, no matter what, she could take it. That's how she'd been my whole life."

A small smile threatens his mouth when he says, "I was so proud of her for how she walked into that appointment. The way she was ready to fight anything, head on, no questions asked."

Even in the darkness, I can see his face drop. The memory of that day coming back to him.

"But it only took a minute with the doctor to understand how bad it was. They tried to soften it. Prognosis, timelines..."

My hand pushes through his hair slowly. I move the hair from his forehead, over and over, until I let my hand rest at the nape of his neck.

His words are rushed, like they're trying to step on each other. "I had all these questions. I was grasping at straws. Thought if I had the right ask, we could find the answer. That's how she always was."

Sadness punctuates his explanation.

Colson presses his lips in a thin line, closes his eyes for a beat. "The doctor was softly letting me down. My mom squeezed my knee, shook her head, then interrupted me. She looked at the doctor and said, '*Don't whisper. I'm not afraid.*'"

My chest aches, but I don't interrupt. I don't ask questions he's not offering answers to. I simply hold him and listen.

"This is her house. I bought it for her. It was a few months before she got sick, so she never really got to use it. But she did the decorating...everything is exactly what she wanted. She wanted light," he continues, quieter now. "Yellow cabinets. Big windows for natural light." He swallows. "This place was never sad to her. I think that mattered."

Colson has had a rough season. Not just in life, but if his mom died last fall, that would have been right around the start of the NBA season. He escaped here. To the place that his mom had such a heavy hand on... it's her, with walls.

I wrap my hands around his arm closest to me and lean my head on his shoulder. He tips his head, resting on mine, and it feels like his exhaustion is wrapping around us.

"There aren't words," I say, quietly. "But I'd love to hear about your mom. Whenever you want to talk about her."

"Thanks."

We sit there for a while as the storm continues to rage. I'm going over our interactions from earlier this summer—how pissed and bothered Colson seemed. It was so much more than the stuff going on with this team.

I can't help but think about that night at the beach. Him in the water. Us together, sort of like this.

I don't know how long it's been before Colson stands, pulling the blankets back on his king-sized bed, and lays down. I follow suit and when we're both under the thin blanket, Colson lifts an arm.

We don't say anything. Instead, I lay my head on his chest like it's the only option. And in my mind? It really is.

I listen to Colson's heartbeat, feeling the rise and fall of his chest, as I do my best to calm my thoughts. And with every minute that passes, I melt deeper into him until sleep swiftly pulls me under.

Twenty-Seven

COLSON

I'VE SEEN BEAUTIFUL THINGS in my life but this view may be at the top. Sadie is snuggled up to my side, one of her legs over mine, her head on my chest and her arm thrown over me. It feels like she's holding me close–keeping me to herself–and I have to remember that she was sleeping and these were most likely subconscious choices.

Her dark blonde hair shines as the light hits it from the window. I soak in the moment of her breathing into me and the flutter of her dark eyelashes. Birds chirp in the morning and it's quite the contrast from last night.

Last night.

Did I intend to spill my guts about my mom? No. Did it feel like there was another way? Not really. It felt very much like it was the time to tell the story. She was calling out all the things my mom would've loved to hear—would've been music to her ears—how light the house felt. Not many people know those details.

Even when I tried telling May, who was supposed to be the person who could help me through this, she kept telling me to stop. It was too sad. It wasn't the right time. She'd always let me get to the opening pages of a story, details from a doctor's appointment or a visit with my mom, until she'd wave me off.

She told me it was too much.

At first, I was kind of waiting for Sadie to find a way to end the conversation last night. But in the dark, with the storm pounding the house, it was clear she'd let me go for as long as I needed to. At no time did it feel like she was crowding me or waiting for the right length of pause to jump in and pivot.

I've been running from a lot for a while. Maybe this is also part of why this is hitting me so hard. I didn't have many people to talk to about my mom's diagnosis, the logistics of treatment, and—when it came to it–supporting her as she died.

Kevin did his best but it was so hard to open up. Especially after May kept making it feel like I was such a burden. My coaches kept tabs on what was happening, but at the end of the day, they were running a business and had a lot of shit going on with the team.

The doctor suggested therapy and a support group. My mom and I went to therapy a few times together, mostly to make sure I knew the best way to take care of her, making sure she got everything she wanted when it came to worst case scenarios.

She wanted to be prepared because that meant it would be easier on me. My mom may have never said it, but that's how she always was; how she sacrificed for me her whole life.

This place? She made it clear that I was to keep it. Use it. Take the trips. Swim in the lake. Make time for the moments she never got to.

Everything has been so complicated since finding out she was sick. It was all the appointments, therapy, logistics, and then fitting all of it in alongside basketball and my commitment to the team. But one day, she had a setback and never really made it out of it. The end was quick and I was thankful. I never wanted her to suffer.

May left me shortly after, still reeling in a wave of depression and grief. If I was too much for her before the loss, there's no way she could be there for me at that time. Honestly, it felt like I'd lost her a long time before the day she actually left.

Then it was the injury. Everything with the team. The slimy athletic trainer. It feels like I've been punched while I'm down for longer than people should be allowed to.

This morning feels different. Like it's the lightest I've felt in a while. It's not that things are perfect, or simple, or really even all that clear, but it feels like there's a bit of hope for me to grab on to.

Sadie starts to stir and when she picks her head up, eyes on me, I can't help the smile that breaks out over my face.

"Good morning," I say as she rubs her eyes.

"Morning. But your smile is kind of throwing me off," she jokes as she sits up, putting a kiss to my lips and then looking out the window.

"You've definitely seen me smile." I roll my eyes in fake exasperation.

"Whatever you say." She shrugs her shoulders.

Fuck, she's pretty.

She squints toward the window, sunlight pouring in like it's making up for lost time. "Looks like the storm finally gave up," she says, then her smile fades a notch. "I should probably go check on things. Make sure nothing's... floating away."

I catch the hesitation underneath it—the way her shoulders tense like she's bracing for bad news. "Hey," I say, more gently. "I'll come with you."

She looks back at me, surprised, then relieved, like she didn't realize she wanted the offer until it was there. "You don't have to."

"I know," I reply, already swinging my legs out of bed. "I want to."

Sadie stands and puts her hands on her hips, weight on one leg like she's testing me.

I walk towards her. "There isn't a world where I'm staying here and not going with you, so..."

Her smile returns, smaller but real; when she laces her fingers through mine, it feels easy. Like whatever comes next, we won't be facing it alone.

Twenty-Eight

SADIE

I WISH I WERE still in bed with Colson. That would be much better than this disaster in front of me. Instead, I stand there with the door dinged up from something crashing into it, keys still clenched in my fist, staring at the wreckage like my brain... refuses to catch up.

The smell hits first—wet drywall and soaked wood, heavy and sour, like the building is already starting to rot from the inside out. Every step sounds wrong. Glass crunches under my shoes, sharp and unforgiving. Somewhere overhead, something drips steadily, a hollow *plink... plink... plink* that echoes through the open space, each drop stinging as a reminder of the water that doesn't belong in here. Sunlight spills through the broken windows in uneven stripes, lighting up dust and bits of debris still floating lazily in the air.

"Oh my god," I whisper, the words falling flat in the cavern of the room. I expected it to be bad but this is much worse.

Part of the roof is just... gone. Torn open like a can lid, insulation hanging down in clumps, framing a sky that feels way too cheerful for the mess below it. Dark water stains snake down the walls, bleeding into the paint color I agonized over and was so proud to paint by myself a few months back.

I take a few steps forward and Colson reaches for my hand.

"Careful," he says.

I look at the court, which I'm hoping is covered with debris and isn't actually damaged. My chest tightens when I see the cubbies. The wooden ones I had custom built—measured, planned, paid for with money I probably shouldn't have spent—are swollen and warped at the bottom, the grain split and buckled where the water continues to sit.

I let out a shaky breath. "I don't even know where to start," I murmur, more to the room than to him. My throat feels tight, panic buzzing beneath my skin. How am I supposed to fix this? How am I supposed to make this safe, functional, *ready* again?

My knees buckle when I look at the sheer amount of damage, then think about what it will cost. I dip down, head in my hands. I try to breathe but it feels like something is sitting on my chest.

Colson steps closer, grabs me by the arms and lifts me back to standing. He studies the damage like a problem to solve, not a failure to mourn. "Okay," he says calmly. "First—we breathe."

I huff out something that's not quite a laugh. He glances at me, squeezes my hand once, grounding. "We've got a few days," he reminds me. "Fourth of July break. No kids, no programs. Time's not breathing down your neck yet."

I look at him then, really look, and something in my chest eases a notch. "You really think so?"

"I know so," he answers, already scanning the space again. "Roof guys, insurance, cleanup crews. We prioritize—what's unsafe, what's salvageable, what can wait." His thumb brushes over my knuckles. "You don't have to figure it out all at once."

"Even if we could logistically do this... cash is going to be an issue." I blow out a breath and gesture vaguely at... everything. "Believe it or not," I say dryly, "this isn't exactly a high-dollar operation with a giant emergency fund tucked away."

Colson snorts. "Shocking."

"I'm serious," I add, glancing at him. "This place runs on tight margins and duct tape optimism. I'm craftier than I give myself credit for."

He nods once, already thinking. "Okay. Then I'll help take care of it."

I stop walking. "No."

He turns, eyebrows lifting. "Sadie—"

"I appreciate it, but no," I say quickly. "I'm not taking your money."

"You're not taking it. Consider it a donation, or a loan—"

"That's still your money."

"And?" he counters. "You pay me back when you can. Or don't. We'll write something up if it makes you feel better."

I cross my arms, fighting the urge to argue just to argue. "You need it."

A corner of his mouth curves. "I hate to be this person, but I have more than enough. Don't worry about what I need." He steps closer, lowering his voice. "Let's see what's what first before we get lost in the details, yeah? Plus, I don't know if you know this or not, but I'm slated to coach one of the summer teams that's predicted to win a championship. Getting this place up and running isn't only about you," he says while stepping over a piece of the roof that's landed on the court.

A sad laugh escapes my mouth, one I can't help. I rub my hands over my face. "Fine. Okay."

He smiles and it grounds me. "Good. One thing at a time."

The building groans as a breeze moves through the broken windows, bringing in the summer air off the lake, the way it does after a storm. Colson stays steady beside me, solid and sure.

AFTER THAT, EVERYTHING SHIFTS into motion. Not graceful, not easy—but forward.

We start with photos. So many photos. I walk the perimeter while Colson follows, pointing out things I would've missed—the way the roof peeled back, the pooling water near the cubbies, the glass sprayed farther than it should've reached. I spend what feels like an eternity on hold with the insurance company, pacing in slow circles, repeating details through clenched teeth while the place creaks and settles around us like it's still deciding what it wants to keep.

While I'm talking, Colson disappears. I don't even notice at first—too busy explaining square footage and storm damage and trying not to sound like I'm one inconvenience away from unraveling. When he comes back, his arms are full: heavy-duty gloves, tarps, brooms, contractor bags, bottled water. Like he'd been doing this his whole life.

"Green light for cleanup," I tell him when I hang up.

"Good," he replies, already pulling on gloves.

We start with the glass—slow, careful sweeps across the court, the sound sharp and constant, catching sunlight with every movement. We drag out the bigger chunks of debris, stack what can be saved, toss what can't. My shoulders ache, my hands sting, but the work is grounding. It keeps the panic at bay. It feels good to start tackling some of the work—I like the feeling of progress.

We've barely started sweeping when I hear my name.

"Sadie?"

I look up and my chest loosens instantly. "Maren."

She's already crossing the court toward me, ponytail half-falling out, sneakers splashed with mud like she didn't even stop to think before coming. "I saw the weather alerts last night," she exhales, pulling me into a hug. "And then I remembered you telling me about the leaks. I wanted to make sure everything was okay." Her voice sounds like she's answered her own question.

I laugh, a little breathless, pressing my forehead to hers for a second. "Of course you did."

She pulls back enough to look at the damage, eyes widening. "Okay. Wow. This is... worse than I imagined." Then she looks back at me, all business. "What do you need?"

Before I can answer, Colson steps closer. "Hey," he greets, offering his hand. "I'm Colson."

Maren glances at his hand, then up at his face, a brow arching. "Oh, I know," she replies easily, shaking it anyway. "I'm in a fantasy basketball league. And Sadie does not bring just *anyone* around the camp kids."

I groan. "Maren."

She grins, already grabbing a broom. "Relax. I approve."

Colson laughs and asks, "Am I on your team?"

Maren grimaces when she answers, "You were last season. That's when I won the championship. But, someone stole you in this year's draft before I could get my hands on you." She mimics grabbing something.

Colson crosses his arms, nodding. "Well, happy to hear I could lead you to victory."

The way the two of them bounce off each other, it's a nice change of pace, but definitely wish it was in better circumstances.

"Now—where do we start?" Maren asks, rolling out her neck and shoulders, like she's ready.

Colson's mouth twitches and we get back to work. The building still groans, the damage still stares back at me, and nothing about this is solved. But Maren is here. Colson is here. The weight doesn't disappear—but it shifts, spreads out, and becomes something I can actually carry.

Twenty-Nine

COLSON

PEOPLE KEEP SHOWING UP. Maren was here for a few minutes and it was clear she immediately started gathering the troops. There are probably ten locals busting their asses to get all the debris cleared, mopping floors or drying walls. Massive fans have been rolled in, trying to dry out as much as we can.

Everyone's trying to be positive and encouraging but this place is a mess. Broken windows. The roof. Water damage we probably can't see. Sadie is doing her best to stay solution oriented. Fuck, that makes me proud of her.

She has these bursts of energy. Hope. But then it topples when something we didn't foresee becomes an issue. Her and I have our hands on the antique cabinet—the one I helped bring in during my first few days there.

We count down and lift at the same time. I'm walking backwards when I say, "If you want, we can go thrifting or something. Try and find something old and creaky. Just like this one."

Sadie offers a loaded but sad smile. "Colson Burke likes to thrift, huh?"

"My mom used to go a lot when I was a kid. That's how we got most of our things. Single parent stuff."

Sadie nods, taking in the details I'm offering.

She doesn't keep the conversation going; instead we walk the cabinet outside to the place we've designated as trash. Things that are unsalvageable.

Birdie, one of the only people I recognize besides Maren, taps Sadie on the shoulder.

"I called about the windows. My brother had an in, so we have those measured and ordered."

"How much are they?" Panic creeps around Sadie's question.

Birdie says nothing, just looks over to me. I made it a point to let everyone know I would handle anything financial related. There wasn't much that we moved on today, but windows are kind of a must for the center to be able to be open to the public.

Sadie realizes what's happening and gently nods.

Birdie looks at her watch. "I had someone getting my opening stuff done at Cherry Pit but I gotta get over there, okay?"

Sadie and Birdie hug, saying their goodbyes, and you can feel the local business owners are kind of on Birdie's timeline. In a tourist town, weekends like the Fourth of July are massive. They've given what they can and need to get back.

It's amazing how quick people learned of Sadie needing help. How many people came and gave a few hours of their time without question. Golden Harbor seems to show up for their locals.

Everyone sort of dissipates, then it's only me and Sadie sitting outside on the picnic table.

The sun is high and relentless, baking the asphalt and turning the damp air into something thick. Somewhere down by the bay, someone's already testing fireworks like it's their civic duty. The whole town feels wound tight, buzzing with the energy of a holiday weekend.

Sadie sits hunched forward, elbows on her knees, staring at the ground like she'd been running on adrenaline all morning. Now that the crowd's gone, it's catching up to her. She looks exhausted, even though it's barely noon, and quiet in a way that's much louder than the panic.

I shift on the bench. "Okay," I start gently. "Talk to me. What do you need right now?"

She blinks, like I've asked something complicated. Then she shakes her head. "I don't know."

"That's an acceptable answer," I tell her. "We've got time. But let me point out that we haven't had coffee. Or food. That *could* be a start."

She presses her lips together, nodding once, like she's considering it.

I try again. "You want to go home? Shower, crash for a bit. Get some time to yourself?"

As much as I'd willingly spend all of the day with her, I'm not sure that's what she needs.

Her head snaps up. "No."

Butterflies immediately come to life and I fucking love how quick her answer was.

"No?" I repeat.

She sighs, rubbing a hand down her face. "I don't want to be by myself. That's no fun." Sadie stands, rubbing her hands on her shorts. "You need to experience a Golden Harbor summer holiday."

I don't hate that answer.

She lets out a tired huff of a laugh, leaning back on her hands. "I just... I don't want to stop yet."

"Stop what?"

She gestures toward the rec center behind us—the fans humming inside, the smell of wet wood and disinfectant still clinging to everything. "If I stop, then it becomes real. That there's nothing else I can do until insurance shows up. And that won't be until next week." Sadie starts to pace, walking the area in front of the table bench. "What do I do about camp? The kids have already paid. Parents are counting on this for care—"

I glance at my watch out of habit. Noon. The day is wide open, whether she wants it to be or not. "Here's the thing," I offer. "We've officially done everything possible for today. Which means whatever we do next can't make it worse."

She arches a brow. "That's all you've got? We can't make it worse?"

"It's my optimism," I correct. "Midwest-style. So," I continue, "we can come back later, check on the drying, but until then…" I shrug. "It's probably best to take the day. Let this all dry up as much as we can. We can make a plan for tomorrow and knock out a bunch of stuff."

"We," she says, brows lifting into her forehead.

"We," I confirm. "I told you, I've got a stacked basketball roster I'm pretty pumped about." I rub my hands together, carrying through the joke.

Sadie laughs and it almost unties part of the knot in my chest. She keeps pacing for a second, then asks quietly, "Can we… keep hanging out?"

Something warm settles in my chest. "Yeah," I answer easily. "I was hoping you'd say that."

"Good," she says, sounding relieved. "Because if I'm alone, I'm going to agonize over all of this." She gestures to the building behind her.

I hop off the table and hold out my hand. "Then c'mon. Let's find you a distraction that involves food and limited responsibility."

She takes my hand with no hesitation, and when she smiles up at me, it's tired—but real.

Thirty

SADIE

By the time Colson knocks, my hair is still damp at the ends and my skin feels human again. The shower helped—washed away the stale rain smell and the sweat from this morning's hard work. I feel reset, or at least closer to it.

I open the door and he's wearing a backwards hat, a simple white shirt and black shorts. The hat has me about ready to drool. He looks ridiculously good.

He pauses inside the doorway, taking in my apartment, and I watch him do it—eyes moving slowly, deliberately. The space is open but cozy, sunlight spilling across the hardwood floors, plants stretching toward the windows. Everything has a place. It feels like me, and I realize I care a little too much about whether he can tell.

"This tracks," he says finally.

"High praise," I tease, closing the door behind him.

His attention shifts to me then—really lands—and I feel it like a warm brush along my skin. I'm wearing jean shorts and a red ruffled top, the sleeves soft against my shoulders. I suddenly become very aware of my legs. How his gaze sticks around. How I don't want him to look away.

"What?" I ask, smiling.

He clears his throat, not even pretending. "You look... really good."

I shake my head, amused. "You're staring."

"I am," he agrees easily, grin breaking through. "Wanted to make sure you noticed."

He steps closer, fingers brushing my wrist, and for the first time all day, the weight in my chest eases. His lips find mine and the electricity from his touch rushes through my entire body. Every piece of me is touched by him.

Pulling away just far enough, he admits, "I like kissing you." He's close enough that his lips brush mine. "But your stomach growling tells me we have other places to be."

Colson puts a final kiss on my lips and opens the door. I can't remember the last time someone picked me up like this and I simply give up.

Because one thing is for sure: none of them were like Colson Burke.

I'm STILL TRYING TO push away the feeling of dread and this perfectly warm July day is definitely helping. I keep thinking about the way my stomach plummeted when I stepped inside. There's nothing I can do about it *today*, no matter how many times my brain circles back to budgets and timelines and worst-case scenarios. Colson is right. Insurance offices are closed. Contractors won't call back. And the town has fully tipped into Fourth of July mode whether I'm ready or not.

Tourists crowd the sidewalks, sunburned and laughing, coolers stacked high, kids darting between legs with boxes of sparklers they are saving for later. Our perfect lake town is brimming with energy.

So I try to let myself be in it. Even if it's only for today.

My mind keeps drifting back to last night, anyway—the way his kiss felt unhurried, like time had finally loosened its grip. The steam from the shower curling around us, warm and quiet, his hands steady on my back like he wasn't going anywhere. The softness of it all surprises me more than the heat did.

"Hungry?" Colson asks, bumping his shoulder into mine like it's nothing.

On cue, my stomach squeezes, a reminder of our makeshift, no power dinner last night.

"Starving."

He tips his head forward. "Cherry Pit?"

I stop walking. "Cherry Pit?" I thought he had sort of entertained me by going there and wouldn't be itching to go back.

He grins, easy and unapologetic. "We like it here."

We. There he goes again, being all swoony and sweet. Who knew the broken NBA player had all this behind that scowl. My chest tightens in that good, unfamiliar way.

Downtown is packed, every table visible through the windows is already full, and when he reaches for my hand, he does it without hesitation. No pause. No checking who's watching. For a split second, I wonder if he'll think better of it—if the weight of being *Colson* will catch up to him.

It doesn't.

He threads his fingers through mine like it's instinct, like this is already something he's decided.

"We'll probably have to wait," I say, looking around at the crowded streets.

Colson shrugs and asks, "Do we have anywhere else to be?"

I shake my head and he squeezes my hand. Fuck, he's charming.

As we wait, pressed together in the summer heat, I realize I've seen him smile more today than I ever have before.

The hostess tells us it will probably be thirty minutes until a table opens up. Colson leads me outside and grabs a seat at the miraculously open bench near the front of Cherry Pit. When we sit down, he picks my wrist up, kissing the inside.

My god. Is this man real?

Thirty-One

COLSON

News travels fast in a small town. Not in the dramatic, headline kind of way, but the kind that moves faster than texts or social media, carried by conversations and concern and people stopping by "to check in."

We've barely been seated at Cherry Pit when the first person comes over. Then another, and another. They don't interrupt for long. A hand on Sadie's shoulder. An offer of help. Someone asking about the rec center, the damage, what still needs fixing. A guy who I'm pretty sure runs the marina offers to bring tools by later. A woman from behind the counter slips Sadie a chocolate-covered cherry, like a secret treat to make things better.

It's... kind of remarkable. I sit there with my glass of cherry lemonade sweating against my palm, watching Sadie respond to each person with the same steady patience, gratitude tucked into her smile even when I can tell she's tired.

No one pushes. They show up. By the time the third group wanders away, I lean back in my chair and shake my head. "Does this happen everywhere you go?"

She exhales a quiet laugh. "Pretty much."

"They all heard already."

She nods. "The Golden Harbor way."

"It's... impressive," I say honestly. "People don't do this where I live. Well, that's a lie. They spread the news that may or may not be true in record time."

"Where you live has at least two million more people," she points out.

"Still," I say. "This is definitely different."

She lifts her glass, the deep red of her cherry wine catching the sunlight streaming through the front windows. Tourists bustle past outside, the warmth of July pressing in every time the door opens.

"It's how it works around here," she shares. "Something happens, everyone checks in. Even if they can't help, they want you to know you're not alone."

Something tightens in my chest. Not in a bad way—just with quiet recognition of something I didn't realize I was missing.

I glance toward the line forming near the counter. "We're kind of taking up a table."

She follows my gaze, then shrugs. "We'll make up for it in the tip."

Our lunch arrives and some of the people walking in are festive, headbands and hats to match the holiday. After a moment, I clear my throat. "This seems like Golden Harbor's favorite holiday."

"We have fun with it. The fireworks from the beach are always a great time but I wouldn't say it's my favorite." Sadie presses her hand to her chest.

"If this isn't your favorite, which holiday is?" I ask the sort of random question, almost falling into step of the game we played the last time we were here. Trading questions. Learning about each other.

She grins. "Halloween."

"Really?"

"Love it," she gushes. "The costumes. Corn mazes. Haunted houses. Golden Harbor goes all in."

Her eyes light up as she talks, and I can already see it—the town stripped of summer chaos, leaves everywhere, Sadie in a sweater instead of her rec center branded T-shirt.

"It's gorgeous here in the fall," she adds. "You should come back."

I smile. "I'd like that."

It's one of the first times we've brought up the future. Something still so murky for me. A few weeks ago, drifting into that place would've left me with nothing but frustration. Now, that's not the case. The uneasy feeling of not knowing what comes next is still there, but it almost feels like the answer is possible to find.

"So," she says, resting her elbows on the table. "Favorite holiday?"

"Thanksgiving," I answer without thinking.

Her eyebrows lift. "Immediate answer. Interesting."

I roll the glass between my hands. "My mom loved it. Cooking all day. Music on. The house would be warm from the oven and smelling that certain way when you're making a bunch of dishes. It was what I remember most from being a kid—her teaching me something in the kitchen."

Her smile is gentle. "That sounds really nice."

"It was," I agree, then add quietly, "though it's harder to do when I play a sport that's in season during that time but we always found a way to make it work. Even if that meant having dinner on the Tuesday of that week, or a week early."

She studies me for a beat. "That must've been hard. The first one without her."

I nod once and look down at the almost gone lemonade in my cup. "Yeah. It was."

The thing about Sadie is she doesn't seem to push too hard. Or maybe talking about my mom with her is a different kind of experience.

"I'm glad you had those memories," she says. "Hope you find a way to continue. That's the magic in remembering."

I offer her a little smile and nod. I don't tell her that I spent this last one eating takeout on my living room floor and letting my days off from the team kind of run together. There was a break in our schedule that allowed us to be dismissed for a few days. Rare. A cruel fucking trick from the universe to take the one person I'd have wanted to spend it with right before.

Another local waves to Sadie from the door, and she lifts a hand in return.

Small town. Big heart.

Sitting here, watching the way this place wraps itself around her, I can't help thinking how lucky she is—and even though something dark and depressing brought me to this place, I know how lucky I am to be here long enough to see it.

TIME FLIES WITH SADIE. After Cherry Pit, walking around town, even watching the apple pie eating contest, I can't believe the sun is already going down. We leave the main stretch of the beach behind, the crowd thinning as we walk. The sounds of the crowds are still there but it starts to feel muted, like someone turned the volume down.

Sadie veers off the path right before the shoreline curves, ducking between two rocky formations I wouldn't have thought twice about. From the outside, it looks like nothing. Just lake and stone and a sharp bend in the sand. More like the end of the line.

Then she steps past the peak, I follow, and it opens up.

A crescent of beach is tucked behind the rise, hidden enough that if you didn't know it was here, you'd not even bother continuing. The lake stretches out in front of us, calm and darkening as the sun sinks lower, the fireworks barge barely visible in the distance.

"Wow," I say quietly.

She glances back at me, pleased. "Told you."

"You weren't kidding," I add. "This is prime real estate."

She shrugs. "Locals only." She puts a finger in front of her lips, emphasizing the secret.

She drops her tote and shakes out a blanket, spreading it over the sand with practiced ease. I help anchor the corners, the fabric warm from being folded up all day. When we sit, we both stretch our legs out and lean back on our arms, close enough that we seem to touch.

"This is where you always watch?" I ask.

"Most of the time," she says. "Unless someone beats me to it. Which never happens."

"Because no one knows," I say.

"Exactly."

The air's cooler now, the lake breeze cutting through the leftover heat of the day.

Sadie tilts her head towards the sky. "Give it a few minutes. You'll hear the first one before you see it."

I glance at her, at the way the lake light catches her profile, how comfortable she looks here—like this place belongs to her.

I turn toward her without really meaning to. Her hair, almost the color of caramel, drifts down her shoulders. She closes her eyes, letting the light breeze run over her skin. When she opens her eyes, she catches me watching her.

"What?" she asks, almost like a dare.

I lean on one arm and use the other to touch her face, my fingers finding the nape of her neck. Pulling her to me, I feel her melt into it like she was already halfway there. Her lips are warm and lush, tasting faintly of cherries and summer, and the world narrows to the quiet press of her mouth against mine.

She sighs into the kiss, her hand sliding over my shirt, fingers curling like she's grounding herself. I deepen it just enough to make my intention clear, but I keep it slow—like I'm savoring something I don't want to rush. And also, because we're out on a public beach.

My tongue sweeps along the seam of her lips and then I'm tasting her. She moans and it could be my undoing. She kisses me back, sure and a bit charged, her hand still pulling at my shirt like she's afraid I might drift away.

Then she's sitting up, not breaking the kiss, lightly pushing my shoulders back. She pulls away long enough to swing a leg over and straddle me, the movement easy and intentional, like she knows exactly what she's doing.

Sadie kisses my jaw, and then down my neck. Her hands move from my chest to my arms.

"Colson Burke, with those good arms," she teases me, squeezing my biceps. Something flashes across her eyes and puts a hand over her mouth. "Your shoulder. I didn't even think about it. Are you okay?" She looks around to the sight of my arms propping me up, like she can see an injury with her eyes.

When she tries to stand, I move a hand to her hip, holding her in place. "The shoulder is fine. Don't you go anywhere."

Relief shows on her face and she slowly leans in, bringing her lips back to mine. She nips at my bottom lip and a groan spills from my mouth. I can feel her smiling into it, sinking into my reaction, and I love how she makes me feel like this. I doubt she'll ever be close enough.

My skin feels like it's buzzing where she touches, and where I wish she was. The wind picks up a bit, pushing her hair into her face.

She pulls back enough to look at me, tucking her hair behind her ears, eyes bright and lips swollen from kissing. "This," she says quietly, a teasing smile tugging at her mouth, "might actually be the real reason I brought you to my secret spot."

I laugh under my breath, my hands sliding to her hips as she sits back, steadying her there. "I feel incredibly honored."

She leans down again, kissing me once more—slower now, sweeter—but there's still a spark underneath it, the hum of something charged and alive. A firework bursts overhead, lighting up the lake.

Sadie turns, looking at the sky. The light from another firework catches her face in flashes—warm, then shadowed, then bright again—and something about it makes my chest feel tingly in that good, dangerous way.

She moves until she's sitting next to me. I pull my knees into my chest, my arms around them. Sadie loops an arm through mine, leaning into me.

Another burst goes off, closer this time, and the sound ripples through the crowd we can still hear but can't see. Someone cheers in the distance. Here, it's just us, tucked behind the curve of the lake, the blanket soft beneath us.

"Thanks for bringing me here," I say.

She turns her head, smiling softly. "You're welcome."

We sit there, fireworks going off, and I feel like the moment stretches around us. And the way I feel about her is something I didn't see coming.

Thirty-Two

SADIE

I'm in Colson's car and he's taking me back to my place. But I don't want to go home. I should be exhausted from today. Kind of feels like today was a whole week–everything with the storm and clean up all the way through watching the fireworks on the beach.

I keep trying to steal looks at him—he's caught me probably every other time. The dashboard lights wash over him in faint flashes, catching on the clean lines of his face and the muscle packed into his shoulders. His white T-shirt fits like it was made for him, stretched across his chest, sleeves snug around his biceps. Every time he shifts his grip on the wheel, his arm flexes. How can something so obscure like that be so damn hot? So distracting? Someone should really study that.

His hat is still on backward like he knows what it does to me. There's something about the way he fills this space that makes my chest squeeze and something pool in my low belly. His jaw is set, a faint shadow of stubble along it, eyes trained on the dark road ahead.

I feel the pull of him without meaning to, a low awareness humming beneath my skin. The car is quiet except for the road and our breathing, the night wrapped close around us. I should be tired. I should want my bed. But all I can think about is how close he is, how good he looks like this, and how badly I don't want this drive to end.

My hand finds his thigh. It's testing the edge of something. Almost feels a tiny bit reckless. I draw slow circles through the fabric, then give a light squeeze, enough to see what happens. His grip tightens on the steering wheel, the muscle in his arm jumping, and this time when he looks over, he doesn't bother pretending he didn't notice.

His eyes flick to my hand, then to my face. One brow lifts. "What's up?"

My pulse kicks up, nerves buzzing, but I don't pull away. I like this version of myself—the one who asks instead of wonders. "I was thinking," I say, voice softer than I mean for it to be, "what if I didn't go home?

The seconds stretch between us. I meet his gaze, heart pounding. "What if I went back to your place instead?"

He doesn't hesitate. Not even a second. His mouth curves into a slow, knowing smile, and his hand shifts, covering mine on his thigh. "Is that even a question?" he remarks. "Of course you can."

Something in my chest loosens, excitement blooming bright and heady. I squeeze his leg once more, a quiet yes, and he passes the turn that would take us back to my place.

I PUT MY HAND on the car door handle but Colson is there, opening it before I get the chance. The night air rushes in, cool against my skin. Before I can even fully swing my legs out, he's there—one hand braced on the roof, the other steady at my waist. I laugh, breathless, because the way he looks at me feels like a promise.

He doesn't give me time to overthink it.

He lifts me like it's nothing, my legs wrapping around his waist. My back meets the side of the car, cool metal grounding me for half a second before his mouth is on mine. The kiss is hungry and unhurried.

I make a quiet sound into his mouth, fingers fisting in his shirt, and he smiles against my lips like he knows exactly what he's doing.

"Come on," he murmurs, forehead resting against mine, breath warm. "Before you make me forget how to walk."

He carries me the rest of the way effortlessly, like this is just how things are now—me around his waist, the night closing in around us, the door opening to his place and something different. Bold. Brave.

I've never felt like this before. Wanted. *Needed*. People I've been with mostly felt like a decent idea. Not like the *only* idea.

When he steps inside, still holding me, I know I'm exactly where I want to be.

He sets me down and his hands immediately find my body, one at the hem of my shirt and the other tipping my mouth up so he can crash his lips to mine. His fingers dance along my stomach until his hand pushes my shirt up and he's cupping me through my bra.

I move my hips and feel his length pushing against me. I can't hold back the whimper that falls from my lips.

"Fuck. That sound," Colson groans, pushing harder into me. "That's what you do to me."

His mouth kisses my neck, spot by spot, like he's trying to put his lips on every inch of me.

And you know what?

I hope I'm right.

Thirty-Three

COLSON

Being with Sadie feels as right, even as true, as gravity. When she asked about coming to my place tonight, her voice was almost a touch smaller than I expected, I almost told her that she can have anything she wants.

It would've been the truth.

I kiss down the column of her neck, tasting her. We're bumping into the wall down the hallway to my bedroom. Once we're inside, her hands grab for my shirt, lifting it up and over my head. Then it's my turn with her cherry-red top. Underneath, she's wearing an almost matching bra, the fabric smooth and crimson.

We watch each other as we both take off our shorts. She's wearing a matching red thong, the cut showing the curves of her ass. Her eyes move to my briefs and I close the space between us.

I push us onto the bed, my arms caging her body from each side. I kiss the soft skin spilling from her bra. My tongue then traces the path once I've made it from one side to the other. Sadie's nails scratch down my back.

"You smell like summer. Like the sun," I compliment, my nose grazing hers.

Sadie meets me, lifting herself up to kiss me. Her lips are firm and commanding. It's like she wants me as much as I need her.

Then her hand moves down, in between us, touching me through my briefs.

I don't need to be told twice. I take off my briefs, watch her take off her panties, and am back over her.

My lips find the soft skin below her navel. Her muscles clench as I kiss down, my eyes catching Sadie watching me as I move further. She looks like she's holding her breath, waiting for my next move.

I can't help myself—I have to taste her, and I think she knows that.

Kissing her clit, I feel her moan and look up to see her gripping at the sheets. That moan? Fuck. It's the sound of dreams coming fucking true.

Swirling my tongue on her, noticing all the movements of her hips, it's making me want her even more. To be buried inside of her.

I lap at her wetness, tasting her, and when she whimpers, I know she's ready. Moving my body up and over her, I see Sadie chewing on her lip. She's quick to grab my dick and guide it to her entrance.

I push in slowly. She stretches around me and it's tough to keep the pace slow. We keep this up until she's taking all of me, and then her hips are tilting. I roll us so she's on top.

She's so fucking beautiful as she rides me.

"Nice and easy, baby. Whatever you need," I groan, my hands gripping her hips.

Sadie almost whines when she answers, "Okay."

I drift down, digging my hands into her perfectly thick ass as she leans forward, grabbing the headboard. She's holding herself up, getting more confident and picking up the pace. It feels like she's holding back. When she goes to moan, she immediately puts her lips together, trying to dull the sound.

But that's not what I want.

"Sunshine girl, let me hear you," I growl through clenched teeth.

At the suggestion, part of her opens up. Considering. Thinking. She pauses for a few seconds, our breaths tangled between us.

"Sunshine girl," she repeats, almost to herself. It's at this moment I know she loves the nickname I have for her.

Her mouth pulls into a wicked grin when she picks up the pace. She's more confident and I feel like I'm about to go somewhere I can't come back from. She's unlike anyone I've ever met.

I'm closer than I'd like to be, considering I never want this to end. She watches me as she rides through her dark lashes.

She moans, makes these little noises I wish I could bottle up. Keep them somewhere special. I'm practically seeing fucking stars with how tight she is.

I take my thumb and position it so when she rides, it will hit her clit. The first touch has her damn near screaming my name.

"Colson. That—" She doesn't stop and lets her eyes roll back as she really sits into it. "Feels so good," she whines.

Her hair falls in front of her face and she's wonderfully disheveled. My hips start moving with hers, wanting to push us to the edge.

I feel her tighten and hear a breath she tries to suck in. Sadie moves even faster, this time letting go of the headboard and putting her hands right above my shoulders. Her face pulls into this look, and I know she's unraveling.

"Fuck, Sadie—" I groan, slapping her ass as I feel my climax within reach.

My girl has to come first.

And she does.

Her eyes pinch and she leans back, grabbing her tits, and she's crying out my name. I grip her hips, pump into her, and let her pussy strangle me. My release spills into her as she rides out the shocks.

I empty every last drop, as I hold onto her like she's a lifeline.

Finally, when we're both spent, she falls on top of my chest. She kisses me and we're both damn near breathless. I'm still buried inside her as I rub her back.

"That was—"

"Amazing," I answer for her.

"One of the many words you could use. Yes. I'll take amazing." She kisses me again.

In this moment, I know that my bed will always feel empty unless Sadie Becker is beside me.

Thirty-Four

SADIE

"You had sex with him!" Maren screams in the car. I'm thankful it's warm enough that I have the windows up and the A/C on.

Playfully, I swat at her, also thankful that the car is in park. "What is wrong with you? You can't just scream things like that."

She points a finger at me. "You aren't even denying it."

I open my mouth, then close it again.

Maren *loses it*.

"Oh my GOD," she shouts, unbuckling her seatbelt even though we are very much not going anywhere. "Was it good? Don't answer that—your face already did." She beams, her cheeks pink with excitement.

I swat at her again. "Lower your voice!"

"No, the kids aren't coming for an hour," she says, glancing at her watch, vibrating in her seat. "Absolutely not. I need a full timeline. Did you kiss first? Who initiated? Was there tension? *Please* tell me there was tension."

"You are out of control," I admit, putting my head in my hands, feeling the flush of my cheeks under my fingers.

She leans closer, eyes wild. "Was it against a wall? A bed? A *car*? Because if it was a car, I'm never letting you hear the end of this."

I press my lips together, trying—and failing—not to smile.

Her scream is practically deafening in this tiny space. "IT WAS A CAR." She gasps, clutching her chest. "I KNEW IT. I *felt* it. Okay, okay—where were his hands? How big is his—"

"Maren!" I laugh, covering her mouth with my hand. I look around us, relieved when it's still just my car in the parking lot. I don't want someone to overhear us, but the way she's acting is the way I've felt internally ever since that night.

Colson is unbelievable. I can't believe he is a living, breathing, walking man. Not just someone I dreamt up.

She pulls my hand away. "There is no one here. It's summer and we're in a school parking lot."

"Fine. I promise to dish on a high level of detail if you let me get through this practice first, okay?"

She nods, lifting her hands. "Yes, Coach."

In all honesty, I'm ridiculously thankful for her. It was her idea to reach out to the local high school, share details about our out of commission rec center from the storm, and see if they had any space they could share. They were more than happy to help as long as we did our own clean up—they don't have any janitorial staff until August.

But, it's July. It's hot. We're further away from the lake and miss the breeze we're used to. Plus, it may not have been all that efficient, but we did have air conditioning. It never made the courts cold, or like we didn't need the fans, but it would pull the sting of the summer heat away.

So, between Maren and Colson, we came up with a plan. It included our industrial fans, plus some borrowed ones from our local hardware store, a cooler of popsicles, and massive water jugs with lots of ice.

Maren even offered to come and be an extra set of eyes for the few days we'll be here. She and I both know that she mostly wants to spy on Colson and me, but I'm not turning down the help. Kids in a new place? The last thing I need is to lose one of them when they're trying to get to the bathroom or something.

"One last question," Maren asks, bringing me back to the moment. "Did he make you forget your own name?"

I hesitate.

Maren slams her palm on the dashboard. "Say less."

Because the universe has spectacular timing, Colson pulls in next to us. I turn to Maren and give her a look, one that begs her to stay on her best behavior. She laughs and looks away, pretending not to see me.

We get out to help Colson with the coolers. He grins at me, in a way that makes me despise that we're not alone, and pulls me in for a quick kiss. Like we've done it a hundred times.

Maren lets out a low whistle, but when I turn to respond, I realize it's not about the kiss—she's looking in the backseat of his car.

"I forget you got that NBA money," she jokes.

Colson opens the door and pulls out two brand new rolling coolers. They have a hard exterior and match the colors of the rec center—which I'm sure isn't a coincidence.

"It's supposed to be really hot. Solid coolers are non-negotiable," he says, trying to act like he didn't pull out the equivalent of a thousand dollars.

"I thought someone had some we could borrow?" I ask.

"They dropped them off, and they were in bad shape. I'm talking about lids that wouldn't close. There's no way they'd actually keep anything cold."

Colson tries to pull off one of the price tags, but I see the cost before he stuffs it in his pocket.

"These are too much. We can't accept these," I protest, my hand pressing on the pit in my stomach. "We can't afford these."

"I can. Consider it a donation to the center. You'll be able to use these for a long time." He taps his hand on the top of one. "Sadie, let me help you," he insists, quieter this time.

His eyes are lighter blue than I'm used to, the height of the sun the culprit. He has this look that makes it hard to say 'no.'

Maren jumps in. "The man has millions of dollars. Let him buy the coolers."

She's right. I also know the feeling residing in my chest has nothing to do with pride and everything to do with needing help.

Colson doesn't rush me. He waits, one hand resting on the cooler like it belongs there, like *he* belongs here.

He continues. "Sadie, you know you'd do the same for someone else."

He's right and he knows it.

I let out a slow breath and peel my hand away from my stomach. "Fine," I grumble. "But if anyone asks, I bullied you into it."

A corner of his mouth lifts. "Devastating. My reputation may never recover."

Maren claps her hands once. "Great. Now that the rich guy's guilt has been accepted, can we get these filled with ice?"

That breaks whatever tension was left.

Colson reaches for my hand, weaving his fingers with mine. When he squeezes, something in my chest dares to explode. It's sweet, unexpected—sort of like him in general.

He holds my hand like he's not hiding it. Not from Maren. Not from me. And that might be my favorite part.

Thirty-Five

COLSON

WHILE THE SCHOOL HAS been a saving grace by offering a place to hold camp and practice, it's not the same as the courts we're used to. That's why me and Sadie, and even other volunteers, have been putting in work at the rec center whenever we have a free moment.

This camp, what Sadie is doing for this community, feels like something my mom would've relied on when I was a kid. A place for me to spend my summer, being safe and bettering myself in some way. Not to mention it was critical for her to be able to work shifts during the day. That's one of the reasons I kept coming back to the rec center early on. Feels right to help restore it to a workable space.

The professional cleanup crew packs up faster than I expect. The day seemed to fly by. One minute there's the steady grind of machines and voices carrying in and out, the next it's only the sound of trucks pulling out of the driveway.

Sadie doesn't slow down. She rolls her shoulders, wipes her hands on the back pockets of her shorts, and grabs another stack of broken-down cardboard like she hasn't already been at this for hours.

If we want to stay on pace with the tentative re-open date, we knew it'd take some extra work.

We. There I go again. Fuck.

I watch as she works like this is normal—like giving everything she has to a place that isn't glamorous, shiny, or easy is part of who she is. No complaints or dramatics. Just steady, almost stubborn effort.

She's a different kind of productive. The type where you know she has to dig deep, that her muscles ache, the exhaustion is starting to touch her bones. But she doesn't quit.

It makes something in my chest tighten. She's a force and I feel like she barely knows it.

"Hey," she says, glancing over her shoulder. "Don't push it."

I hook my fingers around the edge of a metal folding table and lift it, testing my shoulders before committing. Recognizing how she cares about me.

"I'm good," I reply. "Promise."

She squints at me, the way she does when she's deciding whether or not to believe something. "You say that, but—"

"I know," I cut her off gently. "No heroics."

She hesitates, then nods. "You know what I'm thinking now, huh?" she teases.

This is one of my favorite parts of her. The one where she gives me shit. She carefully makes fun of me.

Truth is, if there's a scenario where I stupidly push the shoulder too far, it'd probably be from keeping up with Sadie.

We work side by side as the sun dips lower, the sky bleeding into that soft late-summer palette—orange melting into pink, pink fading into blue. The air cools enough to raise goosebumps on my arms. Somewhere in the trees, crickets start up, slow and uneven, like they're warming into it.

It's hard not to notice how pretty it is here. It seems like every night, the lake dares the sky to do better than the night before.

Sadie hums under her breath while she gathers trash bags, her movements efficient, familiar. Like she knows this place the way I know the lines on a court.

Watching her makes me want to keep going, even when my arms start to burn. Not because she's watching—but because she isn't. Because she assumes I'll be there, doing the work with her.

That kind of faith sneaks up on you.

We work in quiet silence, doing our best to get as much done as possible. My muscles are tired and my feet are sore, but Sadie shows no sign of stopping and I follow her lead.

It's when I'm carrying a stack of flattened boxes toward the dumpster that I notice it—the first tiny spark of light drifting up from the grass near the fence.

Then another. Then three more. I stop short.

Fireflies.

They blink on and off like they're breathing, rising slowly into the dusk. Little floating embers. It's the sort of thing you forget exists until it's right in front of you.

Sadie follows my gaze. "Oh," she breathes. "They're always out over this way." She gestures to the line of houses and the rec center.

"I haven't seen them like this in forever," I blurt before I can stop myself.

She smiles, a little surprised. "Really?"

"Yeah. Chicago may get a few but not everywhere." I set the boxes down, suddenly careful, like I might scare the moment away. "Or maybe I'm not paying attention."

More fireflies drift up from the edges of the tall grass, pulsing gold and green against the deepening sky. The sound of the crickets becomes the soundtrack for the glowing.

For a second, I'm eight years old again, barefoot in the park with my mom, chasing lights with a mason jar while she sits on the edge of the slide. I remember how she told me not to catch them for too long—that some things are better when you let them be.

Sadie breaks the silence gently. "What're you thinking about?"

"My mom," I admit. "She used to make a big deal out of fireflies. She'd take me to the park where they were always bright. I'd be in my pajamas and we'd go in our flipflops."

Her head tilts. "I love that."

I nod. "Yeah."

She's quiet for a beat, then carefully asks, "What about your dad?"

The word lands flat.

I shrug, easy. Practiced. "Non-factor. Left when I was five. Never came back."

Her face shifts—not pity, not shock–with understanding. Like she's filing the information away, respecting it for what it is.

"I'm sorry," she offers and I swear her voice cracks.

"Nothing to be sorry about," I tell her honestly while sitting down at the picnic table. "My mom made up for him."

She sits next to me, close enough that her arm bumps into mine. Her head tips and she rests it on my shoulder. Together, we watch the fireflies rise higher, their lights blinking, like stars that fell from the sky.

This doesn't feel real. Also, it feels so sweet and wholesome that my teeth should fall out. I don't move, and neither does she. Like we both understand this is one of those moments you don't interrupt. Her weight makes it feel like she belongs here. With me.

The fireflies blink on and off around us, careless and glowing; for the first time in a long time, my thoughts don't race ahead to what comes next. There's no pressure. No noise. Just this—her, the quiet, the soft summer night holding us exactly where we are.

Sadie exhales slowly. "This is, like, sickeningly sweet, yes?"

"Totally," I agree.

Sadie laughs, I feel her shift against me, and even though we're the most annoying people to exist in this montage, neither of us move.

After sitting in the memory of my mom and me at the park, I wonder about Sadie. Where did she grow up? Does she have memories like I do? I want to know everything but that seems aggressive. So, I start small.

"What about your family? Are you close?"

Sitting up straight and turning to me, she says, "They're great. We talk all the time, but my dad has a hard time leaving the college. Ever. Coach Becker identity runs deep. But I'm thankful for them. They love each other, they love me, and they showed me what it was like for a marriage to be full of love."

The way her mouth says the word marriage feels off. Like she doesn't want to think about it. Or it's like when lemon juice is getting too close to a cut.

"Probably great having a dad who knows the game. Understood what it meant when you got hurt."

She looks down, her foot tapping the ground. "For the most part, yes. My dad loved watching me play." Her lips almost turn down, but not quite.

Past tense. Loved.

"Do they ever come visit?"

"Typically at the end of August. Before classes start and my dad has his team to keep tabs on. They like it here, but they don't love it like I do." She looks around, the fireflies still glowing like they're showing off.

"This place isn't what I expected," I admit.

"Those are the best kinds of things if you ask me." Her shoulder bumps into mine.

She hits her hands on her knees. "Okay," she says. "One more trash run. Then we're calling it."

I nod. "Deal."

She walks ahead of me, and I already miss the weight of her head on my shoulder.

"And then I'll take you back home."

"But you'll stay?"

Her eyes are wide enough I can see them in the dusk, the darkness cloaking around us.

"Of course."

And if there's one thing worth staying for, it's definitely Sadie Becker.

Thirty-Six

SADIE

I LOVE HAVING COLSON here. Not just *here,* as in my apartment—but here, in my bed.

My king-sized bed is dressed in matching sheets—soft cotton, light blue with a navy comforter. The bed is one of the things I splurged on when it came to the breakup with Nick. It felt ridiculous to sleep in a bed we shared together, planning a wedding in, after everything.

So, I got a new one. Bigger. Better. Completely Nick-free.

Colson is stretched out across the mattress like he was always meant to be there, one leg bent, one arm thrown over his head. He's shirtless, a pair of basketball shorts slung low on his hips and his muscles are making my mouth go dry. The man has abs. Ones you could count, touch with your fingers.

Seeing him in my bed does something quiet and fierce to my chest. It feels like I'm about to get sucked into his vortex. Jokes on me, though, because I'd probably throw myself in at this point.

The A/C kicks on—I love sleeping in the cold—and I hope Colson doesn't reach for his shirt. Because that would be a travesty. A lamp glows low on my dresser, turning his skin golden, *almost like we're at the beach.* The bed looks right like this. Full.

I lean against the doorframe, arms crossed, pretending I'm not staring.

"You know," I say finally, because silence feels dangerous and I don't trust myself not to climb onto the bed if I wait too long, "this should be a crime."

He shifts slightly, lazy, comfortable. One eye opens. "What?"

"You," I tell him, nodding toward his entire body. "In my bed. Looking like... that."

His mouth curves, slow and knowing. "What do you mean?"

I gesture again, helpless. "I don't think my brain is receiving oxygen right now," I add. "Just wanted to flag that."

His lips pull up on one side in a lopsided smirk, one that makes me ache. Fuck. How does he do that?

My body forgets that it's tired. I've been working all day cleaning up the storm damage from the rec center, trying to keep the project on pace. My muscles and bones should be heavy, but Colson's here, and we have the whole night to ourselves.

I'm at the edge of the bed, lifting one leg up and then the other until I'm straddling him. The way he grins at me makes me feel confident and sure in my skin. His hands find my hips, the side of my ass as I dip forward, putting my lips to his.

I shift instinctively, settling more firmly over him, and the sound he makes—barely there, like he didn't mean to let it out—goes straight through me. The kiss deepens, slow at first then hungry, like we're both testing each other's resolve.

I place my hands on his chest, warm skin under my palms, his heartbeat fast and solid. The kiss isn't gentle. It's pent-up and charged, making up for what feels like wasted time.

His hands move to my back. I love how massive they are—how they cover me. I lean in deeper, trying to get everything I can from this kiss. Colson tastes me, his tongue grazing mine, and I don't know if I'll ever get enough of this.

My lips find his neck and I kiss down until I'm at his chest. The muscles? Unreal. Kind of unfair. Not sure my bed will ever look better than it does right now.

Colson grabs the hem of my tank top, lifting it up and off me.

"Fuck, you're perfect," he moans while putting a nipple in his mouth.

My fingers dig into his scalp, pulling his hair while he works me. He sucks and nips, which has my hips grinding into him. He's already hard.

I'm biting my lip, tipping my head back and pulling his head closer to me, when I say, "Take these off." I move a hand to tug on his shorts.

Slowly, he pulls away. I sit to the side while he does what he's told, which kind of surprises me.

"Good boy," I croon. It's part sarcasm until I realize how hot it makes me feel. Talking to him like that. Watching him take instruction.

Colson's dick springs forward and I don't mean to audibly moan, but something like that deserves audible praise.

"My girl likes being the boss?" His brows lift as he props himself up on his elbows. "Tell me what's next, Sadie." His voice is low and it feels like it washes over my skin syllable by syllable.

"I want to taste you," I reply, doing my best not to lose my nerve.

He growls, pushing his head back into the pillows, the column of his throat veiny and blushed. "You're the boss."

I move between his legs and grab his length with a hand, my fingers barely able to fit around him. His muscles flex at my touch and being able to elicit this type of reaction from him makes me feel powerful.

My mouth is close to the head and before my lips touch it, I look up at him. Colson is biting his lip, and when he sees me watching him, he huffs out a breath.

Maybe I like making the calls more than I thought I did? Because seeing him watch me like this, like he's cataloging every millimeter of movement? I know I'm soaking wet.

He seems to be frozen as I move him in front of my mouth, but don't touch him like that quite yet. A few more seconds pass and when I feel like I can't wait any longer, I slowly place a kiss to the head.

Colson groans, his fingers clenching the blankets.

I do my best to take as much of him as I can. Slow and steady until I'm comfortable. Then I'm licking up the shaft, swirling around the tip, before taking him back in my mouth.

My fingers grip him at the base and I lick down to them until I'm back to the top, a bead of precum waiting for me. I let my thumb touch it, spreading it around his skin.

"Grab my hair," I instruct him. There's not a moment of hesitation—Colson's hands are in my hair immediately and I'm ready to take him in my mouth.

I want so badly to know what he likes. I want to know how to make him come undone.

"Don't take it easy on me," I moan before putting my mouth around him.

"You're in charge." He practically groans as his fingers tighten around my hair.

His words have me so needy for him. Fuck. What is this man doing to me?

I'm moving down his dick, sucking, and he's setting the pace with the control of our positioning. I keep trying to take as much of him as I can, but when he pulls faster than expected, I gag. But I don't stop.

"Sadie. Fuck," Colson moans, "you feel so good. Your mouth. Your pussy."

His words spur me on—I love when he talks to me like this—and I go faster, taste as much of him as I can. Keeping one hand on the base of his cock, I take the other and cup his balls. The seconds my fingers make contact, I look up to see him tipping his head back.

"Fuck, I'm close." His words are low, almost whiny.

I give a tiny squeeze, and I can feel him tightening in my hand. His hands pull tighter, enough of a sting to make this hot.

"I'm going to—"

I interrupt him with an enthusiastic moan, gripping his hard length tighter, and let him come in my mouth. His body shakes with his orgasm; he groans through it while keeping my head right where he wants it. His release hits my throat and I don't quit sucking him until he's a heap of breaths on the bed.

I swallow the saltiness and feel like a goddess.

My hands rest on his thighs as he catches his breath. What a beautiful sight—Colson Burke all climaxed out on my bedding.

I smirk, resting my hands on his thighs. He sits up, kissing me in a way that's fierce. Like he's not done with me.

"My turn," he announces between kisses.

He practically tosses me on the other side of the bed and I let out a little yell from the surprise. He's got my shorts off in the blink of an eye, my bare skin on display for him.

Immediately, his tongue goes to my entrance, tasting me.

He groans. "You are fucking soaked."

His fingers grip around my thighs, digging into the sensitive skin. He pulls them wide.

"This beautiful pussy." He blows on it. "I've dreamed of it."

Hearing him talk that way about me has my orgasm already within reach. I need him to touch me. *Now.*

"You're still in control. Do you want me to take my time or are you ready?"

His mouth being this close is *torture.*

My voice is almost a yell as I gasp, "Ready, Colson. I'm ready."

I'm not even done answering when his fingers replace his tongue, filling me as his lips go to my clit. His massive hands, long fingers work me—hitting the right spot. His lips suck on me before pressing his tongue into me.

I move my hips, one hand grabbing the back of his head, and I start fucking his mouth. It's only a few thrusts before it hits me. A tidal wave of pleasure. There are no sounds, the room spins as he goes faster. Harder. I feel the explosion in my low belly and I pull his mouth to me as he pulls the orgasm out of me.

The yell that starts in my chest, comes out all guttural and raw. "Colson!" His name on my lips and his tongue on my clit has the tremors rocking me from the inside out. My entire body feels like a vice, energy zapping through the whole thing.

When I'm finally able to see straight, Colson climbs over me. His arms are on each side of me, my breathing still shallow and quick.

"You are fucking unreal. Like—"

I interrupt him with a kiss, saying all the things my orgasm-strained mind can't formulate into words. He doesn't rush it; his kiss is slow, full, and more than I could've hoped for.

I knew Colson was different. But this thing between us? It's unlike anything I've ever experienced.

And I can't get enough.

Thirty-Seven

COLSON

THE NEXT DAY, MY eyes burn from reading all the fine print of my contract and at this point, my eyes hurt. Basically, if I want to play in the NBA next season, I should be able to do that.

Though I was dismissed, the structure of the deal means I'm still getting paid, am still movable, still valuable. Productive player. Still would start on most rosters. Plus, my shoulder injury isn't going to be an issue. It's rare that I even feel the twinge, the one that would flip my stomach on a whim a few months ago.

There are roster spots out there. I know that. My agent knows that. Hell, half the league probably assumes I'll land somewhere without much trouble.

The problem is I don't know how picky I'm allowed to be. Or how honest. Teams will want to know what happened, which means I'll have to open a can of worms.

There's a secret sitting in my ribs like a cracked bone, and every time I think about walking into a new facility, shaking a new trainer's hand, I feel it all over again. The sting of betrayal. The heaviness of trusting someone only to find out they don't have your best interests in mind.

I flip my phone over, then back again. Kevin's name is already pulled up. I haven't talked to him properly since my last game and it's hurt me more than I realized. We were teammates but we were also friends. He was always there, checking in, making sure I didn't go too many days in my depressive hole once my mom was gone.

I hit FaceTime before I can overthink it. It rings twice.

"Holy shit—" Kevin's face fills the screen, eyes wide, grinning. "Colson? Is that really you?"

I roll my eyes in fake desperation. "Obviously."

"Man," he says, sitting up like he just won something. "I was starting to worry. Where are you?"

"Sorry. Didn't mean to put you out or anything," I answer, guilt prickling at the tips of my ears. Kevin's a good guy, one of my real friends, and I left him behind too. "I'm in Michigan. Needed a minute."

His expression softens. "Yeah. I get that."

There's a beat of silence. Comfortable. Kevin's been my guy since my second season—the one who knows when to push and when to leave me be.

"So," he says, leaning back. "What's up? You're calling to tell me you're signing with a rival team and I have to pretend not to be jealous?"

I look down at the table. "I don't know what I'm doing yet."

That wipes the smile clean off his face.

"Okay," he replies carefully. "That's not nothing."

"I keep thinking this is the moment," I admit. "Like... if I don't decide now, I never will."

"Decide what?"

"Whether I'm still in this."

Kevin lets out a short laugh. "Don't say it like that."

"I mean it like that."

He studies me through the screen. "You're a key player in this league. You're still that fucking guy... if you want to be."

I nod.

"Not trying to scare you away or anything, but fuck, what actually happened that night on the bench?" he asks.

The room feels smaller.

I open my mouth, then close it again. My pulse is loud in my ears. This is the part I've been avoiding. The part where staying quiet feels safer than telling the truth.

"Once I tell you, you won't be able to forget it."

He sets his phone up on something in front of him and crosses his arms. "Does it impact me?"

"Yes."

My quick answer surprises him a bit. His brows pushing into his forehead. He looks around, contemplating.

"Yeah, I want to know."

I take a deep breath and try to collect my thoughts. I launch into the long story. My injury. The rushed recovery. The way the trainer tried to get me to come back too soon with injections that weren't approved. How they tried to get our star rookie to do the same thing with his injury in the middle of the game.

Kevin doesn't interrupt. He listens intently from start to finish.

When I finish, he blows out a long breath. "Fuck. That isn't what I thought you were going to say." He pushes his hands through his hair. "Colson, you did what you had to do. Stepping in for someone who felt like they didn't have a voice."

"Maybe? I don't know. Seemed kind of self-destructive."

Kevin nods slowly. "I don't think so."

"I keep replaying it," I admit. "Thinking if I'd spoken up louder, or at a different time, had a conversation with Coach—"

"Colson," he cuts in. "You didn't fail. You were failed."

The words hit harder than I expected.

He leans closer to the camera. "You still love this game?"

I don't answer right away. I think about the sound of sneakers on hardwood. The weight of a ball in my hands. The quiet right before a free throw. The way my body still sparks with energy when I'm coaching the kids, shooting around with them.

"I do," I say.

"You have to keep playing," he almost pleads.

I sit back in my chair, staring at the kitchen table.

"Tell the truth. You'll find the right landing spot. Man, the league is better with Colson Burke in it."

The silence that follows feels different. Lighter.

I nod once. "Okay."

Kevin smiles. "Plus, are you going to give that asshole this kind of power? Nah. You have to come back."

I've not thought of it this way. If I don't come forward with the truth, there's more harm that can be done. The real issue isn't even my reputation but this trainer being responsible for more athletes. Coaching staff trusting them with the physical well-being of their players.

When the call ends, I don't move right away. It feels good to have shared this with someone closer to the situation. Sadie paved the way, listening first, making the whole thing feel valid.

I just sit there at the table, hands flat on the wood. For the first time, I miss Chicago. My friends. The coffee shop I'd go to on my off mornings. It's ironic because there's no way I'll be able to stay there while trying to find a new team.

Or here in Golden Harbor. Not really a big NBA town.

I have one more call to make.

And that's to my agent.

Thirty-Eight

SADIE

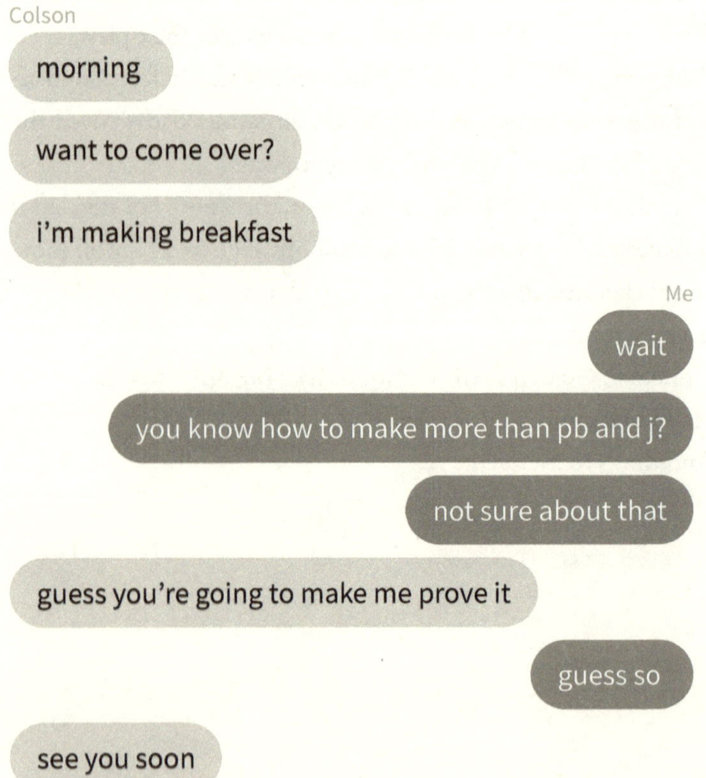

I PRACTICALLY JUMP OUT of bed to get dressed and drive to Colson's. A man offering to make breakfast? Again, it doesn't seem real.

Breakfast is one of my favorite types of food. It's something I had to learn to love again because Nick sort of tricked me into thinking the opposite when we were together. I used to love making breakfast on the weekends, trying new recipes. But Nick wasn't a breakfast guy and typically wouldn't even try what I made.

After a while, cooking for yourself, when you have a partner you live with, gets kind of depressing. So, I stopped. And instead I almost convinced myself it wasn't something that brought me joy.

Spoiler alert, Nick was the joy stealer.

My phone buzzes and I look to see a picture of me and my dad filling the screen. Smiling, I tap the answer button and put the phone to my ear.

"No morning practice? Have you started to go soft?" I tease and my dad huffs a breath. I love getting a rise out of him.

"We're starting in a few minutes. Good morning to you too, Sadie." I can hear him smile and it makes me miss my parents. Part of me wondered if staying back home after everything imploded with Nick would have been the right move, but I simply couldn't find a seed of joy in that idea. Plus, Nick kept telling me how much happier I'd be back home—relocating to Golden Harbor was also partly done in spite.

It was the right move.

I'll never forget the day my mom called, saying Nick had shown up for a quick visit, thinking I'd be there. It was about a month after the wedding was called off and I'd already moved to Golden Harbor. Oh, that was a solid day. He thought his way was always the best way and hated being wrong.

"How's the team looking?" I ask.

A ball bounces in the background; my dad must already be at the court, waiting for his guys to join him. "Young. But the recruitment class seems solid. Should have a chance at making the tourney this year." The hopefulness in his voice carries through and it makes me grin on the other line.

Some of my favorite memories would be when my dad and the team would have dinner together the night of the bracket reveal, learning if they did enough to make it into the tournament. Sometimes, they won their conference championship which cemented their spot, but it was all about what side of the bracket they ended up on.

When I was in college, my mom always made sure to be at our viewing party for women's basketball. I knew my dad wanted to be there, and he did end up making it to one, but it always felt like this thing that brought us closer together.

After my injury, my dad tried not talking about basketball. He was having a successful tourney run but he felt like it would be rubbing it in my face. I begged him to keep me in the loop. To not let my injury take anything else from me.

Now, my dad calls me about his team at least once a week once the season is in session. I love it.

"How's the rec center? Almost ready for you to put the kids back in there yet?"

My muscles ache at the mere thought of the amount of work we've done to try and expedite the process. "Slowly but surely. Shouldn't be too long."

More balls bounce in the distance and I know my dad's about to be pulled in another direction. "Well, Sadie, just wanted to check in. Hope you're having a good Sunday."

"Love you, Dad," I say, hand on my car door, about to get in to go to Colson's for our breakfast date.

I can't help but think about my parents on the short drive to Colson's. After hearing about Colson losing his mom and not really having a dad, it really shines the light on how great my childhood was. How supported I've felt. I've always known I was lucky, but Colson's experience breaks my heart in a way that's hard to try and understand.

I wish he had more.

My chest warms when I think of him, then my cheeks flush when I think of the way he makes me feel when he touches me. It's unreal. Unlike anything else in the world. Nothing has ever made me feel the way Colson does.

My daydream is cut short when I realize I'm already on his porch, knocking on his door. He yells for me to come in. The second I step inside, I stop short.

The house smells warm, like butter melting into something sweet. Like sugar and bananas. But there's also something savory that makes my stomach flip with excitement before my brain can even catch up.

"Wow," I gush, taking my shoes off. "Doesn't smell like PB and J."

Colson laughs from the kitchen. "Rude."

I follow the sound of his voice and find him standing at the stove in only his gym shorts, flipping tiny pancakes. There's a plate stacked with golden mini banana pancakes with steam still rising. Next to it rests an omelet folded perfectly over bacon, parmesan, and caramelized onions—*actual* caramelized onions, not the rushed, sad version people lie about online.

I blink at the spread. "Colson."

"Mm?" He doesn't look up, very focused on not burning anything.

"I was told you only know how to make PB and J."

He finally looks at me, smug. "I never said I only knew how to make it. I said I'm excellent at it."

I laugh, stepping closer as he slides an omelet onto a plate.

I lean against the counter, watching him move around the kitchen and ask, "What's the occasion?"

He shrugs. "I like breakfast. And I overheard you asking Maren about some diner when we were with the kids. You seemed awfully interested in the breakfast menu."

My chest does a small, annoying flip. The thing about Colson is he doesn't miss a detail. Before I can respond, he nudges a mug toward me. "Coffee's almost ready."

I glance down at the French press and freeze. The smell hits me now—rich and familiar, a little nutty, with that gentle sweetness I recognize.

"What kind of coffee?" I ask quietly.

He pauses. "Picked it up at the bakery."

The same coffee I brought the day I watched him paint his address above the garage. When I asked if he'd be interested in helping me with the summer tournament. The day we almost kissed.

Our fingers brush, and he leans in enough to press a quick kiss to my temple before putting his fingers under my chin, lifting before his lips touch mine. Like he can read my mind.

"Breakfast is served," he announces.

I take a sip of coffee, then a bite of pancake, and close my eyes for a second.

"Colson," I groan seriously, "This is so good."

He beams at me and my soul seems to jolt back into place. Colson feels like a key piece in coming back to myself.

WE'RE CLEANING UP AFTER a slow breakfast. Another pot of coffee is brewing in the French press. I open the fridge to grab some cream, and when I close it, I notice there's a short list on the door that seems like a new addition. I'm guessing it's a woman's handwriting and a few bullet points.

"What's this list for?" I ask.

Colson sighs and then says, "Found it. I think it was some of the things my mom wanted to do when I came up here in the summer. Just—" He rubs his face with his hands. "Never got the chance."

My heart. It hurts.

I reach for his hand and hold it. "Well, looks like we have some work to do."

Colson nods, threatening a smile but doesn't let it come through.

"The Basement? Oooh—"

He launches into an almost panicked explanation. "Yeah, I'm really not sure what she means because the basement of this place is fully renovated. She has this projector, and a screen, and all the storage she asked for. A full guest suite. I even called the contractor, there was nothing waiting to be finished. I don't know what—"

I take a finger and put it over his lips.

"I don't think she meant this basement, I think she meant The Basement." I hold back my amusement of Colson trying hard to figure it out.

"What the hell do you mean?" He laughs. "What's the difference?"

I turn, looping my arms around his neck and kissing him. "Colson, The Basement is a place. It's kind of a Golden Harbor secret."

"Okay?"

"It's a speakeasy. Hidden entrance. Cocktails and apps. Something that doesn't really fit with the small town vibe. It kind of started as a joke, but it's sort of perfect."

"A speakeasy? You're kidding me."

"No. Not kidding. We should go tonight."

Colson shrugs his shoulders and says, "Works for me."

Thirty-Nine

COLSON

Sadie doesn't hesitate when we stop in front of what looks like a closed laundromat, but I do.

There's a flickering OPEN sign in the window, but the lights inside are off, and a handwritten sign taped to the door reads *OUT OF ORDER*. I glance down at her, then back at the door.

"This is either a speakeasy," I say, "or we're about to get arrested."

She smiles, adjusting the strap of her flowy black summer dress like this is all part of the plan. The dress moves when she does, light and effortless, and I have to remind myself to keep my eyes up otherwise I'll have a situation that you'd hate to see in public.

"Relax," she says. "Trust me."

"Says every person before they walk into impending danger."

Sadie winks and then steps past me, knocking—not on the door, but on the side of a washing machine visible through the window. Three quick taps. A pause. Then two more.

I blink. "You're kidding."

The machine rattles, then the back wall *shifts*. A hidden door slides open, revealing a man in black, eyebrow raised.

Sadie leans in, completely unfazed. "Need to take cover."

The door opens wider. The guy looks at me once, then steps aside.

I let out a quiet laugh as we walk in. "This isn't what I expected."

She glances back at me, eyes bright. "I know."

We descend a narrow staircase, the noise of the city disappearing behind us. At the bottom, the space opens up into something dark and stunning. Low lighting. Velvet booths. Polished concrete and brass details that catch enough glow to feel expensive.

It's the kind of place you'd expect to find tucked in Chicago—moody and modern, almost luxurious in a way that makes you lower your voice without noticing you're doing it.

My eyes take a second to adjust as we continue our walk. The hostess greets us with an easy smile and leads us past the bar to a booth in the corner, tucked away like it was meant to be found only by people who knew where to look.

Sadie slides in first, crossing her legs and appearing completely at home.

I sit across from her, still taking it all in.

"Okay," I admit, "this is impressive."

She smirks. "I told you."

Before I can say anything else, a man steps up to the table—mid-forties, confident, sleeves rolled up, the kind of presence that says he owns the room without announcing it.

He looks at me for half a second and grins.

"Well I'll be damned," he says. "You're Colson Burke."

Sadie's eyebrows shoot up. Mine probably do the same.

I laugh, instinctively shaking my head. "Ummm, yeah but—"

"Don't worry," he cuts in, waving a hand. "Your secret is safe with me. But it's not because of basketball, no offense."

I sit back, confused. "Then why?"

He leans his elbow on the table. "Your mom. Tracy."

My chest tightens.

"She was in here almost every night during the renovations on the house," he continues, smiling like it's a fond memory. "She'd sit at the bar, order one drink, and send me emails afterward. Pages of them. Ideas for appetizers. Garnishes. Seasonal features." He lets out a quiet laugh. "Some of them were... ambitious."

I groan. "That sounds like her."

"But," he adds, pointing toward the bar, "a few of her ideas made the menu. The smoked olives? Hers. The honeyed ricotta? All Tracy."

I don't say anything for a moment. I just sit there, the low hum of the room around me.

"Really sorry to hear of her passing." His hands are on his hips.

"Thank you," I reply, a feeling of gratitude blooming in my chest. I hadn't known this place existed. Hadn't known she'd left her fingerprints here by being herself. It feels like finding a note my mom left behind without realizing it—tucked into the walls of Golden Harbor, waiting for me to walk in one night and recognize it.

I wouldn't have even known it was here if it wasn't for Sadie.

Sadie reaches across the table and lightly touches my hand, like she knows exactly what I'm feeling without me having to explain it.

The owner straightens. "First round's on me," he says. "For family."

As he walks away, Sadie grins. "That's pretty amazing," she says.

She isn't wrong.

Dipping her bread into the honeyed ricotta, Sadie hums like the flavor surprised her, then looks up at me. "I think your mom and I would've been friends. I'm a big fan of lists. To-do lists, goals, summer lists." She laughs, a little self-aware. "It's how I organize my brain. When things feel... loud."

I tilt my head. "Why the summer list? What's on there?"

She pauses, glass hovering short of her lips. There's a shift—small, but I catch it. That moment where she's deciding how honest to be. Like her sunshine rays are dimming a bit.

"Last summer was rough," she finally admits. "Like, capital-R rough."

I don't interrupt.

"I wasn't sure what my life was supposed to look like anymore," she continues. "The version I thought I was walking toward just... disappeared. And suddenly I was asking questions I thought I'd already answered."

Her fingers trace the rim of the glass. "Do I stay here forever? Is this it for me? Is this my place, my people, my ending? Or am I scared to leave because starting over feels worse?"

Something in my chest tightens.

"I was still healing," she adds quietly. "From the called-off engagement. Things I hadn't dealt with quite yet."

I swallow.

"So I made a list," she says, lifting her eyes back to mine. "Little things. Things that made me feel like myself again. Or things I wanted to feel."

I lean forward without realizing it. "Like what?"

Sadie smiles, softer now. "Sunsets."

"Sunsets," I repeat.

"They're one of my favorite things," she shares. "They make everything feel temporary in a good way. Like, no matter how messy the day was, you get this one beautiful moment that asks nothing from you. So, I wanted to see as many as I could this summer."

I glance past her shoulder toward the dim bar, then subtly down at my watch.

"We can make it."

She's still talking, waving it off. "It's silly. And we don't have to—"

I reach across the table, my fingers closing gently around her wrist. The electricity crackles as her breath stutters.

"It's not silly," I insist. "And we absolutely can."

She blinks. "Colson—"

"You gave me this," I say, voice low. "This place. That connection with my mom I didn't even know existed."

Her expression softens.

"Let me do something for you."

For a second, she looks at me, searching. Then she smiles—slow, warm, a little undone. "Okay," she says.

We settle the check quickly, her knee brushing mine under the table. When we stand, I place my hand at the small of her back, guiding her through the dark room. She leans into it, like it's where she's supposed to be.

Sadie slips her hand into mine as we make our way to the car.

The sky starts to dim but my girl definitely does not.

Forty

SADIE

THE WIND IS STRONG off the lake but the warmth from the sun dulls it, creating the perfect summer night. Colson's hand laced with mine, his thumb rubbing mine. Tonight feels like it's one I'll remember for a long time. Watching Colson listen as he learned of the connection with his mom and the speakeasy. How she made an impact not only on the menu but the owner.

She left a piece of herself in Golden Harbor and that's pretty special.

Thick clouds stretch across the sky—not stormy, but textured—like someone dragged a brush through wet paint.

Colson slows beside me, looking out over the lake. "Damn," he says. "Wish it was a clear sky for you."

I smile, squeezing his hand. "No, you don't."

He looks at me, confused. "I don't?"

I shake my head. "It's a myth that clear skies create the best sunset. Pretty, sure—but flat. You need clouds for this part." I gesture toward the sky, where the colors are already deepening, oranges melting into pinks, streaks of purple beginning to show. "The clouds catch the light. They give it somewhere to land."

He watches quietly, like he's trying to see it the way I do. "I didn't know," he admits. "So this is a good one?"

"This will be a *great* one," I insist, bumping my shoulder into his.

We walk closer to the water until our shoes are abandoned somewhere behind us and the cool lake slips around our ankles. Small waves roll in, calm and gentle, the chilled water the perfect contrast.

We stand there for a while without talking, in a kind of silence that doesn't feel empty. Me, Colson, the sound of the water, and a gorgeous sunset. It's pretty perfect.

Then he quietly asks, "Is this summer better than last?"

The question lands right in my chest. I don't answer right away even though my body wants to scream a resounding "yes!" I watch the sun dip lower, the sky catching fire in slow motion.

"At the start of it, I wasn't so sure. Maybe a little afraid of reliving that rough season I remembered." The honesty burns at my throat a little bit.

I can feel Colson watching me.

"I think I knew it was better before I let myself say it out loud," I continue. "Like my body knew first. I started really laughing again. Sleeping. Wanting things. Seeing more joy in the small things."

I glance over at him. He's looking at me now, not the sunset.

"But to really answer your question, yes, I know it is," I say quietly. "I can feel it right here." I press my free hand to my chest. "And you're... part of that."

His expression shifts into something open, careful, real.

"But it's not just you," I add, because that matters. "It's me coming back to myself. Little by little. Remembering who I was before every-thing fell apart."

He nods, thumb brushing lightly over my knuckles, grounding me.

"I don't feel lost," I admit. "I haven't felt that in a while."

The sun slips beneath the horizon then, the colors stretching one last time before falling into dusk. The lake reflects it all, gold and violet rippling at our feet.

"I get it, I think. I came here because I didn't know where else to go. But now? It feels like this was where I needed to be. I had no idea I'd be next door to a bunch of kids playing the sport that had such a hand in shaping me."

His hand squeezes mine and then he pulls me in, so we're facing each other. Colson leans his forehead against mine, close enough that I can feel his breath. His eyes are drinking this in.

"Had no idea I'd meet you."

Colson takes a hand, tucking my hair behind my ear. Like he did the first day when that spark buzzed along my skin. This time, his hand lands at the nape of my neck and he pulls me close.

The world narrows. The lake rolls behind us, waves slipping in and out like they're keeping time. My breath catches—not because he's rushed, but because he isn't.

When his lips finally meet mine, it's light. A question more than a statement.

And I answer.

The kiss deepens, not fast or desperate but perfectly certain. Like he's memorizing me. Like he's afraid the moment might disappear. His hand stays steady at my neck, warm and protective, and my fingers curl into the front of his shirt, reminding myself this is real. His lips taste me and I can't get enough of him.

I feel it—the way everything keeps shifting and locking into place. Colson pulls back to rest his forehead against mine again, noses brushing, our breaths tangled.

"I love knowing you," he murmurs.

I smile, heart racing, still tasting him. That is quite literally one of the dreamiest things anyone has ever said to me. The words, plus the way he looks at me? Unmatched.

Standing here, waves rolling in, summer wrapping around us, I realize something quietly, undeniably true.

I am falling in love with Colson Burke.

Forty-One

COLSON

THE ECHO OF THE ball against the hardwood settles something in my chest. Makes me feel like I'm at home.

It's been two weeks since I called Howie and told him I wasn't finished. How I was ready to find my next team. Two weeks of waking up sore in the good way, of rehab bands and makeshift ice baths, of trusting my shoulder again instead of flinching every time I lifted my arm over my head.

Today is Sadie's idea, actually.

Invite them to see you, she'd said, like it was obvious. *Let them watch you move. Actions speak louder than words. You know that.*

So now I'm at the rec center, the same one that only a few weeks ago smelled like mildew and rainwater after the storm. The court gleams like it's ready for something new.

I roll my shoulders as I jog through warm-ups, focusing on form, on rhythm. Howie stands near the sideline with his phone up, already filming, his familiar intense expression locked in. Two other guys—contacts he pulled through favors and old relationships—stand a few feet away, quietly taking notes. They work with teams that had expressed interest, before I even made the choice to come back. Howie asked if I wanted to know what teams they were from and I said no. Doesn't matter. The goal remains the same: to show them I'm worth a shot.

And then there's Sadie.

She's on the bleachers with her laptop open, legs tucked beneath her, hair pulled back. She's pretending to be focused on something—camp schedules or some admin—but I know better. I can feel her eyes on me.

A night on my own is rare lately. Somewhere between dinners at her place, mornings at mine, late walks and sunsets at the beach, we've sort of... folded into each other's lives. Easily. The thought steadies me as I move into drills.

I cut hard, pivot, pull up. The shot feels clean. My shoulder doesn't protest. I hear the ball hit the bottom of the net and something loosens in my chest.

You can do this.

I run through another sequence, breathing controlled, body leaning into muscle memory. Every movement feels like proof—not only to them, but to me.

When I glance up again, Sadie's smiling, a bit restrained, like she doesn't want to distract me but can't help it. I swear it gives me an extra inch of lift.

Between reps, I grab my water bottle, hands on my hips, heart thudding. Howie nods at me, with a look that says *this is good* without saying it out loud. One of the scouts murmurs something to the other, scribbling faster now.

This feels doable. The next team. The next city.

But right on its heels comes the ache that's been hanging around for a bit. Golden Harbor has been good to me. Better than I expected. There's a part of me that tightens at the thought of summer ending, of packing this up and leaving—of leaving *her*. The idea sits deep in my stomach, dull and uncomfortable, like I don't want to look at it too closely yet.

One thing at a time.

I head back out onto the court, catching Sadie's gaze for a brief moment. She lifts her chin, almost saying *you've got this* without words.

I *know* I do.

I take the ball at the top of the key, breathe once, then drive.

My feet leave the floor before my brain can overthink it. My shoulder holds. My body follows through. I rise and slam the ball through the rim with a clean, sharp snap that echoes through the rec center.

For a split second, everything goes quiet.

Then Howie claps, loud and sharp. He's on his feet, grinning like he won an argument he's been having for months.

"That's it," he booms, voice bouncing off the walls. "He's back, baby."

I land, heart hammering, a laugh breaking out of me before I can stop it. It feels good—better than good. It feels *right*. Like muscle memory and belief finally lined up again. I know I can fucking do this.

Out of the corner of my eye, I see Sadie clap too, softer, her smile wide and proud in a way that hits me straight in the chest.

I jog back, grabbing my towel as sweat drips down my temples. The two scouts exchange looks now, nodding to each other, one of them already tapping something into his phone. Clearly, they're interested in me.

I walk over, still catching my breath, adrenaline buzzing under my skin.

"Hey," I say sincerely. "Thanks for making the trip. I know it's the middle of summer and not exactly easy to get to." I shake both of their hands.

One of them waves it off. "Worth it. Glad to see you back, Colson."

Howie slaps my shoulder, careful of the bad one like always. "Told you," he says under his breath. "You're not done yet."

"Of course he's not," Sadie agrees, standing next to me. She's wearing that smirk, the one I love to kiss.

Howie laughs; it's the kind that tells me he immediately likes someone. We've worked together long enough that we know all of each other's tells. Believe me, I get it.

Having her in my corner like this? Giving me the time and space here? It's everything.

He nods to her. "That's what I've been saying!" He's enthusiastic and clearly excited.

Honestly, I realize I missed him more than I let myself believe. Howie's always been in my corner. When I told him everything, came completely clean on the questionable care, and the reckless behavior that had me losing my shit.

I could hear in his voice how sorry he was for me, so getting him to show up here was easy. He truly supports me. He's currently working with my lawyer to discuss how to share this with new teams who may ask.

It's clear the information most likely has to be made public. It's what will keep other athletes safe and help get me back on track.

The guys pack up, reiterating they're happy with what I had to show them, and then it's just me and Sadie.

"You were so good!" she exclaims, wrapping her arms around my neck.

I try to keep a little space between us and say, "I'm so sweaty. You want me to shower."

She slows, putting her nose to mine, and then kisses me. "You think I care about a little sweat? Wrong girl." She puts her lips to mine again. "But it's Thursday. You know what that means."

"I'll never look at a Thursday the same way ever again."

"You'll start doodling little cherries in your planner. I can see it now." She presses herself into me, making writing gestures with one of her hands.

"You know there's no way I have a planner." I must do something with my face because her eyes go wide and she pushes a finger in my chest.

"Oh my god! There it is! That signature Colson Burke scowl... or something close to it." Sadie puts both hands on the sides of my face, lightly tapping my cheeks.

I playfully roll my eyes and try not to let the grin get the best of me. "Come on, I do have to shower if you want to get to Cherry Pit tonight."

"Can I come, too?"

That devilish smirk on those perfect lips. Her eyes sparkle like the fireworks on the Fourth of July. Before she can tell what I'm doing, I pick her up, throw her over my shoulder—the good one—and carry her outside the rec center, right into my house.

She's laughing so hard I can feel it while holding onto her. I swear, that laugh, the light she brings, has brought me back to life.

Forty-Two

SADIE

"I don't get it," he says, leaning back in his chair. "Cherries are dessert."

"Don't be a hater until you try it. I'm telling you..."

We're out on the patio at Cherry Pit, string lights zigzagging overhead like constellations someone took the time to map out. The lake is beyond the railing, waves rolling in like a lullaby, the air cool enough now that my shoulders goosebump every once in a while.

Birdie drops off the salsas with a grin. "Okay," she announces, pointing to the dishes. "Cherry jalapeño, cherry street corn, and—what seems to be the crowd favorite—smoked cherry with lime."

Colson squints at the lineup like it personally offended him. "This feels like a prank."

Birdie snorts. "You say that now. What? They didn't have fancy salsa in Chicago?"

"Not where I'm eating..." he replies seriously.

I roll my eyes. "Ignore him. He's about to eat his words."

She laughs and slides the basket closer. "Let me know which one converts him."

When she walks away, Colson picks up a chip, dips it cautiously into the cherry jalapeño, and takes a bite.

I watch his face change in real time.

"Oh," he muses.

"Mm-hmm."

He tries the smoked cherry next, then the corn. "Okay, hold on. Why is this... actually good?"

"Because it's perfect," I boast, dipping my chip again, carefully selecting the one with the most visible salt crystals.

He laughs, shaking his head, and I notice—again—how unfairly attractive he is when he does that. Dark brown hair falling into his eyes, shoulders filling out the sleeves of his T-shirt, muscles earned, not styled. He looks relaxed tonight, open, like the court earlier loosened something in him.

"This one," I say, nudging the smoked cherry salsa toward him. "Trust me."

He does, and groans. "Okay. Fine. I was wrong. I'm kinda pissed this is so good"

I grin. "Say it louder."

"I was wrong," Colson repeats dramatically, "about cherries."

We're cozy, knees brushing under the table, his arm resting along the back of my chair like it belongs there. The lights sway slightly overhead, the lake murmuring behind us; for a moment, everything feels easy.

The wind whips through, almost feeling like the start of fall. It's way too early for that but try telling that to my over-analyzing brain. No part of me thinks there's a world where Colson Burke stays in Golden Harbor. He's going back to the NBA. And he should.

"End of summer's coming fast," I say quietly, dipping another chip.

He nods. "Yeah. Faster than I'd like."

There it is. The thing we keep circling.

"I don't even know where I'll land," he adds. "If a team gives me a shot—"

I look at him. "Someone is definitely picking you up. You're damn near your prime."

He nods, smiling at me. His eyes search mine as he leans forward, resting his elbows on the table. "I want this to work too. Whatever this is."

He rubs his hands together while my brain makes sure that I'm actually awake, not dreaming.

"I'm serious, Sadie. You're like... the light that makes everything make more sense."

Something warm settles in my chest. "I believe you."

My phone rings then, sharp and out of place.

Colson winces. "Who leaves their ringer on?"

"I know, I know, all elder millennials everywhere are screaming," I groan, grabbing it automatically—and freezing.

Nick.

The name sits on the screen and hasn't lost its power. It stops ringing. No voicemail.

Then it rings again. This time, I leave it on the table, Colson reading the caller ID.

He watches me carefully. "Everything okay?"

I exhale, silencing it. "Yeah. If it wasn't, he'd leave a message. Or text."

He nods slowly. "You can answer it if you want."

"I absolutely don't want to do that. That man wasted years of my life. He doesn't get tonight." I smile and reach for Colson's hand over the table.

There's a drawn-out pause before Colson asks, "Does he call a lot? Like, are you guys friendly?"

I start laughing before I answer, "No. No way. I don't want anything bad to happen to him or anything like that, but he isn't someone I could be friends with. After everything."

Colson waits. We've covered the fact that I was engaged to someone named Nick, but that's basically it. Not because I have anything to hide; more like it was a waste of my time.

I stare at the table for a second.

"Nick was supposed to be the guy who didn't hurt me. He came into my life when I needed something. It was the one thing that felt like the universe gifted me for… take away the basketball career, but give me the love of my life." I sigh then press my lips together, trying to buy a little time. I hate talking about this, only because the honest version makes me feel a bit pathetic.

"He called it off because he was in love with someone else," I reveal, my voice steady even if my chest tightens. "Someone he'd been friends with almost his whole life."

Colson's jaw sets, but he doesn't interrupt.

"When we first started dating, I asked him straight up if he loved her. It was maybe the third time we had all hung out and they had this… weird pull to each other. And he told me over and over that it wasn't like that."

I look up at Colson now, who answers. "But it was." He reaches across the table, his hand covering mine—warm, solid, grounding.

"I'm really sorry," he says quietly.

"Don't apologize for things not in your control." My voice is quieter than I mean.

"But I am sorry that happened to you. I can't imagine thinking you're going to marry someone and then it's like… no… no thanks."

"Yeah, it hit me harder than almost anything. For some reason, it felt like it was my fault. Like I couldn't see it sooner."

He tenses. "No fucking way was any of that your fault. I don't know what he did to make you feel that way, but from here, it looks like you have the wonderful ability to look for, and believe in, the best in people. Sometimes they let you down."

"And sometimes they don't," I finish, leaning over the table, reaching far enough to kiss him. It's slow and sweet. The type of kiss that feels like the best hug, one that makes you feel safe and planted.

I sit back in my chair as Birdie brings us drink refills. She sets the glasses down with a knowing smile, the ice clinking. "Looks like you two figured out the salsa situation," she teases.

Colson laughs, slipping his hand back to mine under the table. "I've been humbled."

I smile, content in a way that feels rare and earned. The night hums around us—the low rush of waves, the glow of string lights, the easy warmth of his presence beside me.

For once, I'm not thinking about what comes next or what might end.

I'm right here. And right now is enough.

IT'S LATE AND WE'RE some of the last people at Cherry Pit. I'm sitting next to Colson as we look out over the lake. We're the only ones on the patio when something catches our attention from inside the restaurant. A dropped glass. People sort of yelling, or at least getting loud enough to carry out here.

Then I definitely hear Birdie say something like, "What the hell are you even doing here?"

My body reacts before my brain does.

My shoulders tense. My stomach drops. There's a sudden, sickening awareness in my chest—like a pressure change before a storm. I know that voice. I know it the way you know a song you haven't heard in years but still remember every word to.

Colson and I both turn to each other at the same time, our backs still to the entrance. He looks curious.

I feel frozen. My pulse is hammering in my ears. I don't want to turn. I already know.

Then I hear him say my name. Like he's asking a question. Like he's agitated.

Too familiar.

I turn slowly, dread curling tight around my ribs, and there he is—standing inside the doorway, jaw tight, eyes already locked on me like I was the only reason he came.

Nick.

A full year disappears in one breath.

Birdie is squared up in front of him, arms crossed, visibly pissed, but he's half a step past her, like he pushed his way into the space.

"Oh my god," I whisper, more to myself than anyone.

Colson's body shifts beside me immediately. He doesn't step in front of me, simply gets closer. Protective without being possessive. His hand finds mine, grounding me when my knees threaten to lock.

Nick looks... wrecked. Thinner. Edgier. Like someone who hasn't slept enough or thought anything through.

"I called," he says, voice rough. "You didn't answer."

My chest tightens. "You didn't leave a message."

Birdie snaps, "Because she doesn't want to talk to you!" She takes a breath then asks, "Are you drunk? Did you drive here like that?" She jabs a finger in his chest.

Nick doesn't take his eyes off me. "Sadie, I need a minute."

Colson steps a little bit in front of me, not all the way, but enough to make a statement. He finally speaks, calm but unmistakably firm. "It's late."

Nick's gaze flicks to him then, really seeing him for the first time. The way Colson stands. The way his hand is still wrapped around mine.

Something flashes across Nick's face—maybe surprise or regret—but it's gone fast.

"I didn't know you were seeing somebody," Nick sneers.

I straighten, anger cutting through the shock. "How would you know? You're not part of my life. You don't get to ambush me," I state, voice shaking but loud enough. "Not here. Not ever again."

For a moment, it feels like everything is about to tip.

Standing here with the lake behind me and Colson at my side, I realize this isn't just the past showing up.

It's a test. But I'm not the same girl he left behind.

Forty-Three

COLSON

I DON'T KNOW HOW the night flipped so fast.

One minute it was string lights, lake air and Sadie smiling across the table like she'd finally exhaled. The next thing is this terrible sound creeping from the main restaurant area, ruining the vibes.

I didn't recognize the guy at first. I knew he didn't belong here.

He's standing too close to the patio entrance, half past Birdie like he pushed his way into the moment. His eyes are locked on Sadie in a way that makes my stomach drop. Possessive. Familiar. Like he thinks he still has a right.

Sadie goes still. Not frozen exactly—more like bracing.

Then it clicks. This has to be him. Nick.

I take him in quickly. He looks strung out. Not falling-over drunk, but wired and loose around the edges. Jaw tight. Movements jerky. Birdie's tone tells me everything I need to know. This wasn't a friendly pop-in.

He keeps trying to step closer, angling around Birdie, eyes never leaving Sadie.

"Hey," I say, stepping in front of her without thinking. Calm voice. "You need to take a step back."

He scoffs like he's offended. "I just want to talk to her."

Birdie snaps, "You don't. And you're not."

I glance back at Sadie for half a second, checking in. Her hand grips the edge of the table, knuckles white. That's enough for me.

"Birdie," I say quietly but firmly, "go inside."

She hesitates, clearly torn, then nods. "I'm calling this in," she mutters, pointing at Nick. "You don't go anywhere."

Nick bristles the second she leaves. "Who the fuck are you?" he snaps at me.

I keep my voice even. "I'm not telling you anything. I'm asking you to lower your voice and give her space."

He laughs, sharp and humorless. "Yeah, okay."

Sadie shifts behind me, and I feel it—her fear, her anger, the way this guy is dragging her somewhere she didn't choose to go tonight.

Nick tries to move again. I block him easily, not touching him, just existing in the way that makes it clear he's not getting past me.

"That's enough," I insist. "You've made your point. It's over."

He opens his mouth like he's going to argue. Like he's going to push.

I don't wait. I turn slightly, reaching back for Sadie's hand. "Let's get out of here."

She doesn't question it. Just stands and grabs her bag, fingers threading through mine like she's been waiting for permission to go.

We move fast past Nick.

Inside the restaurant, heads turn. Chairs scrape. The air is thick with tension. I keep my body angled so Nick can't get close, guiding Sadie through the narrow aisle toward the door in front of us.

Birdie's voice rings out, loud and furious. "Nick! Give me your keys!"

There's shouting. Someone swears. I don't look back.

The only thing that matters is getting Sadie out of there—away from him, away from the noise, back to where she can breathe.

As the door swings open and the night air hits us again, I tighten my grip on her hand.

I hear him before I see him. Nick's voice cuts through the night, loud and wild, carrying way farther than it should. Tourists slow on the sidewalk. A couple near the street actually stops.

"What the hell are you doing?" he yells. "Sadie—seriously?"

I keep us moving, my hand firm around hers, my body angled so I'm between them. My heart is pounding now, not from fear—anger. Controlled, but sharp.

Then he says my name.

"Nah—what the hell are you doing with *NBA loser Colson Burke*?" he shouts. "What is he even doing here?"

That's when I stop. Not because of the insult. Because Sadie's grip tightens, like the words landed somewhere that hurts.

Nick staggers closer, frantic energy pouring off him. Too loud. He smells like alcohol when the wind shifts. "You really just replace me with *this*?" he keeps going. "You think this is better?"

Birdie bursts out of the restaurant behind him, keys in her hand, voice already raised. "Nick! Stop it! You're done. Right now." One of the bartenders comes outside with her, following close behind.

I turn fully toward him, planting my feet. "Hey," I say, calm but unmovable. "Enough."

He jabs a finger in my direction. "You don't get to tell me—"

"Shut the fuck up," I cut in. "You're drunk. You're embarrassing yourself. Go home. Sleep it off."

People are definitely watching now. A group across the street has gone quiet. Someone pulls out a phone.

Nick laughs, unhinged. "You think you're tough because you're Colson Burke? All washed up?" And then he shoves me.

It's nothing but words. Intentional. When I don't react, he does it again.

Everything in me wants to react. Wants to end it. My fists clench on instinct. But I don't.

I take one step back, putting even more space between him and Sadie. "Do not touch me again," I say, low and clear.

He keeps yelling, like volume equals control. "Colson! You hear me? You think you're something?"

I don't rise to it. I don't give him what he wants.

Instead, I glance back at Sadie and murmur, "We're going. Now."

She nods immediately.

I guide her away, my body blocking his line of sight, my hand steady even though my pulse is hammering. Behind us, Birdie keeps shouting—calling him out, telling him to stop.

Nick's voice follows us down the sidewalk, chaotic and cracking, echoing off the buildings. When there's a few seconds of silence and I think we've finally lost this asshole, Sadie's name rips through the night.

Not shouted—*torn* out of him.

It's loud and guttural and full of something ugly, something raw enough it makes me flinch before I can stop it. Heads turn again. A couple tourists actually freeze mid-step. I feel Sadie tense next to me, like that sound reached straight into her chest.

Something in me hardens. I stop walking and turn back around.

Nick is still yelling, backing toward us, arms wide like the whole street owes him attention. Rage is rolling off him now, unchecked. This isn't confusion or heartbreak—it's entitlement.

I step toward him. Not fast or threatening. Controlled.

He's still spiraling. "You hear me? You think you—"

When I'm right in front of him, I put my chest to his. "Hey." My voice cuts through it and it's raw like gravel.

He falters.

I take another step forward and he has to step back. "I'm going to tell you this one more time."

The street goes quiet enough that I know people are listening.

"You do not get to talk to her like that," I say evenly. "You don't get access to her. You don't get any of her."

He scoffs, still retreating. "You don't know anything about us."

"I know enough," I snap. "Lose her number. Forget about this place. Anyone who shows up drunk and acting like this doesn't deserve a second of her time."

He takes another step back and his heel catches the curb. He goes down hard, landing on his ass with a startled grunt, and some of the tourists gasp.

I take another small step until I'm standing over him.

"This is where it ends," I say quietly. "Leave her alone. Or I will fucking end you, okay?"

For a beat, all I hear is his breathing. Then I turn away and I don't look back.

I go straight to Sadie. She's shaking. Not visibly crying, just... rattled. I pull her into me immediately, one arm around her shoulders, the other at her back, holding her close enough that she can feel how solid I am.

"You're okay," I murmur, just for her. "I've got you."

She nods against my chest, fingers gripping my shirt like she needs something real to hold onto. A few seconds later, police lights reflect off the lake.

Forty-Four

SADIE

WE'RE TUCKED INTO THE back of Cherry Pit while the officers sort through this mess. The place smells like citrus cleaner and fryer oil that's finally gone cold, an end-of-night scent that usually means relief. Tonight it just makes my stomach roll.

When Nick came in—clearly drunk, loud in a sloppy way that's meant to look charming but never is—and Birdie clocked it immediately, she didn't hesitate. One look at the way he swayed, the way his voice cut too sharp through the room, and she was already on the phone calling the police.

I'd basically begged them to move us out of sight from the front windows.

One: this is humiliating. Two: I'm painfully aware that Colson probably doesn't want a single extra photo floating around out there.

When I saw the tourists across the street, phones half-raised the moment someone whispered his name, my chest dropped straight to my feet. Golden Harbor has been different for him. Quiet. Normal. No spotlights, no performance. Just lake water and fireworks and easy smiles.

Now it feels like I've ruined it.

Maren slides onto the stool beside me, the vinyl squeaking in the empty bar. She was walking to her car from putting in some late night hours at the flower shop and stumbled onto the disaster that was Nick. Cherry Pit is officially closed—servers stacking chairs, the dishwasher humming in the back—while the cops talk to Colson and Nick near the storage hallway.

"What the hell do you think he was even doing here?" she asks, knocking back her vodka soda like she's mad at the glass. The bar might be closed, but Birdie didn't even pretend this wasn't an exception.

My hands shake as I lift my drink. I notice Maren's doing the same, which somehow makes it worse. "No idea. I haven't heard from him in over a year. Like... truly nothing. Out of sight, out of mind." My throat tightens. "Until he called tonight. And then just showed up."

Nick was a lot of things, but aggressive had never been one of them. Not like this. He specialized in passive-aggressive digs, in rewriting reality until I questioned my own memory. He could convince me the sky was green if it served him, and could suck joy out of a room without ever raising his voice. I didn't even realize how small I'd become until I was already gone.

"I can't believe he just showed up, like a bad wish granted by some shitty genie," Maren mutters. "Where is he even living?"

"Downstate. Hours away." I stare at the condensation ring my glass leaves behind.

Maren shakes her head slowly. "I'm *shocked* Colson didn't punch him square in the face."

"Oh, he wanted to." My chest aches at the thought. Colson's fists clenched so hard his knuckles went white, then shoved behind his back like he didn't trust himself. Like he needed to physically restrain the part of him that wanted to protect me.

Fuck. It stings.

Tonight had been so good before all of this. We'd even recovered after the random phone call—laughed it off, settled back into the quiet. One minute we're watching the lake, his arm pulling me close like it's instinct, and the next? Total, awful chaos.

"Nick's lucky I wasn't here," Maren says fiercely. "I'd have kicked him straight in the dick. Apologized. Gained his trust back. And then done it again."

Her eyes shine, angry tears collecting there, the kind that always surprises me. Not sad. Furious. Protective.

Birdie leans across the bar toward me, voice gentler now. "Babe, you okay? Looks like they're wrapping things up back there." She tips her head toward the officers, toward Colson standing stiff and contained a few feet away.

"What can they even do?" Maren asks, glancing between us. "Colson didn't do anything, right?"

Birdie shakes her head. "This happens sometimes with tourists. Not usually locals." She sighs. "They can't do much without catching Nick in the act, driving or even holding his keys. A few of us gave statements. Told them he fell on his own dumb-ass accord and Colson kept his hands to himself."

What a nightmare.

"It's messy. Annoying." Birdie wipes down the bar with a little more force than necessary. "But they'll make sure Nick gets somewhere safe for the night." She snorts. "Not that he deserves an ounce of grace."

I stare down at my drink, at the ripples still trembling inside it, my hands the culprit.

I hate the way I can still hear Nick screaming my name like that, like his words left a mark where no one can see. Like he was ripping through this happy place. The city I call home.

And I have no idea why. What does he even want? I kind of hate that I'm thinking about it but how could I not?

The sound of footsteps grab our attention and we walk as a cop leads Nick out, followed by the other cop and Colson. The sight of them has me standing.

Nick slows as he approaches me, and before anyone can say anything, Maren jumps in.

"I wish I could say it was good to see you but that would be a lie. Gross behavior, Nick." She rolls her eyes and turns back to face the bar, not even giving him a chance to respond.

His face drops a bit and his eyes look at mine. The man I fell in love with years ago is nowhere in sight. Like, not even a glimpse of him.

"Sadie. I just wanted to talk." His head almost hangs but he's being pushed from behind.

I don't even have a chance to respond. Not even sure I want to.

Tom, the town deputy, says, "Keep going, Nick. We talked about this. Now is not the time."

Colson wraps me up in a hug, his arms strong and substantial. I put my head in his chest, so thankful this night is almost over. He doesn't say anything but instead holds onto me, swaying us back and forth. One of his hands draws circles on my back.

When they're out the front door, Maren jumps in. "Spill, Colson. What happened?"

He blows out a breath, looking around to make sure no one else is nearby. "I mean, he tried to say that I pushed him. He was in there, throwing a fit, and then the deputies let him know they already had statements from other people." He rubs his hands over his face. "And then he finally told the truth."

"What a dick," she says.

Colson looks at me when he continues, "He just kept saying he came to talk. Didn't say why. Or what about. They didn't do anything about the drinking and driving, except they're going to drop him off at one of the motels nearby. Awfully nice." He rolls his eyes.

"I brought him here a few times when we were together. Maybe that's why," I contemplate, doing my best to make sure it doesn't sound like an excuse—that's the last thing he deserves.

"Well, at least he's out of your hair." Maren stands from the bar. "You got her?" she asks Colson.

He nods and responds, "Of course."

She puts a hand on his shoulder, which is kind of funny because he's so tall, but Maren has that energy to go toe-to-toe with him. "Thank you for taking care of her tonight. I appreciate it." She pauses and then points at him, "And, I expect it."

"You got it," he assures her.

Maren leaves and it's only me and him.

I lean, my back hitting the bar with the weight of the evening.

Colson doesn't say anything at first. He looks at me, which is somehow worse than if he'd started talking. His jaw is tight, shoulders stiff, like he's holding something back. I can feel his anger without him naming it, the way it hums under his skin.

He steps closer, close enough that I can smell his peppermint soap, something familiar and grounding. Then he kisses my forehead.

It's simple and soft. But needed.

"I don't really know anything about him but I'll tell you one thing," he says quietly, like it's been sitting on his tongue all night. "There's no way he knew what he had." He swallows, his hand flexing at his side. "The way he stole your light? Never again."

My throat tightens. I stare at the floor because if I look at him, I might cry, and the thought of doing that in an empty Cherry Pit bar is too depressing to take.

Colson lifts my chin gently with one finger, forcing my eyes back to his. "You are incredible."

The word lands warm in my chest. I don't quite believe them yet.

"Sunshine girl," he adds, like it's a truth he's reminding me of, not a nickname.

Something in me melts. Enough to catch my breath.

"Come on," he says, exhaling like he's made a decision. "Let's get out of here." He grabs my hand and leads me outside.

Minutes later, I'm in his passenger seat, exhaustion settling into my bones as the remaining downtown streetlights blur past the window. Colson's hands are steady on the wheel, his presence solid beside me.

I rest my head back, eyes closing.

Sunshine girl. I can't get over it. The way he sees me? Tonight, it's everything.

Forty-Five

COLSON

I WAKE UP BEFORE the sun, the house still and quiet. Sadie's curled on her side beside me, hair fanned across the pillow, breathing slow and even.

I ease out of bed carefully, like the floor might betray me if I move too fast. I grab a pen from the bedside drawer and tear a corner from a page in an old notebook.

Went to the bakery. Back soon. — C

I slip it onto the bed where she'll see it if she wakes up, right by her hand.

The drive to the bakery is short, but my mind won't shut up. It keeps replaying last night on a loop—Nick showing up like that, uninvited and aggressive. *What a dick.*

The anger flares again, hot and familiar, but it's different now. Sharper. I end up gripping the steering wheel harder than I need to. I can't help but think about how small she looked at the end of the night. With people in her corner, she still was a shell of herself.

I keep thinking about the way Sadie froze when she saw him. The way her shoulders pulled in, like she was bracing for something. It really surprised me.

Because Sadie doesn't dim rooms—she changes them.

I think about the little things. The way her whole face lights up when someone recognizes her out in public. How she always stops to talk, even when she's in a hurry. The way she plays with her hair when she's listening, really listening, like nothing else exists. The way her smile is honest and grounding.

She makes *people* feel important.

By the time I get back to the house, my hands are full—two lattes balanced carefully along with a bag warm with pastries. I push the door open with my shoulder.

Sadie's up, sitting at the counter, hair messy and wearing one of my T-shirts like it belongs to her. Fuck, she's gorgeous.

She looks up and hits me with that smile I was thinking about in the car. It hits me square in the chest. Like something gears into place, another click I didn't know I was waiting for.

"You didn't have to do that," she muses, standing, already reaching for the bag.

"I wanted to," I insist, and realize how true it is. How I want to do everything for her.

She looks genuinely thankful, like I've given her more than coffee and sugar.

"I'm the one who should be thanking you—"

"Stop," I interrupt, dipping down and kissing her mouth.

If she's kissing me, she can't be telling me how sorry she is or how she's grateful I stepped in. We went through this last night and I thought I made myself clear. She has nothing to apologize or thank me for. There was no other way.

Each time she tries to talk, I kiss her harder, until she's in a fit of quiet laughter.

"Fine, fine. I'll drink the coffee and eat the treats." She lifts her arms in fake surrender.

A few seconds later, her eyes light up. "Oh! I almost forgot. Today is Harbor Blooms day!"

That's right. Another thing on Mom's list. My chest tightens, but it's the good kind—with purpose, not grief.

"Did your mom like flowers? I mean, all moms like flowers, but I feel like this has to mean something." Sadie points to the list on the fridge.

"Yeah, she did. We made friends with a few shop owners, and they'd sell her the leftover loose flowers for cheap when I was a kid." A smile creeps onto my lips thinking back to those days. "She'd come in and be glowing. She was always so excited. Sometimes it was a bunch of greenery and like three flowers, but they always made her happy."

Sadie puts a hand to her chest. "That's such a lovely story. Ugh, we're going to have so much fun today."

It's not the first time I thought it, and Sadie has even said it before, but my mom would've adored her. Her and Sadie would've been something together. It's a bittersweet feeling, because I'd love to see them meet, but I know how happy she'd be that I found someone like her. A love like this.

Love.

The word slipped right into my thoughts; it makes my gulp past the tightness in my throat. I wish I could say it was surprising, but it's absolutely not. Last night cemented it; if there's one good thing about that asshole showing up uninvited, it's that he proved she's mine to take care of. Mine to keep happy.

I have no idea where life will take us after this, my NBA career a question mark, but I'll do anything I can to keep her.

"Colson," Sadie says, waving her hand trying to get my attention. "Where'd you go?"

I let out a little laugh and answer honestly. "Just daydreaming."

Of her and me.

Forty-Six

SADIE

I LOVE THE WAY Harbor Blooms feels. The space is open, pastel and crisp white walls are the perfect contrast for the bright and bold flowers lining the perimeter. Maren sells premade bouquets, does delivery, and allows shoppers to build their own bouquet or arrangement.

"I'm serious," she insists, her eyes pinning me to my seat. "I don't think I've ever been more scared in my life than I was that winter." She cuts a few stems of fresh daisies that were just delivered. For now, it's just the two of us.

My stomach tightens. I know where she's going. I wish I didn't, but I do.

"That bad?" I ask, even though I already know the answer.

She nods, eyes fixed on the display of lilies to our left. "You weren't just sad, Sadie. You were... gone. Like someone had turned off your lights and forgot where the switch was. Nick stole something from you that wasn't his to take."

The words land heavy, bruising.

I stare down into my cup, my iced coffee melting. It makes my stomach ache—physically ache—to hear her talk about that version of me. The girl who slept until noon. Who forgot to eat. Who answered every *how are you?* with *fine* because it was easier than explaining how I couldn't remember the last time I smiled. How I was basically a depressive pit of nothing.

"I didn't know how to help," Maren continues quietly. "You were so small. And you've never been small. You're... you." She looks at me then, eyes bright and fierce. "You're a light. People notice when you dim."

My throat tightens. I swallow hard.

"It didn't feel like dimming," I admit. "It felt like I disappeared." Might be a bit more honest than I planned to share, but it's true.

She reaches across the table and squeezes my hand. "Exactly. That's why him showing up is the fucking worst. What a loser."

The bell above the door rings again.

Maren's mouth twists as she glances up. "Speak of the devil," she mutters. "Or the really annoying, painfully mediocre man."

Nick steps inside Harbor Blooms like he doesn't belong—to be fair, he really doesn't. His shoulders are hunched, hands shoved into the pockets of a jacket that's seen better days. His hair is longer than I remember. His face etched in exhaustion. He looks... wrecked.

I don't feel relief or anger. It's bone-tired exhaustion. Tired of him popping into my life when he isn't invited.

His eyes land on me, and for a split second, something in his expression fractures. It makes me feel nothing. That's really saying something, considering me a few years ago would've buckled. Not today.

Maren straightens immediately, protective instinct snapping into place. "No," she announces flatly when he opens his mouth. "Absolutely not."

"Only a few minutes," Nick replies, voice low, pleading. "Sadie, please."

My best friend takes a step in front of me, like she's my professional body guard. Her arms cross and she looks around, and for once, is probably content that the shop is empty besides the three of us.

"You have a lot of nerve and I say that as disrespectfully as I can." Her voice is level but dripping with quiet rage. "Go home."

He looks around "I just want a few minutes," Nick says, voice low, pleading. "Sadie, please."

I should say no. I know that. Every instinct in my body is screaming for me to shut this down. But I see it—the way his hands shake. The way his eyes keep darting to the door like he's already planning his escape.

Ultimately, my hope is that if I talk to him, he will leave. I can fall back into my normal self in the town I love. Not worried if Nick is going to ambush me at my next dinner.

"I'll talk to him," I say quietly.

Maren whips toward me. "Sadie—"

"Only a minute," I repeat. "We'll stay inside. You're right here." I'm not sure if I'm reassuring her or myself.

Nick exhales like he's been holding his breath for longer than healthy.

We move just inside the shop, near the counter, where Maren can absolutely hear us pretending not to. The buzz of the floral coolers fills the silence between us.

Nick doesn't say anything at first. He stands, staring at the floor like it might give him instructions. Each second that passes with nothing but silence makes me a little more annoyed. Like, let's get on with it.

"Colson will be here in a few minutes," I say finally. "So if you've got something to say, you might want to... say it."

He flinches at Colson's name, then nods.

"Last night wasn't my finest moment. I didn't mean for that to happen. It just did."

I say nothing because there isn't even an ounce of an apology there. My eyes are going wider with each second that passes and he isn't saying the right thing.

"You didn't mean for it to happen? Why does this feel like you're calling off our wedding again?" I can't help the snarky smile that tugs at my lips. I don't know if he remembers but that's exactly how he started the conversation years ago.

I didn't mean for this to happen. Like it was a spell he was under, no free will to be found, instead of the harrowing truth that he treated me like a thing he didn't need anymore.

He looks at his feet, rocking back and forth, and then starts with, "I'm sorry. For last night. For more than that. I know I screwed up," he says, words tumbling out too fast now. "Calling off the wedding. Falling for someone I swore was just a friend. I—" He rubs a hand over his face. "I didn't mean to hurt you."

I laugh on accident. It slips out before I can stop it. Not cruel but horribly honest.

"You don't *accidentally* break someone, Nick."

His shoulders sag as he looks out the window, like he's trying to distract himself.

"You seem like things are good here," he continues, voice cracking. "Happy. Moving on. And I can't. I'm stuck. I can't take the next step with her because I keep thinking—what if she does to me what I did to you? What if I ruined you? What if I broke something that can't be fixed?"

I meet his eyes then. Really meet them.

"You did break me," I say gently.

He winces like I've struck him.

"But not in a way I couldn't come back from," I continue. "You broke the version of me that was shrinking to fit you. The one who kept making herself quieter so you'd stay."

His breathing is uneven now.

"I didn't see it," he whispers.

"I know," I agree. "That was the problem. Especially because it was ridiculously intentional. You didn't care what I wanted. You seriously molded me in the way that would've fit exactly what you wanted."

I take a breath. This part matters.

"I'm glad you left me," I admit. "Not in the moment. God, not then. Then, I drowned in tears like you had died. The thing you did was horrible and made me question everything about myself." I rub my hands together, almost feeling for the place the engagement ring used to cut into my finger. "But big picture? Looking at it now? Thank you for tossing me the way you did. I'm stronger. Clearer. I know myself now. I know what I deserve. And it isn't someone who chooses me halfway."

He swallows hard, eyes glossy. This isn't the Sadie he remembers—the one who softened every truth for his comfort.

"You're different," he admits.

And so is he. The Nick I used to miss was always so confident in his ways. He knew where he was going, how he'd get there–no questions asked. Now he feels like a walking question mark where just enough breath could sway him one way or the other.

"I'd fucking hope so." I shift my weight, one hand on my hip.

He doesn't know it but he gave me the best compliment. I *am* different, in a way that feels right. A sliver of me can recognize what it took for him to make this trip—the old Sadie would view this as effort when really it's self-preservation.

I take a deep breath and continue, "There's nothing I can help you with. You need to talk to her, but you already know that." I step back slightly, creating space. "It's not my job to help you through this, Nick. You already took enough from me."

His head drops.

"But," I add, because kindness is still mine to give, if I make that choice. "Just because you did that to me doesn't mean someone else will do it to you. Some people are still good."

He looks up, startled.

"That includes me," I finish quietly. "I survived you."

The bell above the door rings again.

I don't turn around. I don't need to. I know exactly who is walking in.

"Good luck. There's still time for you to make better choices," I say, stepping past him toward Maren. Toward Colson, who stands in the doorway, waiting for me. "Safe travels."

Colson doesn't flinch; he opens up an arm, pulls me in. His hand tugs at my shoulder and he kisses my temple, our eyes still on Nick.

Nick looks wildly uncomfortable, like he opened the wrong door and stumbled into someone else's birthday party or something. He doesn't fit here. He doesn't fit with me.

When he realizes I'm not going to say anything else, and Maren is even acting like he doesn't exist, he walks up to Colson. I hold my breath.

He looks at Colson like it's painful and offers, "I'm sorry for last night." His words feel genuine but they're also unwanted. "Do better than I did..." Words trail as Nick has his hands on the door, ready to push it open.

Colson doesn't skip a beat when he replies, "That won't be hard." I can hear the smile in his voice.

And then he's gone. Colson doesn't say anything; instead, he puts his lips on mine, wrapping his arms around me and picking me up. Our kiss doesn't break until he starts spinning us and I can't help the laugh that pulls from my chest.

When Colson sets me down, his eyes are bright and his smile makes me beam back.

Quick, he kisses me again. He pulls back, my forehead to his, and he says, "There she is. Sunshine girl."

I may have been light before, but being with Colson makes it feel like I'm made of the stars, sunshine, and sparks.

Forty-Seven

COLSON

Sadie cheats. Not in a malicious way. Not even in a way she tries to hide. She just... cheats.

I know it the second she grins and drops her shoulder like she's about to drive left, then spins right instead, light on her feet, ponytail swinging. The ball kisses the backboard and drops through the net.

She throws her hands up. "Game point."

"You traveled," I tell her.

"I absolutely did not."

"Pretty sure you traveled," I insist, grabbing the ball and dribbling it back to her.

She steps in front of me, wrapping her arms around my neck and kisses me. Her favorite distraction. Fuck, it's mine, too.

"Fine, fine. You didn't travel. You win." I laugh at how easy I fold for her.

Morning light slants through the high windows, striping the court. We're the only ones here; for a second, it almost feels like a secret. Camp starts in forty five minutes but we've been coming in early for the last few weeks. Sadie says she has admin things to work on, but mostly I think she likes to watch me work out. Which isn't an issue on my side, not one bit.

My agent has let me know there are a handful of teams who have expressed interest in offering me a roster spot this coming up season. Even though everyone told me there would be potential offers, this kind of progress feels good. So, I'm doing my best to stay in shape and keep working on mobility and confidence when it comes to my shoulder.

I work on a few more drills, then let my body sort of cool down before I go into Coach Colson mode. Before I know it, the front doors open and kids practically skip in.

It's always chaotic with sneakers squeaking, voices overlapping, and parents calling out to their kid for the thing they forgot, but I've grown to really like this energy. Appreciate it. It always seems to fill my cup a bit.

Sadie claps her hands once, loud and sharp. "Shoes tied, water bottles in your cubby, and if I see anyone wearing flip flops in one minute, you're on clean up duty!"

I step back, give her space to do her thing. Watching Sadie work with the kids is one of my favorite things. Now that I'm helping more regularly, I let Sadie lead the way and I do my best supporting her.

I'm setting up cones when I feel it. That shift. The way the air tightens before something goes wrong.

I glance up and see Sadie freeze near the scorer's table. A woman stands in front of her—mid-thirties maybe, hair pulled back tight, arms crossed like she's bracing for impact. I know she's Emma's mom. I look and see Emma with her backpack on, waiting by the cubbies.

Sadie's smile is still there, but it's thinner now.

I don't hear what the woman says, but I see Sadie glance toward me. Just once. A flicker of something in her eyes I don't like. Then she nods toward the far end of the court.

I jog over, heart thumping with nervousness, "Everything okay?"

The woman's gaze slides to me, sharp and assessing. Not curious but definitely concerned.

"I was hoping to speak with Sadie privately," she says. I can tell she's trying to soften her tone but it barely works.

Sadie jumps in fast. "But if you're asking me about Colson, I'd like to give him a chance to respond."

Asking about me?

The woman's face pinches, like she's uncomfortable with this already, before she exhales. "I didn't know who he was at first," she says carefully. "I mean—I recognized him, but not like that."

My stomach tightens.

Without saying anything, she holds out her phone. On it is a picture of me standing over Nick, after he fell over the other night. Between the headline and the caption, it looks like I hit him.

Fuck.

Sadie looks at and her face pales. She stands up tall, tucking her hair behind her ears and says, "This is a misunderstanding. There was no fight or anything like that—"

She nods, but it's hesitant. "I understand that things like this don't always show everything. But it's getting around and I wanted to bring it to your attention."

Sadie's voice is calm but firm. "Colson didn't touch him. He didn't push him. He was trying to de-escalate the situation."

She's trying to stand up for me, and even though she's telling the truth, I'm not sure that's the move. I look up and watch as the kids get ready to start their warm-ups in a few minutes. How many other parents saw this? All of them?

"I'll be the first to say, this doesn't look good. But Sadie's right. I didn't put my hands on anyone. He literally tripped—"

The seconds the words come out, I know it sounds like a piss-poor excuse.

"My husband told me they dismissed you from your NBA team. Is that true?"

My stomach drops; it's so jarring that it's almost hard for me to stand. It only takes a second for me to realize how bad this will fucking look to anyone who sees this. Like it's normal. Like I'm out of control.

The woman shifts her weight. "I just think we need to talk about this as a family before Emma continues."

She's kinder than I expect. I can't say a single thing because I know how awful this looks. *Me.* How awful *I* look.

Sadie tries to jump in; I can feel the wave of her trying to convince the woman to change her mind. I put up a hand and say, "It's okay. Whatever you think is best."

Emma offers us a sad wave as her mom holds her hand, taking her back out to the car, and it stings.

For a second, the gym noise swells back in but it feels like I'm underwater. I don't know what to do.

Sadie puts a hand on my shoulder, "Let's get through this practice and then we'll figure it out, okay?"

I nod, trying to push down the disappointment and hurt. Right now, it feels like I let Sadie down. But leaving right now would be worse than staying and helping the kids have the experience they deserve.

I commit, mentally, to stay for this practice. Pretend I'm not panicking.

Other decisions can be made later.

Forty-Eight

SADIE

I'm standing in front of my fridge, pretending to think about what I'll make for dinner, when I'm really going over everything that happened with that parent before practice.

I'd been sure Colson was going to leave *before* practice even started. The moment that mother pulled Emma aside, the way her mouth tightened when she mentioned the article, the careful distance she kept from him—I'd braced myself. I'd watched Colson from the corner of my eye, waiting for the shrink of his shoulders, the defeat to ring out.

When Emma left early, I thought that would be it. I really thought he'd leave.

No part of me thinks he'll stay here forever. That's not practical. And I certainly don't have that good of luck. I know he wants to play for another team, and he'll have to go wherever that is, but that seems like something to worry about when the time comes.

Today's event made it feel like his decision is infringing on our time. About to pop the summer bubble. My stomach flips, nervousness pricking at me.

So when Colson stayed—when he finished practice, helped clean up, joked with the kids like nothing had cracked—I felt something dangerously close to relief.

The article didn't get it right. It never does.

He hadn't been aggressive. He hadn't been reckless. He was there taking care of me. Making sure I wasn't cornered, wasn't scared, wasn't alone. And now Colson was going to pay for it.

I could tell he was more reserved, like his mind wandered more than we're used to, but I couldn't blame him. No way.

My apartment feels like it's choking me. I'm up grabbing my keys before I have a chance to recognize the panic. That this is my fault. Nick is my baggage; if it weren't for him, this wouldn't be happening.

I close the fridge, grab my keys, and am practically running back out to my car. I drive straight to Colson's place, my hands tight on the steering wheel, my heart pounding with worry and nerves.

He's in the driveway when I pull in, lifting a duffel bag from the sidewalk and setting it carefully into the trunk of his BMW, still dented from the first day we met. There's another bag by his feet.

My stomach drops.

I get out of the car slowly, like if I move too fast I'll spook him into finishing whatever this is before I can stop it.

"Colson."

He freezes but doesn't turn around.

I walk closer, every step heavier than the last. "What's this?"

He stays quiet long enough that my chest starts to ache. Then he closes the trunk.

"I'm going back to Chicago."

The words hit hard and clean, like a punch I didn't see coming.

"What?" I whisper.

"My agent called. The photo is on every significant sports news outlet and it's making the rounds. I'm going to try and get ahead of it. Or something. I don't know."

"You can't leave," I say, like the only words my brain can produce.

"It's better for you. For the kids. You won't have any other parents afraid to leave their kids with you if I'm back in Illinois."

I shake my head. "You didn't do anything wrong. This isn't fair."

"I don't know what world you live in, but mine has never been all that fair," he replies, short and to the point. He still hasn't even looked at me. "You saw it today, firsthand."

"That doesn't mean—"

"It means it's better if I leave now. Before all the parents band together and tear down the thing you've worked your ass off to build," he cuts in, not harshly but tired. "I can't cost you this."

"This?" I gesture wildly. "The rec center? The league? I can handle a nervous parent, Colson."

"I can't handle being the reason you have to," he argues.

My chest tightens painfully. "This is my fault."

He stiffens. "No."

"It is," I insist. "If Nick hadn't shown up, you wouldn't have had to step in."

Colson pauses for a second, his hands resting on his hips. It takes everything in me to not wrap him up with my arms. Kiss him until my words make sense. Until he has to believe that I don't blame him. That I need him to stay.

He sighs a breath and continues, "Part of this is Nick's fault. Definitely not yours."

Hearing Colson say my ex's name is like lemon juice on a cut you forgot about. It fucking stings.

"You know what? I'd do it again," he says instantly.

That almost breaks me.

"I know," I agree softly. "That's the problem."

He looks away, jaw clenched. "To be fair, this is what I was worried about. Letting you down. Disappointing you."

I take a step closer, "You did not let me down. Why are you falling on your sword like this? Running away? Why don't you fight?"

He hesitates. That scares me more than anything. I wonder if I pushed too far when he keeps quiet.

My voice is bold and strong, it almost surprises me. "You can't just run every time something gets hard. You of all people know that."

"I'm not running away. I've got a career to try and salvage," he says, a little more of an edge to his voice. Good. It means there's something to grab and hold on to.

Lifting my hands in fake surrender, I press, "You're not playing for Chicago. You know you don't have to go back."

"That's where my agent is—" he tries to reason.

"Colson, there are phones. Quit making excuses." I almost stomp my foot, the rage bubbling in my belly. I want him to hear me. There's no room for Sunshine Sadie right now.

He looks away, then back to me, his eyes dark blue like stormy waves. "I'm not making excuses."

"No?" I keep pushing him. Each word has brow furrowed, knitting tighter and tighter.

"No! I'm trying to let you keep your life here, untouched. You were fine before I got here and I'd imagine you'll be fine when I leave." Colson's words are plain but cut like a knife.

"Sounds like another excuse." I cross my arms over my chest, holding on as if I'm keeping myself together.

"Sadie, I promise that you don't need me," he laughs, completely self-deprecating. "I'm the storm cloud. The one that ruins the beach day you've been planning for weeks."

I hate how he's trying to convince himself that I'm better off without him.

"You don't need me. See, you're like the sun. Bright. The perfect summer day that people wish for." His voice fades; I hate that's how he sees himself.

Colson shakes his head, eyes on the ground. It seems the small piece of ground I may have gained is slipping from my fingers. I can feel the waves of disappointment rolling off of him. I can't imagine him leaving like this.

There's no way. This can't be it.

I take another step and we're close enough that I could reach out and touch him. "Fine. If we're making excuses, can I try?"

I swallow past the lump in my throat, it tastes like risk and feels like I'm about to crumble.

His hand cuts through the summer air, telling me, "Go ahead." He says it like a joke. Like he's on the verge of annoyance.

Pressing my lips into a thin line, tears prick at my eyes and I look up. The sky is gorgeous. Whispers and puffs of color dance together, shades of pink and pieces of lush orange, as the sun is setting. It feels like a sign.

Wiping my eyes, I plead, "How about this? You can't run away, because, you see, I'm completely and ridiculously in love with you. You're wrong—I do need you. And if I'm the sun... that means you're the sunset. All those gorgeous colors, changing the entire sky, making the wait feel so worth it."

It feels like time stops and I'm having an out-of-body experience. I feel the words leave my mouth, I hear them, but it's like I'm watching this play out. Like a movie. My stomach ties a knot so tight I press my hand to it, to see if I can feel it.

Colson looks like he's frozen in place. The seconds drag, pulling me through gravel without any shoes on.

"What did you just say?" His voice is lighter than I expected.

I take a breath, filling my lungs to try and get the words out. "I said that I love you." The words tumble and fall on top of each other.

He closes the space between us, his thumbs wiping away rogue tears I didn't know I'd given up, and then his lips are on mine. I sink into it, let him hold me up, the way he's done more than once since being here.

When he pulls away, he says, "Sadie, I—"

"You don't have to say it back. It's... I needed to tell you the truth and—"

His lips find mine again, interrupting me in the best way. When he pulls away this time, his finger replaces his lips and he says, "Sadie, I love you."

I kiss him like he's leaving. I kiss him like he's staying. Mostly, I kiss him in a way that makes me feel like I can't get enough.

We break apart and I damn near beg, "Let me help you. I can help you fix this." I act like my voice isn't shaking and continue. "Stay. Don't leave. Please don't run."

His forehead presses to mine. He locks his eyes on mine, intentional and true, and it's a look that could bring me to my knees.

Without breaking eye contact, he reaches into the trunk, grabs the bag and drops it on the driveaway. He shuts the trunk, the sound of it latching making my heart squeeze. I feel like I can catch my breath.

"Okay," he agrees. "I won't run."

"You won't?"

"How could I when I have my very own human version of sunshine telling me she loves me?" It's like he's trying to make a joke, make light of the heavy words we've exchanged, but I see right through it.

He grabs a bag, I take the other, and then he grabs my hand. Colson squeezes it once before we walk back to the house.

It feels like my heart might trip over itself. Because under the most beautiful sunset, one I never even planned to see, it feels like my key finally found the lock it fits in.

The truth is clear and promising: I love Colson. And he loves me back.

Forty-Nine

COLSON

"You can't leave," Sadie says for what feels like the tenth time since I've dropped my bags.

I don't answer right away. My house feels different with her in it—smaller somehow, like the walls are listening. Her shoes sit by the door as if they belong there. She holds my hand like she's afraid if she lets go, I'll be back out to the car.

Fuck, the guilt creeps up. Even when I was considering leaving as a viable option, part of me knew it was bullshit. I wouldn't feel great about doing it but watching that parent put Sadie on the spot for something I did? Well, I didn't do it. But it feels like this is still my fault.

We'll figure it out. I keep telling myself that. We have to.

Sadie's standing in the middle of my living room, arms folded like she's bracing herself, waiting for me to change my mind. Her eyes search my face, steady and hopeful and terrifying all at once.

"You can quit watching the door. I'm not going to leave," I try to tease as I close the steps between us.

"I really want you to stay." Sadie taps her foot, watching it, before catching my glance at the last moment.

My hands cover hers, which are clasped like she's trying to hold herself together.

"I know. I'm here."

She nods like she's trying to believe me. "I just... everything with Nick? That's not on you. Or me. That's on him. And I can't let him take any more of me." Her words hit me as she almost runs out of breath. "He's taken enough. He doesn't get this."

Sadie lifts her hands until they're in front of us. I still hold onto hers, feeling the faint tremble of her fingers. Her wide eyes are a deep amber, darker than I've seen before.

Fuck.

"You're right. He doesn't." I let the words fall from my mouth before I kiss her. I feel her melt into me and it makes me feel worse about my lapse in judgement. Especially when I'm this lucky.

To know her. To fall in love with her.

"Honestly, I've been waiting for the reason why this won't work. That's been my norm. Losing my mom in a matter of months. The injury. The fall out with the team. And when I saw that parent looking at you, that picture of me, it felt like the reason. The universe being like... 'told you so.' I panicked. And I'm sorry."

Her voice is soft when she says, "I get it. Really I do. But, believe me when I say you have nothing to be sorry for. You were there for me in a way that no one will ever understand."

She leans in and puts her lips to mine. This kiss is slow and patient. It's as if I'm trying to kiss the doubt away. Maybe I am? When she stops shaking, I pull away and take a few strands of her golden hair, rubbing it between my fingers.

"I could say the very same thing about you. You've shown up for me since I arrived here. And you didn't have to do that."

Sadie nods in understanding.

"I love you," I repeat, quietly but without hesitation. "I mean it." The words feel solid. True. Like something I've been carrying and finally set down. They feel good to say.

Her breath catches, and then she's smiling through it, the kind of smile that makes my chest ache. "I love you. And I know you do."

She leans in, kisses me again, and there's no question about it.
I have to stay.

Fifty

SADIE

I feel like I can finally breathe. We're out of the shower and I smell like peppermint—evidence of Colson's body wash. But, he did buy my shampoo and conditioner. He must've looked at what was in my shower at some point during one of our sleepovers.

It makes me smile much bigger than it should. Like, the joy reaches the corner of my soul. He cared enough to do something like this without being asked. I've never complained about staying over at his place but he keeps finding ways to make me feel like I'm welcome.

Like he did with buying coffee beans from the bakery.

He's thoughtful and doesn't make me pay for it. It doesn't feel like he's keeping score. Expecting me to match it, just because.

"Where'd you go?" Colson's voice brings me back to the moment. Us wrapped in our towels, ready to get something to sleep in from his closet.

He sits on the edge of his bed, hair damp, his hands holding on to his towel around his waist. He looks way too fucking good to not be kissing me.

I drop my towel and his eyes go wide for a second, before his hands reach out for me. Putting one leg on each side of his, I straddle him.

His hands immediately are at my lower back, feeling like they take up most of my skin with those massive palms. Colson tips his head, looking up at me, and he bites his lower lip, but smiles through it. Looking at me like I'm something worth keeping.

I kiss him, slow and deliberate, hoping he feels even a fraction of what his gaze did to me. His hands pull us closer together. Shifting, I kiss his neck, leaving my lips on long enough that I can feel his pulse quickening, matching the heartbeat in my chest.

Colson moves his mouth to my sternum, kissing between my breasts. My head goes back and I push forward, giving him as much access as he wants. I love the way his mouth feels on me. Not sure I'll ever get over it.

His mouth covers one of my nipples, sucking. He pairs that with these little moans and I know I'm about to be a puddle. Then his tongue flicks and swirls.

I can feel his length pushing against me through the towel. Putting the weight on my knees, I lift my hips and he follows my lead, pulling the towel and tossing it.

Straddling him again, his dick pushes against me. The pleasure catches me off guard, hitting me just right. It teases a whimper from me and I can't help but rock my hips, again and again.

"This is so good," Colson says, watching me.

I feel him try to tilt himself, getting more of the tension he's looking for. Fuck, I don't know if anything has felt this amazing. I roll my hips again and again before Colson's hands are at my waist.

He lifts me. Those fucking muscles. And I reach down, grabbing him and putting him at my entrance. Slowly, he sets me on top of his hard length. I can't believe how easily he slides into me. He gives me the time to get situated, stretching to fit him. It's also like my brain needs to catch up to Colson, to what we said earlier.

I love you.

He said that back. And I know he means it.

Colson's so patient, with his flushed cheeks and eyes that look like he could devour me whole. I sigh out a breath as his hands run over my skin, feeling all of my curves.

Smirking into it, I kiss him. His tongue dances at the seam of my lips and I let him taste me. My breasts press into him, and his fingernails scratch down my back.

Slowly, I start rolling my hips, needing to give into the craving that's pulsing in my low belly. He guides us together, his hands at my hips helping me move on top of him.

It's euphoric.

I put my hands on the sides of his face and kiss him like he has the air I need to breathe. We pick up the speed and I can't get over the way this feels. The way he hits the right spot. We match each other's intensity, working together.

"Fuck, Sadie," He groans my name and it tips me over.

The sparks fly and I close my eyes.

Colson grabs my chin. "No, no. Eyes on me."

I do what I'm told and cry out as the orgasm has me seeing stars. It's like a wave from the lake, hitting me, every inch of my skin.

"You—" Colson says as he rocks me forward, "Are. Mine." His eyes are fire and ice, almost burning white-hot blue.

It's only a few seconds when he locks in and he's coming with me. I feel his release fill me as he rides the tremors and shocks.

I fall into him when I can't hold myself up any longer. My chest presses to his front and his hands wrap around me. My chin rests on his shoulder as he turns and kisses my cheek.

Once we've caught our breath, I stand and feel him running down my leg.

"Wait," Colson says suddenly, grabbing my hip and pulling me to him.

Then he takes his fingers, running them up my thigh, gathers his release and pushes the cum back in. I've never had someone do that before. It feels intimate. Close. Absolutely perfect.

My belly drops out and the sound that huffs out is unlike anything I've been responsible for. Needy. Desperate.

"You are mine, Sadie Becker."
And I've never been more certain of anything in my life.

Fifty-One

COLSON

"You have bad fucking luck," Howie taunts, his face filling my phone screen. "How are you getting into trouble in a city called Golden Harbor? Seems like a joke."

Scrubbing my hands over my face, wishing I wasn't having to have this conversation, I say, "You know what happened. Quit torturing me... What's the deal with the teams?"

It's been a few days since the sports news cycle got hold of the grainy rendition of my interaction with Nick. Sadie heard from another parent, asking a few questions, before she decided that being transparent was the way to go. After an email providing enough detail without making it awkward, and reiterating that parents are always welcome to sit in on practice, things seem better than I predicted.

Even Emma came back to practice, her mom offering me a slight smile and a wave when she dropped her off. It's not that I need everyone to like me, but it'd be nice to know they didn't think I was so out of control I couldn't be trusted with their kids. A few parents sat in during camp and my anxiety was damn near crippling every time one of them was waiting for me at the end of practice, but it turns out they wanted to introduce themselves, some of them only just realizing I was "that" Colson.

My agent continues, "Well, you're going to need some preliminary interviews. AKA, they want to know what happened at that last game."

I nod, knowing this was coming in one way or another. "That makes sense."

Howie continues, "Some of the offers are gone. After the photo. But—" he lifts his hands like he's trying to keep me calm, "there's enough interest from other teams that I'm still confident you'll find a spot. They're requesting visits this weekend. I can work on the travel plans if you're cool with that?"

"I can do early next week but not this weekend. Rec center things." It's the first weekend of the tournament and our team will play on Friday night.

"You mean Sadie things…" He wiggles his eyebrows.

I'm not hiding this thing with her from him. It's not worth it. My hope is that she's going to be part of my life for a long time—fuck, maybe forever. In order to do that, I can't hide. Can't run. And can't act like she's not one of the best things that's been mine.

This thing with Sadie? It's high stakes. And I'm all in.

"Yes, Sadie things." I agree to get him off of it. "I made a commitment to her and the kids. The teams will have to wait. I hope they understand." It's a youth basketball camp, for crying out loud.

"I'll let you know if I hear otherwise," he says before ending the call.

The thought that teams want to pass on me over some trash tabloid is bullshit. But I can't do anything about it. The thing that's always been the case is there are two sides to every story—including the night on the bench I still haven't publicly commented on.

So, here's the plan. I'm going to meet with the teams who are interested and I'm going to tell them the honest, cross-my-heart-and-hope-to-die story–start to finish. From my injury to the rushed recovery, questionable practices, and the on-court blow up that was really me protecting one of my favorite rookie players.

Then, I'm going to call my head coach. Or, my ex-head coach. He was always decent to me and I find it very hard to believe that he was in on anything like this. He deserves to know and understand why I acted that way. Why I waited to come forward.

No matter what, I don't want to play for Chicago. I'm not trying to get my spot back or anything like that; I want to be an honest man. I've been through a lot of shit and I feel like a fresh start with a new team is what I need right now.

And lastly, there will be a public statement. I want everything out in the open before I make a decision, if it's my choice, on a new team. This might sway the public opinion, or it might look like I'm trying to save my ass with this tall tale, but I know I'll have enough people that back me up to give me a fighting chance.

Sometimes, you have to fight. That's what this is: me showing up, trying to move forward.

Hands press into my shoulders and then arms hold onto me from behind.

"How was the call?" Sadie asks, dipping down and setting her chin on my shoulder. I swear, I can feel her grinning.

I kiss her cheek and give her the highlights.

She hums behind me, arms tightening, like she's holding the pieces together just by being there. Her chin shifts, settling more comfortably on my shoulder, her breath warm against my neck.

I turn my head enough to catch her smile out of the corner of my eye. It's soft, almost like a promise. One that makes me believe the universe has a hand in our lives.

"What if it doesn't work?" I ask quietly.

She straightens, her chin lifting from my shoulder before she steps closer so she can lean in again—this time her cheek brushing mine. "Then we deal with it," she answers simply. "But it will work. Maybe not in the neat, movie-montage way. But you're telling the truth. You're showing up. That counts for something."

Her fingers squeeze my shoulders, grounding me. "You're not the guy people are trying to make you out to be. Anyone who actually listens will see that."

I swallow. My chest feels too full, like everything is pressing outward at once.

"Hey," she murmurs, nudging me gently. "Look at me."

I turn to face her, knees brushing hers. Sadie cups my face with both hands, thumbs warm against my jaw, eyes steady and bright.

"You're going to be okay," she says, like it's not a guess but a promise. "I have no doubt in my mind."

Something in me breaks open at that. Fuck, it's been breaking open since I met her. The fear starts to evaporate, replaced by this overwhelming, almost dizzying affection.

I stand before I even realize I'm moving. Her hands slide down to my shoulders instinctively, laughing a little in surprise when I scoop her up.

"Hey—" she starts, but it dissolves into a grin as I lift her like she weighs nothing and set her on the counter.

She settles there easily, knees bumping my hips, arms looping around my neck. We're eye to eye now, close enough that I can see every tiny fleck of color in her irises.

"I love you," I say, the words spilling out without hesitation. They feel solid. Certain.

Her smile is gentle, something tender and shining in it. "I love you, too."

I lean in, pressing my forehead to hers, hands firm at her waist, and for the first time in what feels like forever, the future doesn't scare me.

It feels like it might be worth it after all.

Fifty-Two

SADIE

His fingers dig into my sides and it almost tickles. A laugh starts up in my chest; when I hear it, it sounds like true happiness. It's hard for me to think back and remember a time when I felt like this. Recently, or ever.

Colson does that to me. Makes me feel like I can fly. I keep thinking back to the first day we met. The dent in his car. The deep grooves in his pissed-off face. Grooves I like to try and kiss, like finding the start of our story.

His lips find my neck and I tip my head back, giving him all the access he needs. Colson stands, my knees on each side of him.

"Hey," I try holding the giggle back, "I thought you were hungry." I look to the cutting board I'd pulled out to make us lunch.

"Oh, I'm starving."

"Then let me down so I can help with that." I grab the front of his shirt, pulling him to me.

He drags his tongue across his bottom lip and then says, "You *can* help with that." His hand starts at my knee and his fingers press into my upper thigh beneath my skirt. "I think I'll have you for lunch."

My belly flips. The fuse lights, and I swear, something buzzes on the surface of my skin.

Colson's fingers reach up higher, hooking the band of my thong, and he pulls. The fabric dragging against my skin, torturously slow, has my muscles clenching.

He holds up my light pink and lacy panties before tossing them. His eyes pin me in place, deepening the ache of needing him to touch me.

I hold my breath as Colson gets on his knees, his face level with the counter. With me.

"Show me that perfect pussy," he croons. I've never wanted to do something more.

I grab the hem of my skirt, one of my favorites for summer, and pull it up. The coolness of the counter pushing into my skin. Then I spread my legs, one at a time.

"Fuck. What a sight," he moans, before kissing the inside of my thigh.

Colson settles between my thighs and I don't know if I've ever seen anything more fucking beautiful. What feels like a millimeter at a time, he kisses up my leg. Covering the sensitive skin of my thigh, he then places the softest kiss to my clit. I cry out, arching my back.

His tongue gently licks me. "You're wet. So wet for me, baby." The vibrations from his lips are close enough that I can feel them, almost like he's edging me. "I love tasting you."

Tasting me? *Fuck.*

His lips drag over me before landing at my clit. He sucks and devours me like he's starved, his fingers joining in by slowly pumping into me. Colson uses his other hand to grip at my ass.

My hips try to move, chasing his touch, the pressure I need. There's no teasing here—Colson is giving me everything I want. I can't keep still, my body trembling and moving on the counter as he inches me closer and closer.

"You going to come for me? All over my mouth?" he asks, but diving back in.

My pussy throbs at his coaxing. My hands pull at his hair and he groans against me. HIs tongue swirls against me and he adds a finger. Heat threatens to push through my veins, the edge of my release so close.

I whimper and whine, tugging his mouth just right. And that's all it takes. He keeps working me with his fingers, his mouth, and I come for him. I choke back a cry as my orgasm runs through me. My thighs clamp against his head, keeping his mouth right where I want it. Colson doesn't try to pull away; he eats me until the shocks simmer and run out.

"You're so fucking gorgeous when you come." His voice is soft and ragged.

I'm still trying to catch my breath, get my head back on straight from serving myself as a snack. And then he says something like that. The audacity—the kind I hope he never loses.

The world feels like it's still spinning and I need something to keep me anchored. I throw my arms around Colson, kissing him, letting him have all my weight.

The way he has all of me.

Fifty-Three

COLSON

Friday comes faster than I expect.

By the time I pull into the park, the sun is high and bright, baking the outdoor court until the blacktop shimmers. There are balloons tied to the fence and a hand-painted banner stretched crookedly across the entrance that reads **WELCOME TO THE SUMMER TOURNA-MENT!** in uneven bubble letters.

I slow to a stop, genuinely surprised. People are everywhere.

Not only parents, either. Folding chairs line the edges of the court; beyond them, there are townspeople standing with coffees, kids on bikes hovering nearby, and a couple of older guys in lawn chairs who look like they've been here since dawn. Someone's set up a little table with a cooler and a sign that says *FREE ORANGES* like this is the biggest sporting event the town's hosted all year.

For nine-and-ten-year-olds, it kind of is.

I grin to myself as I grab my bag and head toward the court. Worth it doesn't even begin to cover it.

Sadie's already there, clipboard tucked under her arm, hair pulled back in a low ponytail that makes her look all business. When she encouraged me to get my workout in and that she'd get the team started with warmups, it was her small way to support me. I love how she finds a way to put me first in all types of ways.

She spots me from across the court and her face lights up in a way that still catches me off guard. Fuck. I'm going to melt into this court.

We don't touch—nothing obvious, anyway—but when I stop beside her, our shoulders brush. Her pinky sneaks into mine for half a second before she pulls away. Our little secret.

"You seeing this?" she murmurs, eyes scanning the crowd.

"I am," I reply. "I think half the town canceled their Friday plans."

She looks to the kids, proud and happy. "They deserve it."

The other team arrives a few minutes later. Kids are piling out of vans, nerves and excitement written all over their faces, some cheeks still red from the warm August day. They're from a town about forty-five minutes away, close enough to be familiar, far enough to make this feel like a *real* tournament game.

When the opposing team is all together, putting their shoes on, I go and introduce myself. Since the photo leaked, there have been more photos of me in Golden Harbor making their rounds. Things like me walking on the beach with Sadie, us at Cherry Pit, just living our normal life.

Anyone who cares knows I'm in Golden Harbor. I wanted to wish the other team luck but also saw some of them pointing at me, like they knew who I was, so I thought I'd go and make their day.

After I'm done saying hi, wishing them luck, and even taking a few photos, it's time to get going. Warm ups start. Whistles blow. Sneakers squeak against the court.

And then the game is on.

From the opening tip, it's clear both teams came ready. Passes are crisp. Defense is tight. The kids dig deep in that way only kids can—no pacing themselves, no holding back. Just heart and hustle and the kind of effort that leaves nothing on the floor. They'll be getting good sleep tonight.

The score stays close the entire first half. Every basket gets a cheer like it's the winning shot. I find myself clapping until my hands sting, shouting encouragement until my voice goes hoarse.

I'm so damn proud I can barely contain it.

Then it happens.

Late in the second quarter, one of the boys from the other team—a small kid with bright red shoes—gets the ball on a fast break. He trips over his own feet going up for the layup. The ball bounces off the rim, straight into the hands of one of our players, who takes off the other direction.

The kid freezes. Some of the kids, and even parents, snicker.

He doesn't chase. Doesn't turn. He stops in the middle of the court and brings both hands up to his face, covering his eyes like if he can't see anyone, no one can see him.

My chest tightens.

He's supposed to get back on defense, but he can't. He's shaking his head, shoulders hunched, standing there while the game moves around him.

I get the ref's attention and call a timeout.

Both teams jog to their benches, water bottles already being shoved into hands. While the other coaches start talking, I jog back out onto the court. The kid's still there.

"Hey," I say gently, crouching in front of him. "Sweet shoes."

He peeks at me through his fingers, eyes wet and furious with himself.

"I messed up," he blurts. "Everyone saw. I'm so stupid."

My heart cracks a little.

"You know what I saw?" I ask.

He sniffs. "What?"

"I saw a kid who hustled down the court faster than anyone else. I saw courage."

He frowns, processing that.

"The important part," I continue, keeping my voice calm and steady, "is what you do *after the fall*. You don't stop playing. You don't hide. You keep going. Because you're more than one play. Right?"

His hands lower slowly.

"You're still in this game," I say. "You hear me?"

He nods, swiping at his cheeks with the heels of his hands.

I hold out my fist. "Deal?"

He hesitates for half a second, then bumps it with his own, fighting a smile.

"Good," I praise, standing. "Now don't run the score up on us or anything."

He runs back to his huddle, people cheering him on, with his head high, wiping the last of the tears away. When I glance up, the other team's coach catches my eye and gives me a grateful nod.

I nod back.

As I turn toward our bench, Sadie's looking at me. She doesn't say anything. Just mouths the words—clear as day.

I love you.

My heart skips a beat, I swear. And I can't help the way it feels to have her by my side.

Fifty-Four

SADIE

THE BUZZER SOUNDS, THEN it's the best kind of chaos. Kids are yelling, slapping hands, bouncing on the balls of their feet like they've won at everything in life. They swarm each other first, then the scorers' table, forming a crooked, impatient line that keeps breaking apart because none of them can stand still.

Medals aren't typical for these games. Everyone knows that. But when you ask nine-and-ten-year-olds to show up all summer, to run drills in the heat, to learn how to play as a team? You give them something they can hold that tells them they mattered.

The medals are bright, catching the last of the sun as they're passed out, one by one. The kids beam like they've been crowned royalty, lifting them to their mouths, clinking them together, throwing their arms around each other.

We only won by three.

You wouldn't know it, considering the other team is still laughing, still running, still proud in the way only kids can be—like the score doesn't define the night. Parents pour onto the court, phones out, calling names, crouching low for photos, scooping sweaty kids into hugs. Everyone is pink-cheeked and full of life.

I step back a little, letting it all wash over me.

That's when I see Colson.

He's standing to the side, hands on his hips, watching everything like he's trying to memorize it. The kids with their parents. The way one dad lifts his son straight into the air. A mom brushing hair out of her daughter's face before snapping a picture. The way everyone seems lighter than they did two hours ago.

He looks... happy. His eyes sparkle in a way that makes my chest ache. I wonder if he's thinking about his mom. About summers when things felt this simple. Like showing up and trying hard were enough to make the world feel the way it should be.

It's a Friday night in the middle of summer, and for a moment, everything is exactly as it should be.

When the chaos finally settles, I step up beside him.

"Good job, Coach," I say, nudging his arm.

He turns to me, smiling like he's never scowled in his life. "Right back at ya."

Before I can respond, I notice a man walking toward us with a boy at his side. The boy's got red shoes—the same ones from earlier—and Colson's smile shifts, his brow furrowing slightly, like he's trying to place a memory.

The man stops in front of us and holds out his hand. "Darren Jones."

Colson takes it automatically, then freezes.

"You're the head coach for the Detroit Wolves."

Darren grins. "Guilty."

I swear my heart stutters.

He gestures toward the boy beside him. "We've got a summer place about an hour from here. My kid missed the tournament last year. No way we could make that mistake two years in a row." He laughs, squeezing his son's shoulder.

"This is DJ," he adds. "And I wanted to thank you. For earlier."

DJ looks up at Colson, eyes wide. "Thanks, Colson! Can we get a picture before I leave?"

Before anyone can answer, he takes off toward his friends, already calling out, and Darren laughs, shaking his head.

Then he turns back to Colson, expression shifting slightly. Still friendly but a bit more focused.

"So," Darren says, casual as anything. "Heard we're meeting next week? I'd love to tell you about how the Wolves are making a real run at the championship next season."

Colson's mouth drops open.

"Yes, sir," he manages. "I mean. Yes. And I want to make sure I give you the full story about everything that happened at my last game and—"

Darren lifts a hand, waving it off. "Don't worry about it. I'm sure there's a reasonable explanation. I'm looking forward to hearing all about it next week."

Then he glances around the court again, smiling. "But for now? Enjoy this."

He reaches for my hand and says, "Great work on this. I heard this was your brain child. You should be proud."

The kind words wash over me and it makes me feel like this is even more worth it. There's something special about the opposing parents being thankful, even when they lost, for the opportunity. To build something that people look forward to.

"I appreciate that. Thanks for being part of it. Good luck next weekend." I say.

He steps back, already turning away. "Colson, hope to see you in those Detroit City Blues next season. Talk soon."

And then he's gone. I stand there, stunned, my brain absolutely scrambling to catch up with reality.

Colson turns to me slowly. "Oh my god," he gapes. "Did that just happen?"

I don't even think before moving. I grab his face with both hands and kiss him—right there on the court, surrounded by kids still buzzing with adrenaline, parents snapping photos, someone yelling about medals and oranges and where the car is parked. I don't care. I don't care if anyone recognizes him. I don't care about *anything* except the way he freezes for half a second and then melts into me, hands finding my waist like that's where they belong.

The kiss isn't careful or quiet. It's full and feels like summer magic.

When we pull back, he's laughing under his breath, forehead pressed to mine, eyes shining.

"Everything okay, Coach?" I tease softly.

He exhales, shaking his head. "I'm so happy. With you. Here. All of it."

I laugh, still holding his face. "So... does this mean I'm never going to see the famous Colson Burke scowl ever again?"

He grins and dips his head to brush his nose against mine. "Baby, I'll scowl whenever you want."

My heart feels so full it's almost unbelievable. I lean in for one more kiss—slower this time, sweeter. He holds me tight to him and I catch a glimpse of the sun, the kind of blue sky you'd see on a postcard.

This doesn't feel real. This level of happiness. The way Colson and I crossed paths, over pain and grief and tough pasts.

I know it won't always be easy. Love like this never is. But wrapped in his arms, beneath a sky too blue to be anything but honest, I know one thing with absolute certainty...

If I'm the sun then Colson is my sunset.

The kind of ending you wait your whole life to find. And you know what? This was definitely worth the wait.

Fifty-Five

COLSON

Two Months Later

I feel like the human version of a sparkler, nerves and energy buzzing on my skin. Christmas morning has nothing on opening night in the NBA. Looking down, the light blue and black warm-ups remind me that it's my first game on a brand new team.

No matter the result, I feel like I've already won.

I met with Darren a few days after seeing him at the kid's summer tournament. He didn't ask me what happened that night everyone's been speculating; instead, he invited me to simply shoot around with his assistant coach. They watched me move, warm up, and it felt like I was catching up with old friends.

Once they saw I was moving like Colson Burke, pre-injury, everything became a formality. Flat out, they asked if I wanted to play for them, and I answered honestly—more than anything. This was my home team when I was a kid, where the dream of playing in the league started.

I told them about the night on the bench—start to finish. How I was going public with this in a few days. Darren shook his head and the hurt that crossed his face didn't go unnoticed. They apologized for things that weren't theirs to apologize for and promised me the medical staff didn't operate like that in Detroit.

I cancelled the rest of my team meetings after that one—there was no reason to act like I was going anywhere else. My agent was reviewing my offer a few hours after I left the facility.

The athletic trainer was fired from my previous team and they've not been able to get another position in the league. Thank god. After everything came to light, I heard from everyone at my old team. The grateful rookie I went to bat for, my other teammates, and even the general manager. Everyone wished me luck and reiterated that there were no hard feelings.

I didn't need their approval or understanding, but it definitely didn't hurt.

When I walk out on the court, my heart jumps in my throat. I'm fucking proud of myself. I made it back. The tunnel is lined with eager fans, my jersey hanging, asking to be signed. Joy fills me and I make it a point to sign something for every single fan waiting for me. They take selfies. They tell me how happy they are to see me in their team's jersey. I try to give each of them that moment we'll both remember.

Darren catches my eyes from across the court and he tips his head. We have a great relationship and we're only getting started. I know we're going to have a great fucking season and I'm so excited.

We run through warm m-ups, and even though I'm still getting to know all the guys on the team, we've become fast friends. No ego on this team and I think that's my favorite.

Fans are filling the stadium and I keep checking the courtside seats, literally the first row on the floor, that I bought for tonight. Every few minutes, my eyes wander, the perfect distraction as the nerves rush through my body.

I feel her before I see her.

Sadie. In my jersey. My number on the front and my last name on the back. Fuck. She's gorgeous.

I jog towards her. The way her face lights up when she sees me? Fucking unmatched.

"Sunshine girl," I greet her with the nickname that feels like it's the only thing close to giving her justice.

Sadie wraps her arms around me before giving a quick kiss. Excitement rolls off her as she takes me in.

"Boy, you look damn good on a basketball court," she jokes.

Maren jumps in with, "Colson, what are the odds I get smoked with a basketball tonight?" She keeps looking down at the court.

"Definitely possible." I answer.

"Very cool," she says, which I know means thank you in Maren.

Sadie puts a hand to my chest, "Go warm up. Enjoy! Go Wolves!"

I cover her fingers with mine. "I love you. Thank you for being here."

"I love you," she says back, her words pulling at my rib cage. No matter how many times she says it—proves it—it never gets old.

I jog back out to shoot around as a wave of calmness surrounds me. I wish my mom were here but I know she'd be so proud. Excited for this next adventure—both with the team and with Sadie.

Sadie was approached, personally, by Blair Miller—the first woman to ever play in the NFL. Sort of randomly, she became the kicker for the Upstate Cosmos this past season. A complete bad ass. Before she was on the team, she owned and ran a functional fitness gym, and is looking to expand the brand and mission. Blair was tagged in a video from one of the girls in our summer rec league as she made twenty free throws in a row... all the boys cheering her on. It had Blair looking at the team, looking at Sadie, and connecting with her for an opportunity.

Ember and Ashes, the gym brand, is coming to Golden Harbor. Sadie will help open it this winter and stay on staff, helping the day-to-day operations and finding more ways to get girls and women involved in sports.

It's perfect for her.

I know this next season will be challenging, while Sadie still lives in Golden Harbor and I'm almost five hours away in Detroit. I did buy an apartment downtown, only a five minute walk from the arena, that has more than enough room for me and Sadie, as well as any guests she may want to invite for a home game.

We're obviously keeping my mom's place in Golden Harbor and we'll spend as much time as possible there in the off season. The city that changed my whole life. The one that sort of felt random when this house went on the market but turned out to be the thing I needed most.

A place to heal. A place to learn. A place to love.

I shoot the ball and watch it fall through the net. Right now, the shots are easy but I know that won't always be the case. Last season, I was so riddled with grief and trying not to drown that a bad night on the court would have me spiraling.

But I'm not worried. Not with Sadie by my side. Being with her makes it feel like we can accomplish everything, Her light is something to be bottled, studied,

The only thing that comes close to Sadie is the diamond ring I have tucked away in my sock drawer. The black velvet box holding the most sparkly engagement ring I could find. The one I bought a few weeks ago.

I shake my head on the court because the version of myself, from before Golden Harbor, would absolutely riot if he knew I was so open to making Sadie my wife. It wasn't necessary. I didn't understand it. Never felt like a need.

That was before meeting Sadie Becker.

Because when you find someone who shines like Sadie does—even when you're a walking storm cloud—you do everything you can to keep her.

THE END

READY FOR MORE COLSON AND SADIE?

Scan for bonus content!

WANT TO KNOW MORE ABOUT BLAIR MILLER, THE FIRST WOMAN IN THE NFL?

READ FROM THE SIDELINES – A STANDALONE FRIENDS TO LOVERS, SPORTS ROMANCE, WHERE IT'S ALWAYS BEEN HER.

What's next for
Rachel LaBerge

Scan for upcoming preorders!

ACKNOWLEDGMENTS

I don't know if I should divulge a secret like this, but... this was the easiest book I've written to date. Colson and Sadie's story hit me in the best way possible and watching it play out through my words was unlike anything I've experienced this far. Seriously. It was the kind of story that broke me and put me back together. I loved it.

As always, I have people to thank who made this possible. The story may have been easy but it wouldn't be possible without the support from these people.

First, to my readers, thank you. The fact that you're holding this book brings me so much joy. Like, when Sadie sees the perfect sunset or when Colson is looking at Sadie. Thank you for taking the time to read my words. There's no way I could do this without you.

Ambar, you get a little shout out at the front, but I'm so thankful for our friendship. For the little moments, the ones where we're together, and the way we cheer each other on. Thank you for being there for me.

Mollie and Carly... we are spiteful and we are mighty! Kidding. Kind of. I love you two! Thank you for everything, especially when I am panicking at the disco.

Abby, your support made me feel like I could do this. That this was the right move. My pearl, so thankful for you and all the advice you bestow.

For my alpha and beta readers, the ones who made the time and space to read and help get this book to where it needed to be: Stephanie, Rose, Danie, Amber, Emma, Ceilidh, Ashley, Casey, Keona, Georgia, Cassie, Dawn, Emily, Lina, Tiffany.

Kendra, my editor, friend, and hype woman, thank you. Please don't ever leave me.

Robby, my lovely husband, for all the trips we've taken to Traverse City, one of my favorite places in the world, and the inspiration behind Golden Harbor. I love you.

ABOUT THE AUTHOR

Rachel LaBerge is best known for writing love stories where the characters' brains are spicy, just like the plot...

When she's not reading or writing, she's probably watching a sporting event, thinking about donuts, sour candy, or looking for her next hyperfixation. She lives in Michigan with her husband (Roberto), her two Frenchies (Rafa and Ruby), and cat (Riley).

You can connect with her on Instagram, TikTok, and Threads @rachellabergeauthor (no 'R' name required).